ABSOLUTION

ABSOLUTION

(A FATHER JAKE AUSTIN MYSTERY)

by John A. Vanek

coffeetownpress

coffeetownpress

A Coffeetown Press Book published by Epicenter Press

Epicenter Press
6524 NE 181st St.
Suite 2
Kenmore, WA 98028
For more information go to: www.epicenterpress.com

This is a work of fiction. Names, characters, places, brands, media, and incidents are the product of the author's imagination or are used fictitiously.

Cover and book design by Rudy Ramos

Absolution

ISBN: 9781603816236 (trade paper)
ISBN: 9781603816243 (ebook)

Printed in the United States of America

For the many fine authors who have guided me on my writing journey, and for friends, family, and the readers who have supported me throughout.

ACKNOWLEDGMENTS

I am extremely grateful to my wife, Geni, for her advice and patience, and to Jessica & Randy Dublikar, Jen & Matt Vanek, Father Thomas Winkel, Sterling Watson, Michael Koryta, Laura Lippman, Les Standiford, and Dennis Lehane for their help and encouragement. Special thanks to Abe Spevack, Susan Adger, Barbara Schrefer, Ann O'Farrell, Lee Summerall, Jeanne Hirth, and Richard Erlanger for their brutally honest critiques over the years. I am grateful for input and support from: Patti & Ron Poporad, JoAnn & Jim Gavacs, Mary Winter, Kathy & Emil Poporad, the Pinellas Writers, and the Oberlin Heritage Center. I wish to thank Jennifer McCord and Phil Garrett at Coffeetown Press for guiding me through the morass of the publishing world. I also want to express my gratitude to all of the readers who supported the first two novels in the series, *DEROS* and *Miracles*, by recommending them to friends and posting kind reviews online.

The poem entitled "My Universe" (Copyright © 2009 by John Vanek), and the poem entitled "The Children's Ward" (Copyright © 2019 by John Vanek) are both my works. "My Universe" was originally titled "Pediatric Oncology." It first appeared in my book of poetry, *Heart Murmurs: Poems* and was revised for this novel. It is used with permission from Bird Dog Publishing. "The Children's Ward" appears for the first time in *Absolution*.

The characters, settings, and all of the events in *Absolution* are fictional and entirely the product of the author's imagination. If you enjoy the Father Jake Austin Mystery Series, please tell your friends. Word of mouth is the lifeblood of independent presses and their authors.

PROLOGUE: SEEKING REFUGE

Sunday, December 1, 2002, 10:00 p.m.

The old man shuffled through ankle-deep snow farther into an abandoned freight yard. An angry wind howled in over Lake Erie and slashed at him, sharp and cold as a knife blade. His toes were frozen and his cowboy boots weren't worth a damn on the ice. Hostile faces glared at him from what was left of a dilapidated boxcar, so he walked on. Frigid air clawed at his nose and throat, leaving him wheezing and panting hard, his breath trailing behind him like steam from a locomotive.

There was no doubt in his mind. He never should have come back here, never should have moved to this frozen meat locker in the first place, so many years ago.

Spotting a sheltered doorway in a shuttered warehouse, he tried its graffiti-covered steel door but found it locked. The entranceway was deep and the overhang large enough, however, to shield him from the flurries and sporadic gusts. He heaved his battered duffel bag out of the weather into a back corner and gently set his saxophone case next to it.

He took a few steps from the doorway to survey the train yard. Fifty feet away, a burning barrel cast a small circle of jaundiced light. A raggedy old woman pitched a broken board into the barrel. The wood crackled and spit, sending flickering yellow sparks fluttering upward like fireflies.

In the firelight, he could barely make out a dozen or so homeless folks, hunkered down for warmth around the fire in cardboard boxes and under plastic tarps. Half were probably as crazy as shit-house mice. Getting much sleep tonight with this bunch nearby would be tricky. Christ, he couldn't remember the last time he had slept, really slept. He knew he should hoist his gear and keep going, but his exhausted body refused to move.

A passing cloud drifted across the moon, turning the night into sludge. Retreating back into the warehouse doorway, he snatched a bottle of Thunderbird from his coat pocket and took a pull. The familiar glow warmed his gut and eased his mind. He took another swallow and set the bottle on the concrete step.

A mournful wail pierced the night, growing louder and more urgent. The ground began to tremble, rattling the wine bottle. The vibration grew into a roar, exploding into a waning thunderclap as a freight train hurtled past the forgotten Ohio rust-belt town, its caboose lights fading into the distance.

His eyes swept his surroundings as he leaned against the building and softly sang the chorus of "Born Under A Bad Sign," snapping out the rhythm with his fingers.

Truer words were never spoken, he thought. Summed up his life, that's for sure. No, truth be told, it was more than bad luck. At every fork in the road, he had chased the green of money, filled his nose with happy white powder, and his head with neon dreams. Now, his only way out was a shallow grave. Hell, he hadn't even made it out of Louisiana before they torched his car and almost barbequed his ass.

He stomped his frozen feet, sat on the step, removed a tattered blanket from his duffel, and slipped under it. His whole body ached. Too many days on buses and thumbing rides, too many nights sleeping on park benches and doorsteps. He tried to fluff up his duffel bag; it remained lumpy and stiff.

Under the blanket, his hand found the saxophone case, his ticket to a fresh start, a new life. He hugged it to his chest. The case was cold and hard. But after sixty-six long years, his sax was the closest thing he had to a friend or kin. His eyes teared.

A small, hairy critter skittered across the frozen ground in front of him. A dog yelped in the distance. Something rustled to his left. *Footsteps?* He scanned the area again, drained the last swallow from his bottle, and grabbed it by the neck as a weapon.

A battered van drove slowly into the yard and parked on the other side of the burning barrel. Two men stepped out. The taller man leaned against the van and lit a cigarette. The shorter one wandered over to warm his hands at the fire. He appeared relaxed, but something about him was off. He did not belong here, not in that leather coat. The guy was either clueless about where he was, or he was a hired gun and didn't give a damn.

He looked Hispanic, not like one of Big Angie's gym-rat greaseballs. His right coat pocket, however, bulged and hung low. Could Angie have hired some local Ohio talent? The big fella' yelled something at the guy in the leather coat, called him "Santana," then vanished around the side of the vacant warehouse.

The old man sighed, wondering if his son would put him up for a couple weeks. He doubted it. Not after what had happened.

Maybe a friend from the old days would help. Somebody he trusted. No one but Jimmy Sole came to mind, and he was room temperature on a morgue slab.

Out of money, out of options. Without a plan, he was a dead man.

The wind shifted again, launching snow into the air like a swarm of white gnats. An old newspaper rose up, sailing over the van into the sky. Flames leaped from the burning barrel, but that Santana guy was now nowhere in sight. *Crap! Where'd he go?*

Son of a bitch! They had outflanked him, one in front and one behind. If he tried to run, he would probably catch a bullet.

Another rustling nearby. A quilt of clouds blanketed the moon again, the train yard fading to black. He tightened his fingers around the neck of the wine bottle and waited.

CHAPTER ONE

Monday, December 2, 2002, 8:30 a.m.

Finished with my twenty-four-hour shift at St. Joseph's Hospital, I tried to prop up my eyelids with caffeine. The cafeteria coffee smelled and tasted like tar, and my head seemed to be stuffed with used Kleenex. No question about it, on the wrong side of forty-five with a lot less sand in my hourglass, I felt too damn old to be pulling all-nighters supervising a bunch of rookie interns and residents. The full moon often ushered in a traumafest, and the emergency room had stayed as full as the moon my entire shift.

As I pitched the Styrofoam coffee cup into the trash, a soprano voice erupted from the PA speaker, repeating the phrase no physician ever wanted to hear.

Code Blue—Third Floor South. Code Blue—Third Floor South.

I was sprinting to the nearest staircase when the Code Blue team rolled its equipment into the elevator. The elevator door started to close, and I yelled to the code leader, "Need any help?"

He waved me off. "No, we got this, Jake."

I stopped, grateful to be spared. Although I was trained in advanced life support, the code team was a well-oiled CPR machine, and my presence would have added nothing. Exhausted after my overnight shift, I began heading toward the parking garage, relishing the idea of spending a pleasant afternoon with my young nephew—until the damn PA speaker reawakened again.

Code Blue—Urgent Care. Code Blue—Urgent Care.

Mother of God! Another patient in cardio-pulmonary arrest. I prayed no one else in the hospital would choose this exact moment to try to leave this world. With the Code Blue team unavailable, time with my nephew would have to wait.

Rather than navigate the maze of hallways in the hospital, I opted for the shortest distance to Urgent Care and crashed out an exit door into a raging blizzard. Nearly taking a nosedive as I slid across a patch of ice, I regained my balance and snow-plowed my way past an old car parked on the sidewalk with its passenger door open. The Urgent Care Department's pneumatic doors hissed apart, and I hurried inside.

The room was the usual frenzy of organized chaos that accompanies every resuscitation. A young boy, maybe eight or nine years old, lay on a steel hospital gurney, his skin ashen, lips a dusky blue. Both of his skinny arms were extended to the sides at ninety degree angles, resting on arm boards. Two nurses struggled to insert IVs into the slender veins in his hands. With his legs crossed at the ankles, it looked as if I had walked in on some sort of twisted Salvador Dali crucifixion scene. One intern was pumping on the child's chest, and another performing mouth-to-mouth.

When they noticed me, relief lit their faces as the responsibility for the boy's life shifted to me.

I charged over. "What's the story?"

Raj Patel blew another breath into the boy's lungs, and the child's chest rose and fell.

"I'm not sure, Dr. Austin. His older brother carried him in." Someone handed Patel an Ambu bag, and he placed the mask over the boy's mouth and nose, squeezed it, and delivered another lung-full of air. He pointed toward the triage nurse and an adolescent standing in the corner. "The brother didn't say much. He's pretty freaked out."

One nurse finished taping her IV to the boy's arm and peered up at me.

"Get the crash cart and defibrillator stat." She was gone before I finished speaking.

As I approached the brother, he was babbling through his tears. I heard only snippets: "Can't be … just for fun … oh, Jesus … didn't think …."

"Nurse Ochs, what do we have?"

"This one," the head nurse said, pointing to the acne-ravaged teenager, "was partying with his buddies last night, passing out pills like Halloween candy. He and his younger brother, Ethan, played hooky today after their parents left for work. Ethan found the stash and decided he wanted to be *all grown up* too."

I grabbed the teen by the shoulders. "What kind of pills?"

"Donno." His speech was slurred, eyes unfocused, pupils constricted. He wobbled and leaned against the wall.

"Where are they?" I shook him. "Where are the pills?"

His eyes drifted down. I shook him again. He hesitated, yanked a plastic baggie from his pocket, and handed it to me.

Two green tablets marked OC on one side, 80 on the other: Kickers. Controlled-release oxycodone. Eighty milligrams—enough to knock *me* on my butt—and the boy on the gurney couldn't have weighed more than ninety pounds.

"Did your brother chew these?"

The teen nodded.

Damn it! *Uncontrolled-release*, opioids flooding the boy's system.

"How many did he take?"

A shrug, a whimper. He examined his sneakers.

I refocused on the interns. "It's an Oxy overdose. Patel, do a tox screen to see if the child's got anything else in his system."

"Already on its way, doctor."

The second nurse finished taping down an intravenous line in the child's other arm. I sent her for portable oxygen as the first nurse returned with a crash cart and quickly set up the defibrillator.

"Load him with Narcan." I estimated the child's weight. "Push two milligrams IV now, and repeat that every two minutes. Keep me posted on the total."

Sick to death of dealing with drug overdoses, I whirled around, gripped the older brother's arm hard, and waved the bag of pills. "Where the hell did you get these?"

He looked down, mute.

The last of my self-control went up in flames. I stepped nose to nose and screamed, "Tell me, for God's sake! Who gave you the drugs?"

"Guy named Razor. Sells 'em near school."

I gave Nurse Ochs the baggie of pills and asked her to locate an NG tube and stomach pump, then sat the teen on a chair in the corner where I could keep an eye on him. "Stay put, son," I said, unable to hide the anger in my voice. I couldn't deal with him yet, but didn't want him leaving the hospital before I made sure that he too hadn't overdosed.

The intern performing chest compressions was doing a piss-poor job. I tapped him on the back and said, "Switch on three. One, two …" and I was pumping on the boy's bony chest. His skin was ice cold and his face as pale as a Kabuki mask. The child's irises had expanded to compensate for his pinpoint pupils, and his huge, motionless chocolate-brown eyes gazed right through me. I hoped he was not staring at God Almighty.

The sluice gate of time closed, and the seconds slowly trickled by. I locked into the rhythm of the chest compressions, but instead of the usual *one one-thousand… two one-thousand … three one-thousand* I normally relied on, my mind switched from numbers to words: *Our Father … who art in Heaven … hallowed be Thy name …*.

We attacked the child's lifeless frame with a singular purpose. Patel deftly guided an endotracheal tube down the boy's throat, past his vocal cords, and into his windpipe. He was cool under pressure, and I rewarded him with a nod of approval.

My near-tumble on the icy sidewalk while hurrying to Urgent Care had ignited an old injury in my right hip and it protested loudly as I leaned over Ethan, pumping on his chest. Sweat rolled down my cheeks. My arms and back ached. The tiny silver crucifix I always wore under my shirt seemed to weigh me down like an anchor. It felt as if I had been working on the child for days and I needed a break, but we would get no relief. With the Code Blue team resuscitating a patient on the third floor, we were Ethan's only hope.

Raj Patel attached the Ambu bag to the endotracheal tube and the other intern took over bagging the boy. Patel snaked a nasogastric tube through the child's nostril into his stomach. It returned a thin greenish-brown liquid tinged with flecks of blood.

"Come on, kid," I whispered, "stay with me!"

The defibrillator's monitor showed a jagged, saw-tooth EKG pattern. We shocked Ethan repeatedly until I thought I smelled seared flesh. His mouth remained frozen in a grimace around the endotracheal tube, his blank stare mocking our efforts as the life slowly drained from his eyes.

When the EKG finally flat-lined and stayed that way, I said, "That's it. I'm calling it." Nurse Ochs signaled her agreement. I checked the wall clock. "Time of death, 9:41."

I had completely forgotten about Ethan's brother in the far corner of the room. He heard me, slumped in the chair, and shrieked, the sound as piercing as shrapnel. But the long silence that always follows a failed CPR seemed louder than the scream.

As Raj Patel began the paper work, I went limp. Nothing eroded my faith in God more than the death of a child. Not wanting to lose both boys on my watch, I told the other intern to take the teen into an exam room and begin a workup for possible overdose.

Ethan's corpse was pin-cushioned by tubes and needles. Blood spattered his clothes and mine. In his face, I saw my young nephew and wilted. Unable to find the strength to move, I whispered a short prayer.

Out of nowhere, a geyser of anger erupted in me. This scumbag Razor, the guy who sold narcotics to kids, wasn't a drug dealer. He was a damn *murderer*, sure as if he had put a gun in Ethan's mouth and pulled the trigger!

I called my buddy, Tremont Macon, at the Sheriff's Office. He headed up the county's Drug Task Force, so I told him everything.

"Be there in fifteen minutes, Jake. I'll meet you in Urgent Care. Don't let the dead boy's brother leave." His voice took on a menacing edge. "And don't *you* go anywhere. I got a whole bunch of questions for you too."

A click and he was gone.

Questions for me? What the hell! I didn't like the sound of that.

I drew a deep breath and was heading for the doctors' lounge to change out of my bloody clothes when Nurse Ochs stepped in front of me. She ran shaky fingers through short, coal-black hair and cleared her throat. Her eyes glistened and she wiped them. We were friends, and I wanted to hug away her pain.

"Ethan's mother will be here any second. I called her at work," she said. "The poor woman's terrified. Ethan's brother told me the family is Catholic." When I didn't respond, she added, "Can you ... talk to her? Please, Father."

I had seen my share of death as a medic during the war and later as a physician treating terminally ill patients in the hospital, and I had dealt with grieving families even more since my recent ordination into the priesthood, but none of that made comforting a parent over the loss of a child any easier.

Some days, I hated my jobs—both of them.

CHAPTER TWO

Monday, December 2, 2002, 10:00 a.m.

Instead of changing out of my blood-spattered clothes, I hurried to the chapel, grabbed Holy Oil and the ritual book, and returned to Urgent Care. As I performed the Last Rites, whispering prayers over Ethan's lifeless body, Raj Patel's mouth dropped open. Apparently, he was among the few people at St. Joseph's Hospital who didn't know that I was also a priest. Or maybe he knew the sacrament was actually called the Anointing of the Sick and intended for the living, not the dead, and he was wondering what the heck I was doing.

Breaking Church protocol made me feel like a charlatan and a fraud, but I wanted to provide Ethan's family with at least this small comfort.

Nurse Ochs peeked in the door. "Ethan's mom is here. She's in room two. I didn't tell her he died, I ... I couldn't. Only that he'd had a terrible accident. She's scared to death."

When I had finished the prayer, I slipped on a clean white coat, buttoned it to cover the blood on my shirt, and entered the exam room. A stocky, young woman wearing olive-colored slacks and a matching striped top stood near the window wringing her shaking hands. She had draped her fur coat over a nearby chair.

I introduced myself and seated Ethan's mother before breaking the news of his death. Her expression twisted and distorted until she resembled Edvard Munch's painting "The Scream." She released a keening wail that would echo in my nightmares for months, hugged herself, leaned forward, and folded into the fetal position.

After a minute, she sat back up and gazed out of the window into her own personal Hell, softly mumbling, "No, no, no! Not possible. *Can't* be true."

Without warning, she jumped to her feet. "Where's Kyle? Ethan's brother. Is he okay?"

The last hint of color in her complexion drained away and her knees buckled. I caught her and eased her into the chair.

"Kyle's fine and will be with you soon."

But I knew for certain that his life would never again be the same.

She crossed herself and whispered a litany of Hail Marys, entreating the Mother of God for mercy. But there would be no mercy for her that day.

No words could ease that kind of pain, and all the platitudes and condolences I had been taught rang hollow, so I said nothing more and let her pray. When she finished, her cheeks were lined with makeup-streaked tears. I handed her a box of tissues, asked if she wanted to call anyone for support, and offered my cellphone.

She shook her head and pulled a mobile phone from her purse. "But … my husband's out of town. Dear Lord! How can I tell him?"

When I didn't answer, she dialed St. Anthony of Padua Church and asked her parish priest to come.

I cleared my throat and said, "You should know that Ethan did receive Last Rites." I had intended this to afford her some comfort, yet the finality of the phrase crumbled her dam of denial and she again burst into tears.

Reverting to my seminary training, I offered what solace I could, feeling completely useless as a doctor, helpless as a priest, and emotionally drained. I should have stayed with her, tried to comfort her in that stifling, clinically-sterile room. Instead, I bolted the instant the hospital grief counselor arrived and wandered to the Urgent Care nursing station as Sheriff Tremont Macon arrived.

He wore an old sweatshirt and jeans instead of his uniform, indicating he had been called in to work from home on his day off. His demeanor, however, was all business.

He and I had been close friends since junior high. I gave him a weak smile. He volleyed with a scowl. I walked over.

"Thanks for hustling here, Tree. Did you speak with the dead child's brother? He told me he bought the pills from some guy named Razor at the school. Please tell me you'll arrest the S.O.B. who kills kids for money and that he'll be going to prison *forever and ever, amen.*"

"Got a deputy with the brother now." He stared at me with dark eyes as cold as black granite. "But it's *you* I want to talk with. Now. In private."

We were standing near the nursing station, and the conversations around us abruptly ceased. Nurse Ochs set down her chart and looked over.

I led Tree into a vacant exam room. "What's up?"

He closed the door. "You know a guy named James Sole?"

"No. Why?"

"He's been a low-life drug dealer in the county since we were kids, mostly selling weed." Tree crossed his massive arms over his chest, his broad shoulders stretching his white Lorain County Sheriff's Department sweatshirt taut. He frowned. With his shaved head, he resembled a disgruntled African-American version of Mr. Clean. "We found Sole's body in a dumpster with a bullet in his brain, execution style ... and both hands chopped off and missing."

"What? Why do that? To prevent IDing him from his fingerprints?"

"Doubt it. That's pretty extreme." He shrugged. "More likely somebody used Jimmy to send a message."

"That's one heck of a message. What's it mean?"

"No clue. Maybe ... *We catch you with your fingers in the till, you lose them.* Beats the hell out of me. Wish I knew."

He went silent.

My sore hip was throbbing and I leaned against the exam table. "Okay, Tree. So?"

"So we identified him from his dental records. It's definitely Jimmy Sole. Here's his most recent mugshot." He handed me a photo. "You sure you don't know this guy, never saw him?"

"I meet a lot of people here and at the church, but I don't recognize him."

"Well, ol' Jimmy knew you, Jake. We found a pile of cash and a list of names hidden in his apartment. You're number two on his list." He gave me a penetrating glare that nearly drew blood, then stepped into my personal space. "Don't BS me. Tell me what you know about this clown."

"Honest, Tree. I never met him and have no idea what you're talking about." I didn't like the way my friend was staring at me, and my mouth went dry. I walked to the sink, filled a paper cup with water, and took a sip. "This makes no sense. Why would he have *my* name? You don't suspect me of hanging around with drug dealers, do you? I've only been back in town six months, and I sure as heck wasn't selling grass in the seminary."

"Where were you Saturday night between five and midnight?"

"Offering Vigil Mass at Sacred Heart Church. I was filling in for the pastor who wasn't feeling well. Afterward, my housekeeper, Colleen, had dinner with my nephew and me. Ask her. When she left, I put R.J. to bed, watched Ohio State beat the Wolverines, and went to sleep."

"What was the score?"

"Really? The score?" I downed the last of the water, crushed the paper cup, and hurled it into the trash. "Come on, buddy, give me a break!"

"The score, Jake."

"Thirty to twenty seven. The Buckeyes won it with a last minute field goal. What the hell, Tree. You can't suspect me. You *know* me! Are you kidding?"

"I never found mutilated bodies anything to joke about. And you're damn right I know you—warts and all. I *also know* about your past fondness for drugs. Not many folks ever really get their shit totally together."

"It took a lifetime, damn it, but I got *mine* together!" I was angry and had raised my voice. I dialed it down a notch. "You want the truth? Here it is. There must be thousands of people in the country with my name, and you're eyeballing the wrong one, Tremont."

The only people who called him *Tremont* were his wife, complete strangers, and me when I was pissed off.

"Sorry if I came on strong. Been up all night with this shit. I'm only doing my job and had to ask. Better I question you than have one of my troops grill you. I just wish I knew how your name got on Jimmy Sole's list."

Tree leaned against the wall and cleared his throat. "Lemme give you a glimpse into my world. For three years, drugs have been pouring into Ohio. Crank, crack, and weed, but also prescription drugs." Tree retreated briefly into his thoughts. "We got more overdoses in this county from prescription drugs than from heroin or cocaine. More deaths from drugs than from homicides. Grandmas sell their prescriptions to supplement their social security. Kids swipe pills from medicine cabinets and pass them out at school like candy. And the Dark Net and Black Sites online sell drugs and every illegal service you can think of, and a few you can't even imagine. Christ, we're completely out-numbered and under-manned!"

Tree pushed off the wall. "Before you came back to town, we had a doctor who ran a pill-mill east of Oberlin. He actually had a valet, who doubled as an armed guard. The guy even had one of those take-a-number machines in his waiting room. Folks would pay him $300 per visit, cash of course, and walk out twenty minutes later with their ticket to ride—Valium, narcotic pain-killers, and Xanax mostly. Hell, it didn't take Sherlock Holmes to figure out what was going on. His office looked like a damn amusement park, with folks lined up outside his door waiting to get onboard for their next trip on the Topsy-Turvy Reality Coaster."

"That's rather brazen. I can't imagine why any physician would be stupid enough to risk losing his license and going to jail. It's not as if doctors can't make a decent living."

"Decent yes, but that's not enough for some folks. Greed's a powerful motivator, Jake. When the doc picked up our scent, he changed tactics. He began hiring homeless guys, bankrolling them, and sending them to fill the prescriptions at local Mom-and-Pop pharmacies—along with a couple thugs to insure that no one bolted with his money. When they returned to his office with the pills, he would pay them in cash or with their drug-of-choice."

Tree released a derisive snort.

"Everyone was happy, except those of us who had to clean up the collateral damage. ODs, DUIs, brawls, knifings. Stoned kids, robberies, and drive-bys. Problem was, shutting the dirty doc down didn't even slow the influx of pills.

"At first we suspected other doctors around here were dealing, hiding behind patient privacy laws, but the sheer quantity of drugs made it obvious we were dealing with a well-organized street gang—and I'm not talkin' the Little Rascals here. I'd give my left nut to blow up *that* operation."

For a moment, Tree was deep in his nightmare. Finally he said, "Okay, okay. Let's drop it. I'll check out your alibi and we'll be all good. We still on for Monday Night Football at your place tonight? I'll bring pizza."

Although I'd completely lost my appetite, I said, "Sure buddy. See you at six."

CHAPTER THREE

Monday, December 2, 2002, 11:00 a.m.

Between watching a child die under my hands and my best friend indicating that I was somehow involved in an on-going drug ring investigation, I was frustrated, dazed, and wanted nothing more than to go home.

Walking toward the parking garage, there was little that could have brought a smile to my lips, though seeing our hospital administrator, Harvey Winer, came close. Maybe it was the lack of sleep from my twenty-four hour on-call shift, but the sight of him pacing in the hallway reminded me of Santa Claus on guard duty—well, the same physique, beard, and cherry complexion. Winer, however, was Jewish and wore a yarmulke and tailored business suit. He brightened when he saw me and waved me over.

"Ah, Jake. Excellent. I was afraid you'd forgotten about us."

Overcome by Ethan's death and physical exhaustion, I *had* forgotten. A meeting was the last place on earth I wanted to be. Hospital committees were as interesting as watching C-Span and about as productive, and I doubted that this one would be any different. My only desire was to drive home, play with my nephew for a few hours, and take an afternoon nap when he did.

Winer began shepherding me into the conference room. I knew it would probably be easier to convince Santa to cancel Christmas than to talk my way out of the meeting. Nevertheless, I gave it a try.

"Come on, Harvey. Don't saddle me with this. I promised my sister on her deathbed that I'd care for her son, and I'm struggling to rebuild the boy's shattered world. I don't have time or energy for committee meetings. Besides, I've been working all night and can barely keep my eyelids up. Please let me go home to my nephew."

"I realize you've been through hell since you got back to town, and I'm very sorry about your sister's death. But it has been months and it's time you got involved, Jake. Our Medical Ethics Committee *needs* a physician with your unique background."

There was no fight left in me, and I raised my hands in surrender. "Fine, you win."

We entered the meeting room, and all heads turned toward us except one. Emily sat at the far end of a long conference table. Sunglasses masked her eyes, and her fingers danced across a page of braille. She wore a long-sleeved blouse in a rich cabernet sauvignon color, which nicely contrasted the white coats and gray pinstriped suits sitting around the table. A tall, elegant Asian woman took the seat between Emily and a well-dressed balding man.

Dr. Marcus Taylor, the committee chairman, greeted us. "Glad you're here. We were about to begin." He was a large man with a soft, pear-shaped body. His white hair matched his pale skin. He gestured toward me. "Everyone, allow me to introduce our newest member, Dr. Jacob Austin."

Emily raised her head and flashed a megawatt grin that warmed the room.

Taylor continued. "Jake's an internist and has been a real asset in the short time he's been at St. Joe's. You may remember my patient with tick paralysis. He made the diagnosis and saved that girl's life. Jake was a physician for many years before entering a seminary and becoming a Catholic priest." A few eyebrows around the table lost their gravitational pull and drifted up. "He brings a new dimension to our committee. Emily Beale is our patient advocate, and Jake adds the spiritual perspective."

I glanced around the room and nodded a greeting.

"Oh, for Christ-sake! Really? A priest?" A burly man in his early thirties with large hands and hairy knuckles spit out the word "priest" as if he had bitten into something rotten. His old-fashioned crew cut was the color of motor oil, and his pencil-thin mustache was trimmed with precision. He was built like a linebacker and probably could have bench-pressed the rotund Dr. Taylor. His name tag read, G. GLADE MD, GENERAL SURGERY.

His beeper chirped. He checked the number, silenced it, and snapped it back onto his blue surgical scrubs. "Why add a priest to the committee? This is a hospital. Our decisions are medical, not religious." His voice was surprisingly high-pitched for a muscular, athletic-looking man.

Glade eyed me, awaiting my response, but I was not going to take the bait. My day wasn't finished and fatigue had already draped a heavy arm over my shoulder. If Glade somehow managed to get me kicked off of the committee, I would have been eternally grateful. I remained silent.

Taylor's face flushed. "Really, Dr. Glade. Having another principled member can only *strengthen* our Ethics Committee." His tone invited no debate. He opened a manila folder and passed the agenda around.

We first discussed an elderly woman with multiple metastatic tumors in her brain. All appropriate diagnostic and therapeutic steps had been taken, and we agreed that further aggressive measures were futile and it was time for Hospice to assume end of life care.

"Let's move on." Dr. Taylor checked his agenda. "Next up is drug abuse. Harvey?"

Our hospital administrator's usually cheerful expression abruptly became somber. He opened his suit coat and loosened his tie.

"Illegal prescription drugs are flooding the county," Winer said. "The DEA suspects a local physician has opened a pill-mill. They're asking us to call in any suspicious behavior."

"They want us to *spy* on our colleagues? That's pretty dicey," Taylor responded. "Most of us prescribe Schedule Two drugs, and no one wants to be investigated for doing their job. The Joint Commission on Accreditation recently declared *pain* to be the fifth vital sign, and patient advocacy groups are pushing us to treat it vigorously!" He furrowed his brow. "It's a damn Catch-22. We're criticized if we under-treat pain, and risk sanctions if we treat it aggressively."

Pain management was a significant part of my practice, and I knew I would be on the DEA's radar, if not in their crosshairs. I cleared my throat, but Glade jumped in first.

"Listen, I'm not interested in being my brother's keeper." He pointed at me. "That's the padre's job. And I don't want to play Big Brother." Glade's voice grew louder and higher in pitch as he turned toward Taylor. "On the other hand, I've seen too damn many lives snuffed out by uppers and downers, and if I ever find out who's dumping those pills on the street, I'll personally put his ass out of business. Hell, I think oxycodone and fentanyl cause more harm than good and should be banned."

The morning's Code Blue had left my emotions erratic, and the memory of Ethan's death-mask stare ignited my rage. Heat flared in my cheeks. Glade was right. I, too, would be damned if I'd allow some pill-pusher to endanger lives. I fought to regain my composure.

"You're throwing the baby out with the bath water, Glade," Taylor retorted. "Some patients require powerful pain killers. Used as directed, the drug companies insist they're perfectly safe." He took a sip of water. "And why's DEA picking on us? Physicians aren't the only problem! Dentists prescribe lots of narcotics, and pharmacies have no incentive to be vigilant. Prescription pads get stolen and signatures forged. There are lots of weak links in the chain."

When no one responded, Taylor raised his voice. "Patients with chronic diseases develop tolerance to pain meds and demand higher and higher doses for relief. What should I do? Throw them out? They'll simply hop from one office to another."

Harvey Winer tried to interject, but Taylor was on a roll and continued.

"Without a state reporting system, how can I possibly know that one of you already prescribed a narcotic to my patient earlier the same morning? And what should I do if I catch a patient altering prescriptions or doctor-shopping? If I dismiss them from my practice, they'll find another doctor or just fill up the ERs. Do I report them to the police? If word gets out that they're arresting my patients, who in their right mind would come to my office?"

Glade slammed his fist on the table. "That's your concern, losing business? Why're you so defensive, Taylor? Hell, there's always a line of patients at your office door. Maybe there's a *reason* you don't want the cops involved. What's to discuss? It's a felony, so call the police! End of story."

"What are you implying, Glade? How *dare* you suggest that I—"

Winer waved his arms to interrupt Taylor. "Please, gentleman. I wanted all of you to understand that we're part of a major investigation. Keep your eyes open. Use your judgment. I'll send out a staff memo."

"Fine, fine. Moving along." Taylor ran a plump finger down the agenda. "I have to give you some follow-up. Despite the mixed reaction at our last Ethics Committee meeting, the board of directors has decided to establish a Department of Alternative Medicine and place Dr. Guo in charge."

Glade threw his pen on the conference table. "You gotta be kidding! A Department of Leeches, Spiders, and Voodoo?" He groaned. "It's bad enough that the Cleveland Clinic's gnawing at our borders. This'll destroy our hospital's credibility."

It appeared that Dr. Glade woke up in the morning pissed off. I leaned back in my chair, hoping his operating room skills exceeded his social ones.

Every village has an idiot, and ours was not done raving. Glade leaned forward and glowered at the Asian woman seated next to Emily.

"Listen Guo, you can perform all the damn hocus-pocus you want in your private office, but keep your traveling medicine show out of the hospital. This is the twenty-first century, not the twelfth."

"That's enough, Dr. Glade," Taylor interrupted. "We're all painfully aware of your opinion." He gestured to Harvey Winer. "The administration refuses to leave market share on the table by not offering alternative medical options."

Dr. Guo stood slowly. Her thin frame was wrapped in an ornate silk dress, a celebration of violet and maroon flowers that accentuated her regal bearing. She swept a hand around the conference room.

"We are part of the same community. I wish us to be like the paper lanterns strung around the village square where I was born—all lighting the darkness together. We have much to learn from each other." She faced

Glade. "Maybe it is *you* who should join the twenty-first century. Herbs and acupuncture have healed for generations. And as I already told you, MDT would benefit Mr. Meacham."

"That's total bullshit," Glade shouted, "and exactly what I'm talking about."

"Whoa," Taylor said, holding up his hand. "What's MDT?"

Glade banged his fist on the table. "Maggot Debridement Therapy. She wants me to put god-damn *maggots* on my patient's leg wound! Not a chance in hell."

"It is simple biology." Guo returned to her seat. "Debridement is what *you* do with a scalpel to make antibiotics more effective. Maggots eat the small amount of dead tissue you surgeons leave behind. MDT is better than gangrene, better than amputation."

Glade threw up his arms. "Can you imagine the publicity? Front page photos of the Cleveland Clinic's state-of-the-art MRI machine next to a picture of Dr. Guo proudly displaying St. Joe's new bag of maggots."

Clearly enamored with his own wit, Glade conjured up a malicious smirk. With his soprano voice and his muscular physique, I wondered if he had a bodybuilder's fondness for anabolic steroids. Were his volatile emotions indicative of so-called "roid rage?" Maybe. Or maybe he was simply a jerk. The guy, however, was half pit bull, half Doberman, and I wanted no part of this dog fight.

The balding man seated across the table wearing a pricy wool suit, power tie the color of arterial blood, and a matching pocket square looked up from his yellow legal pad.

"Cease and desist, Glade! Dr. Guo is a staff member here and will be treated as such, or your tenure on the committee and at this institution will be short-lived."

Harvey Winer leaned over and whispered in my ear, "That's Rudy VonKamp, Esquire—of Blake, VonKamp, and Martin. He's the hospital's legal counsel, a board member, financial donor, and all-around majordomo. Kissing his ring is optional."

Taylor clanged a pen on his water glass hard enough to rattle the ice cubes, ending round one. "It's nearly lunchtime. Let's set the joys of squirmy things aside for now."

"May I add one final thing, Dr. Taylor?" Emily asked as she stood and removed her sunglasses.

Since our time together in high school, she had maintained her youthful figure. Her auburn hair was now shorter and it caressed the curve of her face. A few silver strands managed to reach the surface, catch the light, and blaze like electrified wires. To avoid the impending flood of memories, I let my eyes drift to the snow flurries outside that whispered against the windowpane.

Emily continued, her velvet voice sounding like a prayer. "Though I'm not a physician, as the hospital's Patient Advocate it's clear to me that people need alternatives when their treatment plan fails or is unacceptable to them. Otherwise, they do desperate things—such as substance abuse or suicide."

"Great! Now we've heard from the Far East *and* the uninformed public." Glade gestured from Guo to Emily, drumming his fingers on the table in exasperation. "Those of us trained at the Mayo Clinic want hard science, not BS."

It sounded as if he had also completed postgraduate training in arrogance and cruelty.

Emily's lips formed a tiny "O," and her cheeks flushed as if she had been slapped. She sat without a word, her chin dropping to her chest.

I had bitten the bullet the entire meeting as I watched this man's mean-spirited belligerence, but his attack on Emily provoked me to fire off a few rounds.

"Maybe the Mayo Clinic should have taught you some manners, Dr. Glade."

Glade became as motionless as a department store mannequin, then sprang up like a switchblade. His hands were fisted, arms big as logs. I was already standing.

He edged closer as we exchanged glares. "And maybe you should have taken a vow of silence, Father!"

Taylor banged his pen on his glass so hard that water splashed onto his notes, ending round two. "Sit down, both of you. Dr. Austin, do you have anything *constructive* to add to this discussion?"

Glade flopped into his chair, swiveled in my direction, and fixed me with his bird-of-prey gaze. I conceded the staring contest to him and directed my comments toward the others.

"I saw some Eastern Medicine as a medic in the Army. My concern is that herbal products lack quality control and government oversight. Some contain unlisted ingredients or lead-based dyes. There are also lots of possible side effects and drug interactions. The spice turmeric, for example, contains a blood thinner, which may cause severe bleeding if taken with prescription anticoagulants. St. John's Wort can make birth control pills ineffective."

Glade rolled his eyes and chuckled. "FYI, Father, it's the horizontal mambo that causes babies. And I didn't think priests cared about birth control."

It had become clear that Glade was a one-hundred percent guaranteed, double-your-money-back flaming asshole. As I studied him, I could almost hear my father's country-spun wisdom: *Son, there's a lot more horse's asses in this world than there are horses.*

I opted for civility.

"What I *do care about* is neglected and abandoned children." My dad had deserted my mother and me when I was young, and my nephew's father had also walked out on him. "So yes, Dr. Glade, I'm concerned about any product that contributes to unwanted children, abortions, or contains harmful ingredients."

"You're wasting our time, gentlemen, and your diatribe has nothing to do with *ethics*." VonKamp removed the reading glasses perched on the tip of his nose and set them on his legal pad. "The hospital is a business, and the board of directors has already made its decision. Dr. Guo will chair the Department of Alternative Medicine. Period. End of discussion."

Silence followed. Although he had lost the battle, Glade clearly had enjoyed the melee. He leaned back and painted a self-satisfied smile on his inflated ego. I searched for a pin-sharp comment but came up empty.

Taylor checked his watch, eased his plump body up from the chair, and released a sigh that sounded more like a growl. "We'll continue this agenda at our next meeting. We're adjourned."

On my way to the door, I was wrestling with the idea of having lunch with Emily versus going home to see my nephew and taking a well-deserved nap, when Glade grabbed my arm. I turned and braced for a punch.

Instead, he lowered his voice and said, "Sorry I went off, Father. It's just that the stakes are high, and I get … passionate about things." He took a deep breath. "Be careful who you pick for your allies. I have my suspicions about the source of the pills flooding the streets." He gestured toward Taylor. "I haven't got proof yet, but a word to the wise—things aren't always as they seem."

He walked away, leaving me to ponder a child in Urgent Care dead from prescription drugs, the possibility of Taylor's involvement, and my overwhelming urge to run home and hug my nephew.

CHAPTER FOUR

Monday, December 2, 2002, 12:10 p.m.

I followed Dr. Glade out of the meeting. Emily was waiting near the conference room door. She smiled. "Ah, Sir Galahad. Good afternoon, Jake, and thanks."

Glade walked on. I stopped. "For what, Em?"

"Defending my honor, jousting with Glade, and knocking him off of his high horse. No one ever stands up to that abrasive egomaniac. Let me thank you by buying lunch. Do you have time?"

Emily was the complete package of beauty, brains, and wit. My feelings for her had not waned over the years, and our history together drew me to her like a magnetic force—no, more like she was gravity and I was a skydiver without a parachute, watching the ground rush up at me.

But spending time with a woman that I could never have was not only pointless, it was also downright painful. Was I deceiving Emily, the Church, or myself? It was the question I had been asking myself for the past five months, the question that had cost me many dark nights of the soul. The barbs of first love, however, dug deep. Maybe I had already failed my vocation and my vows the moment we reconnected and I did not walk away.

Emily placed a hand on my arm. "Jake? Hello. Lunch?"

The Old Testament warning sounded in my head: *The heart is deceitful above all things and beyond cure.*

Since returning to my hometown in Oberlin, Ohio in July, we had rebuilt a strong friendship. Having once been apart for decades, I now couldn't even imagine *not* having her in my life. I wondered if my heart was beyond cure.

Although I did not want to lie, I fumbled for an excuse to avoid lunch with her. A *prior engagement* sounded aloof and pretentious. I considered telling her that I had to see a patient and couldn't spare the time. I was about to say, *Sorry, wish I could*, but instead said, "Sure, lunch sounds nice."

I had always found it hard to say no to her.

She nodded, extended her red and white cane, and we walked down the hall, her lips moving silently as she reeled off step counts. Away from the hospital, Emily would take my arm and let me guide her. On her own turf, she did not require or want my help. Even before she lost her sight, she had been fiercely independent.

As she turned a corner and sped up, I fell behind. We are all spiritual beings trapped in physical bodies, but sometimes I wondered if all men were this easily hypnotized by the sashay of a beautiful woman, or if I had gotten in line twice the day God dispensed desire.

I picked up my pace, the blind leading the bewildered. I caught up with her near the hospital snack shop, operated by The Society for the Blind and staffed by Emily and her father.

She opened the door and said, "Dad, I'm having lunch with Jake. Do you want anything?"

Her father was behind the counter. He removed his sunglasses. Large bags drooped below his rheumy eyes. "Nope, I'm good. Just relieve me at suppertime."

We said goodbye and as we headed to the cafeteria, I reflected on the hurdles that they faced. She and her father were a study in resilience, proof of the strength of the human spirit. He had been an accountant; she, a journalist at the local newspaper. After their hereditary loss of vision as adults, they had leaned on each other and forged new lives at the hospital. They ran the snack shop and received room and board in exchange for serving as resident advisors to the young interns who lived in the hospital dormitory. Not that Emily and her father hid from life. Far from it. Instead of giving up, they both shook the Tree of Life and gobbled up its fallen fruit. The hospital simply provided them a safe, compact environment.

I entered the cafeteria with my usual trepidation about institutional meals. The entrée du jour was pot roast, which on good days was somewhat edible.

As I glanced around the room in search of an available table, Emily and I drew our usual quota of stares. Although I was not wearing my collar, most of the staff knew who I was. Sightings of the priest and the blind woman together were frequent at St. Joe's—and the fodder for countless unfounded rumors. For many folks, delicious gossip was too difficult *not to share* throughout the hospital—whether it was true or not was irrelevant.

Several of the Urgent Care staff sitting at a nearby table looked at us. Nurse Ochs raised an eyebrow. One of the receptionists who had been in high school with us began whispering, and I wondered how much of our history she actually knew. Not much, I hoped.

Emily and I had been close friends since fourth grade. Our relationship was complicated. We had briefly been lovers in school, long before I joined the Army and entered the priesthood. But we'd never made it to our senior prom because by then, there was no *us*. I cast off the memory.

We selected our food and I carried both trays to a table by the window. Snowflakes sparkled like sequins outside as they fluttered to earth. The bitter cold front that had assaulted Ohio in early November had banished autumn, and I wondered if we would ever see green grass again.

"Is Everett any better?" I asked as we sat down.

Although I did not care for her ex-husband, for reasons I would never understand, she still did. He had been the victim of a shooting, and I asked the question only because I *did* care about Emily.

Since my return to town, we had rebuilt our friendship. During our time apart, we had both endured our own private versions of Hell. Emily had progressively lost her vision and her marriage, and I had physically survived a bloody overseas war, but still carried invisible scars from what I'd seen and done there.

Now, we tried to support each other in every way possible. I was her chauffeur and her eyes when she had to leave the friendly confines of the hospital, and she accepted my strange and stressful new lifestyle, often babysitting for my nephew when his usual sitter, Colleen, was not available. We had even teamed up recently to solve the mystery of a bleeding statue at a church south of Cleveland. More than a friend, she was my sounding board and sometimes my conscience.

"Everett's improving slowly but is weak and confused. He needs a walker to get around, and I doubt that he'll ever fully recover."

Emily drifted into a reverie.

"You okay, Em? The doctors here are doing all they can for him."

"It's not that. I was just thinking about the illusion of control that we all cling to ... the way life throws us curveballs, like with Everett, your sister's death, and you having to care for your nephew." She was quiet for a few seconds before adding, "And how accidentally our fate is made."

"That sums up most peoples' lives in one short sentence. You're getting downright profound, Em."

"Philip Roth, not me. Though definitely profound." Emily's smile returned. "How's RJ doing?"

"As well as can be expected. The poor kid barely knew me before my sister died."

Emily set down her soup spoon. "Honest to God, Jake, I don't know how you do it—two grueling jobs *and* raising a child?"

For centuries, nuns had taught school or nursed the sick, priests had worked as teachers or presided over colleges, serving two masters yet bowing to only one. Over the last few years, I had learned to live in two worlds, juggling medicine and the priesthood. Life was hectic but manageable.

My half-sister's leukemia changed everything. From her deathbed, she had begged me to care for her son. I had sworn to her that I would, a promise I fully intended to keep. My father had deserted me as a child, and I refused to abandon my four-year-old nephew or allow him to be warehoused in the foster care system or an orphanage. But that decision had launched a third ball into the air for me—and I was not sure I could juggle them all. I had become a Jake-of-all-trades, and it seemed a master of none. The only two peaceful times in my once serene life were when I was in the shower and during Mass. No, the truth was that I was floundering. No, I was drowning.

After my sister's death, I began to rebuild my life and resumed my duties at the hospital. The Church allowed me to keep some of my medical income so that I could provide for my nephew. Bishop Lucci wanted me to place the boy up for adoption, but instead I had moved from the rectory into an apartment and hired Colleen Brady, the rectory housekeeper, to be his nanny—and I was now in the diocesan doghouse.

My concerns must have bled through because Emily said, "What else could you do, Jake? You couldn't turn your back on your sister or abandon RJ."

In fact, RJ was my only real family. That didn't matter to Bishop Lucci when I told him I had chosen to be my nephew's guardian and hoped to adopt him. The Church had permitted adoptions by priests on very rare occasions, but not on Lucci's watch—and he was not happy. He had placed me on a Spiritual Retreat, a leave of absence from my parish duties, hoping I would reconsider. A retreat is usually an opportunity to strengthen one's faith through prayer and meditation. In my case, it was the ecclesiastical version of sending me for a "time-out" in the corner to reflect on my ... waywardness.

"The bishop thinks priests aren't capable of parenting, and evidently most people agree."

"Sometimes, Jake, I no longer recognize the world I live in." She cocked her head and a strand of hair drifted across her forehead. "Clearly, gay and single folks can be good parents. Somehow a priest can't be? What utter drivel!"

As if on cue, the strains of "Onward, Christian Soldiers" floated from my cellphone, the ringtone I had chosen for Bishop Lucci. He was my Commander-In-Chief, and I was his foot soldier. In my world, only the archangels and the Pope outranked him.

Emily listened, added two plus two, and said, "His Excellency, I presume?"

Not much got past Em.

I let the call go to voicemail.

"Yup. I swear the good Bishop can read my mind."

"What were you thinking?"

I looked across the table at the face that was etched in my mind. Having been a priest for a very short time, I was still wet behind the ears with the oil of ordination, trying to find my way on a lonely spiritual journey through a secular world. My commitment to the Lord and His ministry was firm, but I was shaken by the feelings I had for her.

I had expressed my concerns to the bishop and had sought his guidance, hence *the other reason* for my leave of absence. Lucci had offered me time to sort out my volcanic life—which had erupted when I'd been assigned to town and was reunited with Emily. He had also made it clear that my clock was running out of ticks.

Dr. Glade strode into the cafeteria, trailed by two surgical interns. He was pontificating loudly. His minions scampered after him, hoping to catch any pearls of wisdom their mentor might bestow.

A frigid gust of wind rattled the window by our table, and Glade noticed Emily and me sitting together. He gave me a thumbs up and marched into the private doctors' lounge.

As a young man, I had been confident that I knew all the answers. Now, I wasn't even sure I knew the right questions. There was a time when I could finish Emily's sentences, but we were no longer the same people we had been when we'd gone to school together. We had spent many hours over the past few months exploring our new relationship. Our decades apart and the priesthood, however, had formed a deep crevasse between us—and something unspoken, a mutual distrust, lurked in its depths. We had let each other down in the past and were both afraid of our rekindled feelings. That lack of trust intermittently rose up like the living dead and gnawed at us.

I had apologized for my past sins; she had not. She'd been my best friend and the love of my life. As an eighteen year old, alone and terrified in the middle of a war, I had written to her every chance I got. After a couple letters, she had stopped writing back. No explanation, no apology. Total silence. Next thing I heard, she was engaged. Even two decades later, the deep wound of her abandonment continued to ache.

I longed to ask her why she had stopped writing. The question pulsed on the back of my tongue. I swallowed it before it could escape my lips. How would hearing her answer or excuses help now? Besides, I could barely juggle the three balls I had in the air, without throwing Emily into the mix by fanning the embers of our youth.

"Jake? Knock, knock. Anybody home?"

My forbidden fruit smiled at me from across the table.

"You zoned out again." She waved a hand in front of me. "What's going on with you today? You never answered my question. What were you thinking when the bishop called?"

Rather than lie, I reshaped the conversation.

"I had to tell a mother that her nine-year-old son died of a drug overdose. It's almost as if the bishop has 'rule book radar' and can tell I broke one."

"What rule?"

"I performed an Anointing of the Sick—what most folks call Last Rites. It's intended for the living; the boy was already dead. That's not permitted." I released a deep sigh. "The child's family is Catholic. I'd failed them as a doctor and wanted to offer the mother some small comfort as a priest."

"Heck, Jake, doctors have been wrong about pronouncing death before. And who can say *when* a soul leaves the body? It was worth a try. What harm could it do?"

"That was my rationale, but I'm sure the bishop wouldn't approve."

"Then don't tell him, or deny it. Sometimes there is *righteousness* in a good lie."

Emily should have been a cardiac surgeon, because she had the God-given ability to *cut to the heart* of any problem.

I paused to chew a piece of shoe leather disguised as pot roast. "So Em, how's your poetry therapy class going?"

A look of excitement spread across her face. "Terrific! The music and art therapists are supportive, and the Psych Department understands that poetry can be healing for some patients and families. They've asked me to add another session on Wednesdays."

"Good for you! I've always loved your poetry." I took a forkful of mashed potatoes, which tasted like the box they had come from. "Are the Ethics Committee meetings always that much fun?"

"Actually, the members usually aren't as pleasant."

"Glade's a real charmer. How the heck did he get on the *Ethics* Committee?"

"No other staff member wanted the assignment."

"The guy's got a god-complex. Guess he thinks his medical degree stands for M.Diety."

"He has more of a Zeus-complex, Jake, flinging thunderbolts from on high at us mere mortals."

"It's a pity he can't surgically remove his own ego." A shaft of sunlight broke through the cloud cover, transforming her auburn hair into quivering gold. "Glade cornered me after our meeting, Em, and said that things at St. Joe's aren't what they appear. I think he meant Taylor. Any clue what that's about?"

"Hmm, I haven't the foggiest." She removed her sunglasses and flashed a self-deprecating grin. "Even with my eyes wide open, I miss a lot."

"Maybe Glade knows something that could damage Dr. Taylor."

"I doubt it." She switched to a low, raspy voice. "Glade's a nuclear warhead. If he had evidence against Taylor, he would have already launched a first strike. That was probably a reconnaissance mission."

Emily had been in all the school plays, and I loved it when she switched personas. Her Scarlet O'Hara impersonation always made me chuckle. This staff sergeant parody, however, was a new twist.

"What's with the military-speak, Em?"

"What's the matter, Private? You don't recognize a metaphor when you hear one?" She smirked, and the velvet returned to her voice. "Hey, I'm multilingual, and even fluent in medical jargondygook." She took a sip of tea. "I hear Dr. Taylor's a very wealthy man. Big car, bigger boat, semi-retired. Maybe Glade's jealous."

I pushed my plate aside, splashed cream in my coffee, and considered that. We sat for a while in a comfortable silence as I watched the flurries outside the window become a blizzard with all the makings of a fluffy version of the Great Flood—only this time, Noah would have to build a giant snowmobile.

"Ever considered getting a Seeing Eye guide dog, Em?"

"I decided against it." Mischief danced in her blue eyes. "I don't need one, now that you're back in town."

She laughed, a sound I had always loved. Our impossible relationship, however, was a childish dream, too painful for both of us. I had begun to accept that we had both moved on. Time to tell her. I hoped to remain friends but wasn't even sure if that would be possible.

Her cell rang, and she said, "Sorry. I should take this."

I nodded and watched the blizzard bury the statue of Saint Francis in the courtyard. Icicles hung from his eyes like frozen tears. A sparrow landed on his head.

"Hi Todd. Thanks for last weekend. That was fun."

Saint Francis no longer held my interest. I refocused on Emily.

"Oh, I wish I could, Todd. Another time, okay? Talk with you soon. Bye."

Apparently Emily had come to the same conclusion about our relationship and was not wasting any time before moving on—and with good reason. *I was the one* who was unavailable.

Emily's *friend* Todd worked in the radiology department. I had met him. He was young, educated, and physically fit with a long blond mane—and their relationship bothered the hell out of me.

Emily finished her tea and leaned back. "How's the good Sheriff? That's a big step up from small town cop. Tree and his family must be very proud."

She steepled her fingers and said, "Of course, shooting a serial killer and saving your helpless behind didn't hurt his landslide election."

"Real nice, Em." Like most humor, her comment was funny because it was based in truth. "Tree's coming to my place tonight for pizza and Monday Night Football. Want to join us?"

I hoped she would come, both because I enjoyed spending time with her and because her presence might prevent Tree from interrogating me further about my connection to the dead drug dealer found in the dumpster.

"Football? That's torture for me. Watching you two play in school was bad enough. Besides, I'm working at the snack shop. Please give Tree and RJ my love."

"Will do." I tried to mask the disappointment in my voice. "I worked last night, so I'm going home."

A filigree of frost decorated the cafeteria window next to us, giving it a festive, holiday appearance. The notion of playtime with RJ drained away my fatigue, and I decided that this was a perfect day to bundle up my pint-sized cherub and teach him the joy of making snow angels. Maybe I would buy a sled on the way home.

"See you tomorrow, Em."

"Let's do lunch again." She reached across the table, found my hand, and patted it. "I hear the roads are treacherous, Jake. Drive safely."

CHAPTER FIVE

Monday, December 2, 2002, 5:00 p.m.

An entire battalion of soldiers advanced on my squad, weapons raised. Bazookas, machine guns, flame throwers. Explosions echoed. Two tanks thundered toward us. We were outnumbered, outgunned, and didn't have a chance, but I was not going down without a fight. What fun would that be?

My brave band of clothespins leaped from the protection of my recliner and opened fire. The outcome was inevitable. Within minutes, my last few troops surrendered to General RJ. Amazingly, his green plastic army had suffered no casualties.

My nephew's face filled with delight under his helmet of red hair. I struggled to maintain the proper military decorum as my skinny, human pogo stick bounced around the room.

"I win! I win! Let's play again."

He bounded over and tugged at my pant leg, and I was reminded of a line from a poem Emily once read to me. To a kid, the world is *mud-luscious* and *puddle-wonderful*. My life had started out that way until my father discarded my mother and me, transforming my childhood into a puddle of muck. Raising my four-year-old nephew, however, had helped me to reclaim some of that wide-eyed awe—but I was also the adult.

"That's enough for now, RJ." I headed into the kitchen. "Clean up your toys, while I make dinner."

"Aw, Daddy. Please?"

I stopped and spun around, my heart racing.

Daddy? In all the weeks since my sister's death, my nephew had never called me Daddy. Hundreds had called me Father. No one had ever called me Daddy.

I felt a warm rush inside. What was that strange feeling? Kinship, connection, fondness, love? God knew that my sense of responsibility had already blossomed into a fierce devotion to RJ. Was what I felt *parental* love? Or was this merely my deep desire to reclaim a family, to share a bond stronger than that of co-worker or confessor? And was his use of the word *Daddy* a simple expression of complex emotions, or the desperate need of a motherless boy, or a child's way of accepting the fate he had been handed?

After leukemia took my sister, RJ and I were left with gaping holes in both of our hearts. His biological father was a married man who did not want his *tawdry affair* to ruin his life. He had gladly signed away his legal rights to his son, and I had become RJ's guardian.

Daddy. The word somehow diminished my dead sister's memory and spotlighted my inadequacies. The warm glow inside me quickly cooled. I was in way over my head and prayed that my sister would have approved of RJ's new home and my feeble attempt to be her surrogate.

"Please, Daddy, please! Just one more game."

Hopeful silver-blue eyes peered up from under his curly red mane. RJ was a miniature version of his mother. My iron will softened. The boy had my number and knew it. I drew a breath and gathered my jumbled emotions.

"Sorry, sport, dinner first. Uncle Tree's coming. If you eat all your food, maybe we can play again later."

And that's exactly what happened. I made a salad and Tree brought pepperoni pizza. After we had feasted in true bachelor style, RJ's plastic juggernaut army humbled our combined clothespin forces, driving us from the living room into his bedroom. "Colonel" Tremont Macon rose to his full six-feet, six-inch height, surrendered his imaginary sword with a flourish, and said goodnight.

I dressed the little general in pajamas decorated with yellow Big Birds and blue Cookie Monsters, certain that wealth and riches came in colors other than green and gold. I tousled his hair and tucked him into bed.

RJ suddenly rolled away and seemed to shrivel. "I want my mommy," he whimpered softly. His tiny chest heaved and he turned back toward me, his pained expression melting me like candle wax. Huge tears rolled down his cheeks. He flung his arms around my neck. "It's not fair! I miss Mommy!"

When I tried to speak, I choked up. In the three months since her death, my nephew and I had both been wandering through a thick fog of sorrow and uncertainty. She would always be his mother and my sister, but there was no name for what I had become. Was I still a brother? An uncle? RJ's custodian? I had no idea. Finally I managed, "You're right, RJ. It's not fair, and I miss her too."

I had tried to explain the concept of Heaven and angels to him in the past with no success, so I searched for words of comfort, but found none. His sobs sliced into me.

"It's okay to be sad and miss your mommy, and to talk to me about her. I loved her too, RJ, and always will." I kissed the top of his head and let the hug linger. "Let's read a story before bed. What do you say?"

He let go of me and nodded.

"Which one?"

He wiped tears on his pajama sleeve, sniffled, and pointed to *One Fish, Two Fish, Red Fish, Blue Fish*. Dr. Seuss was the other doctor in his life.

I began the hypnotic, rhythmic rhyme and RJ snuggled against me. By the fifth page, he was asleep.

I kissed him again, whispered a short prayer, and watched his quiet breathing—but in my mind, I saw the motionless chest and vacant chocolate-brown eyes of the child who had died under my care. He had not been much older than RJ. Dr. Glade's fury about illegal prescription drugs flooding the county, and his suggestion that Dr. Taylor was involved, brought my morning crashing back down on me.

One pill, two pills, red pill, blue pill.
One kid, two kids, live kids, dead kids.

CHAPTER SIX

Monday, December 2, 2002, 8:30 p.m.

I shook the image of dead children from my head, closed RJ's bedroom door, and walked into the kitchen, where Tree stood with a beer in his hand. He looked almost as tired as I felt.

As I grabbed plates from the table and loaded the dishwasher, he said, "We should talk more about Jimmy Sole, the dead drug dealer."

"No, we shouldn't. I already told you, I don't know him, don't smoke weed anymore, and I haven't got a clue why he'd have my name. My house, Sheriff, and my rules. Knock it off."

"Fine. In that case, I'm punching out for the day." He downed what was left of his beer and set the bottle on the kitchen table. "What's with your football jersey? Sixteen wasn't your number in school, and who the hell is this 'John' guy?"

I had changed into comfortable clothes after work.

"That's the gospel in a nutshell, Tree. John 3:16. 'For God so loved the world, that he gave his only begotten Son.' Don't they teach you Baptists anything?" I grabbed two beers from the refrigerator and handed him one. "Fear not, oh heathen, I come bearing gifts of enlightenment and adult beverages."

"What a relief!" Tree took a swig and unleashed a smile. "When you came back to town as a priest, I was afraid you'd given up all your vices."

"Don't let it get around, okay? The bishop might think it's bad for business."

He raised his bottle to the light and inspected it. "Ah, my favorite flavor—Guinness. A powerful dark brew for a powerful dark man."

We clinked bottles.

Between my all-nighter on-call at the hospital, the morning's dustup with Dr. Glade, and my continued state of limbo with Emily, I felt as if one beer could easily lead to a binge. I took a very small sip.

We adjourned into the living room, and I plopped onto my recliner. Tree removed a toy car from a chair, sat, and pointed to Lego blocks scattered across the floor.

"Very impressive what you've done with the place, Jake."

Tree and I often sparred with mindless banter whenever we were avoiding more serious subjects. I had no clue what was bothering him but for my part, I hoped to preempt any discussion of Emily.

"Hey Sheriff, you're more than welcome to clean up this town. The broom's in the closet." I tilted my bottle toward him. "Speaking of powerful men, how's your new job going?"

His shoulders slumped. "If I handed you my piece, would you put me out of my misery?"

"That bad, huh? Not racial flak, I hope."

"Bigots? Hell no. I *am* the Grand Imperial Poohbah. I don't take crap from nobody ... well, except maybe the Governor and my wife. To me, racists are mosquitoes; I swat 'em away or squash 'em. I'm even thinking about getting a white lawn-jockey holding a lantern for my front yard." He downed more beer. "Nah, I just had a bad day. That drug ring I told you about is well organized and hidden deep underground. Got no evidence of who's running the show or where they get their endless supply. Doesn't help that the frickin' DEA and FBI are stomping all over my turf, kicking up dust."

I was no happier to have them nosing around the hospital and eyeballing my pain management practice.

"Far as the job goes, Jake, the money's good. Wife and kids are proud. But being a sheriff is a lot more about paper-shuffling and politics than police work. Instead of calluses on my flat feet, I'm getting them on my backside from too many hours sitting behind my desk. Dunno, maybe I'll be a one-termer. I'm not sure I want to run for reelection."

Tree took a slug of beer and looked directly at me. "How's it going with you and Emily? I get that the bishop gave you time to sort things out, but at some point, buddy, you got to shit or hop off the pot."

"Ah, always the romantic, Tree. Maybe you should consider a career writing happy little ditties for Hallmark Cards."

But I was trapped and couldn't avoid the topic. Tree had backed me into a corner and I knew he wouldn't let me joke my way out of it. He was not merely my best friend; he was my confidant, confessor, and personal shrink—and I was unwilling to lie to him.

"The few months I've been back in town aren't long enough to cover the ground we've lost." I sighed. All that wasted time, all the could-have-beens. "I used to know her every thought before she spoke. Now Em and I keep dancing around each other as if there's an invisible wall between us.

Maybe that's God's way of telling me not to go there. She gives off mixed signals. We both do. I guess I just can't get past …."

"Past what?"

"Emily dumped me during the war. She couldn't even be bothered to write to me. I was half-a-world away with guys dying around me, completely terrified. The idea of being with her again was all that kept me going. I sent her dozens of letters, but after a few weeks she stopped writing completely."

"I'm surprised she wrote to you at all. What did you expect, love letters? After you cheated on her with Marisa during our senior year? Hell, you broke Emily's heart!" Tree dismissed the central trauma of my youth with a wave of his hand and ran his fingers over what would have been his hair, if he hadn't shaved off the remaining fringe. "Ask you a question?"

"Sure."

"Back in school, you were into strong drink, fast cars, and willing women."

I nodded. Filled with drugs, booze, and testosterone, my youth had been a living, breathing cautionary tale that had landed me in the middle of a bloodbath overseas and destroyed my relationship with Emily.

"So what's your question?"

Tree arched his eyebrows. "Celibacy? Really? You never did do things the easy way but …." The big man rapped his knuckles on the coffee table. "Come on, man. That's gotta be near impossible."

"No, it's not easy—that's why it's called *sacrifice*. I took a vow to serve the Lord, forgoing all others. Offering an undivided heart is an important part of the commitment. Heck, everyone's tempted, in many ways. It's *the struggle* to stay on the path that proves your love for God."

As the party line rolled off my tongue, I felt like a seminarian again. I knew that Saint Peter, some popes, and most of the early church leaders had been married, many with children. There had been no mandate of celibacy until the fourth century.

My friend deserved the truth, however, so I stopped spouting the official talking points and slipped on a neutral expression, the one I wear whenever I'm annoyed or threatened.

"I've learned to manage my attraction to women, Tree, mostly by steering clear, avoiding *occasions of sin* as we say. I try to be vigilant without being aloof. Lately though, every time I see Emily, I want to throw my arms around her."

"So, why don't you?"

"You know damn well why!" I had worked hard on taming my fiery temper since seminary, but sometimes I still burst into flames when I was pissed off. "Is that your solution? Chuck my vows and sail off into the sunset?"

"You get ordained and what, you become a plaster saint? Flip a switch and poof, you're a different person? Bullshit!"

We locked eyes and I opened my mouth to respond. Fortunately, the Lord grabbed hold of my tongue. I turned on the television, found the pre-game show, muted the sound, and drew a slow deep breath.

"The priesthood wasn't a whim. Every time I say Mass, hold the body and blood of Christ in my hand, I feel His arm around my shoulder."

In my heart, I knew my life was one giant contradiction. After the war, I had hoped that healing bodies would atone for my past sins and shortcomings, yet my medical practice was not enough. I had been spiraling downward, bracing for impact, until God reached out and literally became my savior. I'd joined a religious order to rejoin the human race—and to save me from myself. If my bizarre journey to the priesthood was not part of God's greater plan, then all those years of suffering and soul-searching had no meaning, no purpose.

But Tree and I had already been through all of that and there was no reason to rehash it. I took a slug of Guinness and watched a muted replay from last week's debacle against the Jets.

How to explain things to Tree? My mind was fuzzy, and the beer and my fatigue were not helping.

"When I entered the seminary, Emily was married and hundreds of miles away. I was certain my passion for her had burned out. Now she's divorced and within arm's reach."

It's strange how the doors you should never open are inevitably unlocked. I studied the beer bottle for a moment, surprised that it was nearly empty.

My frustration flared, and I smacked the arm of the recliner with my fist. "I'm not the reckless teenager I used to be. Rekindled passions aren't enough! Running off with Emily is not even an option, Tree. Her ex may be an invalid now, but he's not dead. The Catholic Church doesn't recognize divorce, so in their eyes she's married. Abandoning the priesthood is a grave decision, but giving up my faith is unthinkable! It's a damn no-win situation."

"Easy, buddy. Don't be blinded by the brilliant reflection off your own halo. I only raised the question because I saw her at a restaurant with a young guy."

"Long blond hair?"

"Yup."

"His name's Todd. We're … acquainted."

"The two acted, ah … pretty lovey-dovey. They a couple?"

I shrugged.

"All I'm saying, Jake, is that I've seen Emily with RJ, and it's clear she already loves the boy. Maybe it's time to focus on your medical practice,

RJ, and Emily—before Todd or somebody else snaps her up. The girl's definitely a catch."

"Things aren't that simple."

"Seriously, your relationship with Emily is really screwed up … and believe me, bizarre behavior is something we cops know a shit-load about."

The glimmer of a smile twitched at the corners of his mouth.

"Am I missing something funny here, Tree?"

"No. It's just a pity Catholic priests can't marry." He laughed. "It would teach you guys the real meaning of humility."

"I'm glad you think this is amusing—"

My cellphone rang and I was grateful for the interruption.

"I have to take this." I walked into the kitchen. "Austin."

"Jake? It's Juan Santana."

Santana had been one of my parishioners before my leave of absence, and we had become friends. I'd never met anyone more devoted to caring for the less fortunate. He embodied the proverb *Happy is the man who feeds the poor.* He not only fed them, he gave them a safe, warm place to sleep and helped turn their lives around.

"Hey, Juan, how're things at the shelter?"

"Unemployment's off the charts, it's freezing cold, and the homeless are pouring in. Honest to God, I don't know where I'm going to put them, or how we can care for them all. I'm a social worker, but all I do now is fund-raising."

I had forgotten to mail in a check. Jesus stared at me from a crucifix on the wall.

"Hey, I'm sorry, Juan. I meant to send my donation."

"Oh, I didn't call about money. We picked up a guy from the freight yard last night. A sickly old man, rail thin, and jumpy as a frog in a frying pan. The guy makes *me* nervous. He keeps asking about you."

"What's his name?"

"Won't say. No ID either, Jake, though that's not unusual around here."

"What does he want with me?"

"He's trying to find you. Knows you're a doctor. How do you want to play this? I haven't told him anything yet."

"Good. Until I figure out what's going on, keep it that way."

What the heck? First a drug dealer in a dumpster, now an old man from the train yard. I gazed out of the kitchen window, uncertain how to respond. The apartment building's Christmas lights dappled its snow-covered shrubbery in ruby and emerald splotches, giving the appearance of scoops of vanilla ice cream covered in sprinkles, but my day had left me neither hungry nor the least bit festive.

"Tell you what, Juan. I'll stop by the shelter tomorrow after work. Will you be there after five?"

"Heck, I'm always here. I don't think the mysterious Mr. X will be going anywhere soon. He was starving and freezing his butt off. I'll give you a call, though, if he bolts for the door. See you tomorrow."

When I returned to the living room and flopped back into my recliner, the Pittsburgh kicker had teed up the ball and the Browns were lining up to receive.

"Game time." I kept the volume low so as not to wake RJ. "Let's see if the good guys can take it to the men in black."

We watched a bone-crushing tackle on the runback. Tree slapped his knee and said, "Now that reminds me of *your* playing days. A young *Jake the Snake* slithering between blockers, uncoiling like a rattler, and hammering the runner into the ground. Hell, half the time, you'd knock their helmets clean off!"

As a free safety in high school, I had been a head-hunter and proud of my nickname. I hadn't heard it in years and loathed it now. With my absent father and boozing mother, the worse things got at home, the better I had performed. Unlike life, the rules on the field were clear. I had embraced both the predictable routine of football and its violence.

After graduation, I had even found the regimentation of the Army reassuring, the valor and camaraderie exciting. War, however, was not the rush I'd expected or hoped. Blood and mutilated bodies soon shattered my childish illusions.

For all the years I had known him, Tremont Macon had always been called "Tree." Two hundred and fifty pounds of giant oak, he had solidly rooted the defensive line on our team. His nickname suited him and he'd always been comfortable with it.

I was not comfortable with mine.

"*This snake* has shed a lot of skins since those days, Tree. I'm not that guy anymore." But I suspected that the serpent always lurked somewhere within us all, waiting in the shadows.

I sighed and let the noise and commotion of the game wash over me.

CHAPTER SEVEN

Tuesday, December 3, 2002, 7:00 a.m.

Colleen Brady wore her short-cropped, silver-gray hair in a no-nonsense style. She marched into my apartment with the demeanor of an Irish drill sergeant. Her troops were well trained. I snapped to attention and RJ immediately climbed onto his chair at the kitchen table and set his stuffed Winnie-the-Pooh next to him, all three of us ready for inspection.

With the portion of my salary from the hospital that the Church allowed me to keep, I had hired Colleen as a nanny to help care for RJ and deliver him to preschool. Our relationship was mutually beneficial. She was widowed and needed steady income. More importantly, she and RJ had formed a strong bond during my sister's illness, and he had become the child she never had. She was God-sent and I couldn't function without her. The second she left for the day, I was lost. I was fumbling through Parenthood 101 and still had no clue how to raise a child. None. I had come to think of her as the patron saint of blarney and blended families.

"Sorry, Colleen." I grabbed my coat. "I'm offering Mass and have to leave early today."

My "spiritual retreat" had limited my religious duties and contact with my parishioners at the church. I had finally convinced the bishop to allow me to say morning Mass in the chapel at St. Joseph's Hospital, which helped to keep the fire of my faith burning. He had agreed only because the diocese had a shortage of priests.

For a change, I felt well-rested and dying to take on the day, fairly certain I could handle anything it threw at me and knock it out by the third round. As I kissed RJ goodbye and headed for the door, Colleen cleared her throat—always a warning.

"I see you've not touched the casserole I made for you, Father." With her strict Irish-Catholic upbringing, she could not force herself to call me Jake. She furrowed her brow. "What, might I ask, is the point of my slaving over a hot stove if you've no intention of eating the food I prepare?"

The edge in her voice told me something more than casseroles was bothering her, but I had no idea what. Colleen was a hard person to read. Her crusty temperament concealed her softer side. She could be as soothing as a summer shower or as unyielding as a stone wall.

"Come on, Colleen! We *love* your cooking." Her meals could feed a small village and we seldom finished them, so RJ and I often had delicious leftovers. "Sheriff Macon dropped by last night and brought pizza. The casserole won't go to waste."

I checked my watch and tried for the door again. Her frown remained.

"We should talk, Father." She aimed her double-barreled stare at me. "About your distressing influence on RJ."

I removed my hand from the doorknob.

"My what?"

"You take your leave of us every morning without breakfast, not even a cup of tea or piece of bread to keep you from the hunger. Now, I cannot get the boy to eat a bite either."

"Colleen, you know I fast before communion."

"I do, Father," she said tapping her foot, "but the lad does not."

This was a problem of my own making, and Colleen knew it. Although the Church now required only a one hour fast, when I was young, we were not permitted to eat after midnight before communion. My mother had been a devote Catholic and after her death, I had resumed the ritual of overnight fasting in remembrance of her.

I watched RJ at the kitchen table through the steam wafting from his uneaten oatmeal. He had placed a raspberry on the tip of each index finger like ruby hats and was entertaining himself with a finger puppet show. I desperately wanted to laugh out loud, but Colleen was scowling and already in a stormy mood.

"You're right, Colleen. I'll explain it to him tonight, I promise. Sorry, I have to hurry now. Attendance at Mass has grown, and I can't be late."

The teapot came to a boil with a shrill whistle. Colleen snapped the heat off and lifted the kettle from the stove. She too was simmering.

"Not to mention one particular member of your new congregation, I'm guessing."

My head snapped up.

"Hit a nerve, did I now, Father?"

So *that's* what was bugging her. Emily sometimes joined us for supper and they had met. Colleen was as staunch a Catholic as my mother, and she saw Emily as my Eve, tempting me from the Garden of Eden.

"Aye, she could charm the birds from the trees, that one." Colleen paused long enough to steep a cup of Earl Grey, its aroma filling the room. "Would I be right in speculating, Father, that the lovely blind lass is there every morning? Sitting in the front pew, is she? Hanging on your every blessed word."

Blood rushed to my face. I threw my coat over the back of a chair and walked to the kitchen table. Besides cooking and caring for RJ, chastising me was one of Colleen's unrivaled talents. She knew all of my hot buttons and was quick to push them if she deemed it necessary for my well-being or the sanctity of my immortal soul.

"The *blind lass* sits with her elderly father and prays, Colleen."

"Ah, but prays for what? That's what I'd be asking."

Colleen had already chiseled the Eleventh Commandment into a stone tablet: *Priests shalt not have female friends.* The problem was that her suspicions had hit close to the mark.

Colleen sensed my hesitation and added, "And, while I'm on the subject, who helps the pair of you avoid occasions of sin when I'm not here after dinner?"

"You must be joking. With old eagle-eye here?" I loaded a spoon with oatmeal, blew on it, made airplane noises, and flew my cargo toward RJ's mouth. He shook his head and refused to open up.

"RJ's asleep by eight, Father, as we both know."

As annoying as she could be, Colleen's love of my nephew had stabilized his world, and I refused to jeopardize that. I gave up trying to reason with her, bit my tongue, and tried again unsuccessfully to fly breakfast into my nephew's mouth.

"Come now, Father! The airplane and hanger gambit? Really? RJ's too grown up for that old trick. He's not a baby anymore."

That was news to me. Time for Plan B. I saluted my nephew.

"Okay, soldier, time for inspection. Let me see those muscles." RJ smiled, came to attention, and pumped up his skinny biceps. I squeezed them and pretended to injure my fingers. "Those are mighty impressive guns, trooper. Soon you'll need a license to carry them." I reloaded the spoon with oatmeal. "I'm promoting you to Master Gunnery Sergeant. Here's some more ammunition."

RJ grinned, returned my salute, and let me land my cargo in his mouth. He swallowed, giggled, and opened wide. I flew in another shipment and winked at Colleen.

Remembering Juan Santana's phone call about the old man at the homeless shelter I said, "I have a stop to make after work today. Would you please pick up RJ from school and stay with him till I arrive?"

"Of course, your lordship. Shall I plow the fields and tend the cattle too?"

I raised my hands in exasperation and shoveled in the last of the oatmeal. "Sorry, I have to go." I gave RJ a goodbye hug, put on my coat, and trotted to my car.

The pewter gray sky hung low and sullen. The roads remained icy, but the blizzard had faded to light flurries. I got stuck behind a city snowplow and crawled slowly toward the hospital, passing two plywood Santa Clauses, a reindeer with a maraschino-cherry nose, and a few colorful puddles of deflated plastic Christmas decorations. The back of the truck started spewing road salt, which pinged off the hood of my car. I slowed even more to get out of range.

When I tuned the car radio to an oldies station, "Precious and Few" poured from the speakers, each note plucking strings of regret and resurrecting memories of Emily and me dancing to the music, lost in our embrace. In high school it had been *our song*. I changed the channel, but the irony was not lost on me. If we had had a song these days, it would be "The Hokey Pokey"—one foot in, one foot out, and you turn yourself around ... and around ... and around.

I stopped at a red light near the hospital. The neighborhood brought to mind a sketchy part of Gotham rather than the wholesome town of Mayberry. Several physicians maintained offices in the area as a convenience for their patients. Dr. Taylor's was a converted concrete ranch home located on the opposite corner. At just past seven-thirty in the morning, his parking area looked like a used car lot and dozens of people were lined up at his door, some wearing gang colors. The crowd appeared tattered and underdressed for the freezing temperatures.

I had never seen that many folks waiting in the cold to see a doctor and was not sure what to make of it. Taylor was a pillar of the community, and a major donor to the county food bank and the community college. He was the grand-old-man at St. Joe's and the president of the medical staff. No one had a bad word to say about him—well, no one except Dr. Glade. Could he possibly be hiding in plain sight, running a pill-mill? Or was I casting doubt on an innocent man?

While pondering questions to which I had no answers, I hadn't noticed the light turn green. A car horn honked behind me. I drove up the hospital parking garage ramp with Emily's description of Taylor echoing in my mind: *A very wealthy man. Big car, bigger boat, semi-retired.*

Given the throng outside his office, the DEA drug investigation, and Dr. Glade's suspicion of Taylor, the apparent conclusion made me more than a tad uncomfortable.

CHAPTER EIGHT

Tuesday, December 3, 2002, 8:00 a.m.

Having entered the Advent season, I dressed in deep violet-colored vestments in the sacristy. Like many Christians, I relished the joyous preparations in anticipation of the birth of Christ. When I finished dressing, I glanced in the mirror and smiled. The teenaged boy that I had once been had enlisted in the Army and never even considered the possibility of becoming a priest. Such was life. Man plans, and God laughs.

I took a moment to muse about Saint Camillus de Lellis, the founder of the religious order to which I belonged. Although he lived in the sixteenth century, I considered him to be the loving father with the gentle guiding hand that I'd never had. In addition to vows of obedience, poverty, and chastity, we Camillians take a fourth vow of service to the sick and wear a red cross on our black cassocks to distinguish our order. To us, hospitals are houses of worship and the cries of the afflicted are prayers of petition to the heavens.

What better place in the Catholic Church for a man of my medical background than the Camillians? It was as if all of the struggles and confusion of my early years were designed to lead me to this vocation. And what better place for me to say Mass than in a hospital chapel?

I walked from the sacristy into the sanctuary and nodded to the three elderly nuns in the front pew. They were dressed in traditional ebony-colored habits over white wimple veils, which had been quite the fashion statement in the Middle Ages. I thought of them as my Three Owls, perched in the front of the small chapel every morning, dependable as sunrise, wearing their oversized round-rimmed eyeglasses. They worked as nurses on the medical floors, and like many nuns, they lived together as one joyous flock. I envied them. Priests usually flew solo.

A shaft of sunlight fell from a window onto their folded hands, adding a sparkle to the wedding rings of these "brides of Christ." As was the case with most priests, I wore no band.

I scanned the chapel for Emily. She was not there. She attended Mass occasionally on weekdays, depending on her schedule. I banished my disappointment and cleared my mind of all worries. The faithful filled much of the chapel, and I owed them my full attention.

As a physician, I derived satisfaction from relieving pain. As a priest, I took pleasure in alleviating spiritual suffering. But when I consecrated the bread and wine, that precious hour with the Lord was the one I loved best. Every time I placed the Host on my tongue, mingled the body of Christ with mine, I could taste the love of God. Although difficult for many people to understand, that was who I am, who I had become.

Statues of the Virgin Mary and St. Joseph flanked the pews, positioned as if gazing at the altar. High above, a small stained-glass window showered Mary in rainbow colors. Seeing her there always reminded me of my days as an altar boy, when my mother had watched me serve Mass.

I inhaled the faint, lingering scent of incense and began the service, letting the ancient rhythms of the Catholic Church wash over me. During my homily, I happened to glance at the statues and was shocked to find that the head of the St. Joseph's statue was askew. Joseph was staring at the wall.

I gave the blessing, bid everyone "go in peace," and walked over to examine the alcove. St. Joseph's neck had been broken and his head repositioned at an inhuman angle reminiscent of someone possessed by the devil in a horror movie. The hand-painted alabaster statue was heavy, and it would have taken considerable strength and effort to wring its neck until the head snapped off. I picked up the fourteen-inch figure and studied it, indignant that someone would desecrate a chapel.

As I pondered vandalism and religious intolerance, the *lub-dub* of an uneven gait approached me from behind. I turned and found Joey Childs gazing at his shoes, looking as guilty as a cat with a mouth full of feathers.

Joey was in his early thirties, but in some ways he *was* a child. He had been born with moderate cerebral palsy, resulting in both a developmental delay and a lumbering gait. People at the hospital avoided him, so I made a point of befriending him. Harvey Winer, the hospital administrator, had found Joey a job busing trays and cleaning the cafeteria. He had also hired the blind to work the snack shop and made Emily and her dad the resident advisors in the intern dormitories, and I respected and admired him for his many kindnesses.

"Don't ... don't hate me, Father," Joey muttered softly, pointing at the figurine. "I tripped when I came in and bumped the statue ... and it hit the floor. Didn't mean to do it." He leaned against a pew to steady himself. Tears streamed down his cheeks. No doubt, he had spent the past hour fretting about the statue, expecting a severe reprimand.

"It's okay, Joey. Don't worry about it. Accidents happen." I took his hands in mine. "I'm sure it can be fixed."

His gaze wandered from me to the statue and back again. "You ... you forgive me?"

"Of course I do. Everyone needs forgiveness once in a while." The memory of a vengeful act I had committed during the heat of battle and the selfish way I had treated Emily as a teenager were my constant companions. "Me too, Joey."

"Even you?" The concept of a priest requiring absolution confused him. "You're still my friend, right Father?"

"You bet. Join me for lunch today, if you have time."

His eyes widened and his hands trembled. "Don't let 'em fire me! Please. I love it here!"

"No one's going to fire you. I promise. What would they do in the cafeteria without you?" I gave him a pat on the back. "I'll take care of everything. Off you go, now. And smile. It'll be fine."

He gave me a quick hug. Over the years, I had received some thank-you hugs from my patients, but an embrace from a special needs person somehow always felt warmer, more heartfelt. I watched Joey leave the chapel and prayed that God held a special place in Heaven for the mentally and physically afflicted.

I carried the broken statue into the sacristy and exchanged my vestments for a white coat, hanging my stethoscope around my neck. I wrapped St. Joseph in a towel, and realized that he and I had a special bond. We had both chosen to raise someone else's child.

Although the world beyond the chapel could have an edge and an ugliness, Mass always left me feeling buoyant and renewed. My faith was the cornerstone on which I had rebuilt my life. I strolled to the doctors' lounge with a spring in my step, put the damaged statue in my locker, broke my fast with a cream-filled doughnut, and headed for my shift in the Urgent Care Center.

Dr. Glade spotted me in the hall and waved me over, darkening my mood. I was already late and searched for an escape route without success, because whenever surgeons are not busy cutting, as a rule they will talk your ear off.

When I did not respond, he walked toward me. His white coat partially concealed blood droplets on his blue surgical scrubs, and his white slip-on clogs were spattered with scarlet polka dots. Some surgeons wore a smattering of blood in public as a red badge of courage.

He said, "Sorry if we got off on the wrong foot yesterday. I care about the toll that drugs are taking in our community, and sometimes my passion gets the best of me. I hear you put your life on the line with the Oberlin murders a few months ago. I admire that."

Glade extended his hand and I shook it, though I suspected he was playing me.

"Thanks, but that was more about my lack of common sense than bravery."

"Not what I heard, Jake. In any case, Harvey Winer's right about the drug problem. Some docs see a pill as the answer to every symptom."

"Spoken like a true denizen of the O.R." I chuckled. "What's the surgeons' motto? *Why wait, when you can operate*, right?" Or my favorite, "*If in doubt, cut it out*! You guys should add a catchy jingle and advertise on TV."

He was not amused. "Yeah, yeah. About yesterday, I didn't mean to be cryptic. I was late for surgery. Got a minute?"

Having already filed Glade away under *Life's Too Short*, I checked at my watch. "Sure, but not much more. What's up?"

"Just wanted to be clear. I joined the Ethics Committee 'cause the powers-that-be here care more about the bottom line than patient care. Everywhere I look at St. Joe's, I see dollar signs and conflicts of interest."

"For example?"

"Rudy VonKamp, our esteemed hospital legal counsel. Remember the balding guy in the thousand-dollar suit sitting next to Taylor at the meeting?"

"Yes."

"That's VonKamp. He donates money to the hospital and folks think he's a saint. That's simply a tax deduction for him. He makes a fortune here." Glade's high-pitched voice raised an octave above its usual mezzo-soprano range as he cranked up the volume, his iron-pumped body vibrating. "The guy doesn't say much but he churns out reams of paper—at $500 an hour. Got a license to steal!"

I wondered again if I was witnessing the rage of an anabolic steroid abuser. He was white water, churning and crashing on the rocks, and talking with him was the same as stepping into the rapids. He scanned the hall, guided me into a quieter corridor, and dialed his tirade down a few decibels. It came out as a growl.

"Seriously? A damn lawyer on the *Ethics* Committee! Can you believe that crap? Most lawyers don't even know what the word means! Same as putting Iran on the Human Rights Council. And VonKamp's brother runs his own law firm in town and get this, the S.O.B. specializes in malpractice cases against doctors. Me included! They're goddamn predators, a pack of legal wolves hunting us down, *that's* what they are."

Most hospitals wanted a lawyer on any committee that had legal ramifications, although having been sued once myself, the physician side of me understood Glade's frustration—and the priest half was fairly certain that malpractice lawyers never went to Heaven.

"I understand what you're saying, but is there a business connection between the two brothers?" I hesitated. "Or is this personal because of your lawsuit?"

His cheeks flashed crimson, and he let out a bitter laugh.

"Hell yeah, it's personal!" He lowered his voice. "VonKamp's brother sued me for nine frickin' million dollars. I got three kids in school. The depositions and other legal bullshit gobbled up my life for two years. Though I won my case, my insurance company spent thousands on my defense and jacked up my premium anyway. Those two are in cahoots. Be careful talking about specific cases at the Ethics meetings, or anywhere within earshot of VonKamp. Any whiff of patient problems in this town, and the malpractice minions come pouring out of their offices like clowns from a tiny circus car."

"I see your point, but unless you can document collusion between the two ...." I shrugged and left my objection hanging between us, then checked my watch again. Subtlety did not work on Glade. He nodded as if we had come to some monumental agreement.

"It's not just VonKamp, Jake. The administration's happy to give Dr. Guo a monopoly as the in-house witch doctor because Alternative Medicine brings in new patients and fills hospital beds. No one's going to monitor her to see what mumbo jumbo she has up her sleeve. Hell, she sells *plant remedies*, pincushions her patients with acupuncture needles, and puts leaches on surgical wounds to make a buck. With an M.D. degree and access to Schedule Two meds, why would anyone think she wouldn't stoop to selling prescription drugs? And don't even get me started on Taylor! He's another favorite son. The guy could take a dump in the courtyard and everyone would pretend not to notice the stink."

"I don't know. Harvey Winer tells me that Taylor's an important ambassador on behalf of the hospital, building bridges to the local community."

With no one near us in the hall, his fury ramped up. "I'm damn sure that every time the greedy bastard builds a bridge, he also puts in a toll booth! Our Ethics Committee chairman's *ethics* lie somewhere between a street corner pimp and a used car salesman. He's the lead investigator on a clinical drug trial, and the more patients enrolled, the more the pharmaceutical company pays him. Guess who refers most of the patients to him—his partners. And *they* get a nice finder's fee too! If you look up *conflict of interest*, Taylor's photo is right next to the definition. I heard the drug company flew him to a meeting in Aruba to give a lecture. He probably spent two weeks eating escargot, sipping Bordeaux, and working on his tan."

Glade removed the stethoscope from around his neck, and I stepped back so that he wouldn't accidently hit me with it as he gestured wildly.

"Listen, Jake, Taylor's office is in the ghetto but he makes more money than the U.S. Treasury. It doesn't add up. He owns a Mercedes and a damn Lamborghini that costs more than my house. If he's not scamming Medicaid or selling drugs, I'm the frickin' tooth fairy." Although Glade's soprano voice resembled Tinkerbell's, when he bared his teeth he more closely resembled a grizzly. "Taylor is dirty! I'm positive, and you can quote me. Hell, you can tattoo it on my forehead!"

I considered Dr. Taylor's resistance to reporting suspicious physician behavior at the Ethics Committee meeting, and the line of patients waiting outside of his office this morning.

"Do you have any proof?"

"Proof? Hell, if I did his ass would already be in jail."

"All right, you have my attention." I wondered if Glade was a righteous crusader, a jealous and vindictive wannabe, or a screaming paranoid. "I doubt I can help, though."

"All I'm saying is be open-minded. Don't pull the monk's cowl over your eyes, *Father*."

I was about to hustle to Urgent Care when an intern came racing toward us waving x-rays.

"Dr. Glade, glad I found you. Dr. Taylor and I admitted a man in a coma to ICU and his belly is real distended. We're worried he may have a bowel obstruction. Dr. Taylor wants a surgical consult stat."

Glade snatched the images and held them up to the fluorescent ceiling light.

"Don't think that's obstruction, but it's a damn weird gas pattern. What'd the radiologist say?"

"The department's backlogged. He hasn't looked at them yet, sir."

Glade stared at the x-rays. "Beats the hell out of me. I'd better examine the guy's belly." He handed the films to me. "What do you think, Jake?"

Glade was right, the bowel gas pattern was bizarre: small scattered collections of air, all the same size and shape, too identical to be random.

I looked at the images again and had an epiphany—though not the kind I had always hoped for. "Wait a minute! I've seen this pattern once before when I was in the Army—in a young girl being used as a drug mule. She was forced to swallow balloons filled with opium. There's always a small amount of air trapped in the balloon, so you get that strange gas pattern on x-ray. One of the balloons burst while she was stopped at a check point. The child died. If the patient in ICU has a slow leak, that could paralyze his bowel, distend his abdomen, and put him in a coma."

"Oh shit! Thanks, Jake, I'm on it." Glade handed the films back to the intern. "Give these to the radiologist *now*, and have him page me with his reading!" he added and took off down the hall like an Olympic sprinter.

CHAPTER NINE

Tuesday, December 3, 2002, 9:30 a.m.

The flu was the malady of the month, with ice-related fractures and fender-benders vying for second place. Nevertheless, Nurse Ochs ran Urgent Care like a well-tuned Ferrari and with the help of a competent resident, we cruised through a waiting room full of patients.

Dr. Glade phoned me at eleven.

"How'd your operation go?" I asked.

"Flawlessly, of course. I have a firm rule. I never operate on a patient on the day of his death." His confidence was only exceeded by his arrogance. "My greatness aside, Jake, that young man will be dancing in a week—but locked behind bars in a prison cell. When I found the heroin, we called the Drug Task Force."

Glade went on to describe in detail how he had removed eight heroin-filled condoms from the drug mule's bowel. One had leaked, but he'd been prepared with an IV dose of Narcan to counteract the narcotic. Although his voice danced with excitement as he recounted every pressure-filled moment, Glade never thanked me for my help. I was not surprised. Many of the surgeons I'd met over the years had failed Charm School and had never heard of etiquette or good manners.

Just before my shift ended at five o'clock, I entered room three to find an eleven-year-old girl moaning and writhing on the exam table. Her mother said the child had awakened with nausea and a belly ache. She had given her daughter an antacid and Tylenol, and kept her home from school. The pain had intensified and shifted to her right pelvis, where the girl had localized, rebound tenderness. Diagnosing appendicitis could be tricky and sometimes required an ultrasound or CT scan for confirmation. This case, however, was straight out of the textbook. I paged Glade and made him a happy man for the second time that day. He came down, confirmed my findings, and whisked the child up to the operating suite.

When I'd finished the last of my charting, I called Santana at the homeless shelter. He confirmed that the mysterious Mr. X was still there asking about me.

I stopped briefly in the chapel and prayed the Liturgy of the Hours from my Breviary, which I did daily to keep my spiritual focus. After I had finished, I asked God to guide me through the confusing maze of my feelings for Emily. If He answered, it was from far away and so softly that I could not hear Him.

Crossing myself, I pushed up from the kneeler, left the chapel, collected the damaged statue of St. Joseph from my locker, and stowed it in the trunk of my car. Ten minutes later, I was cruising through a part of town that belonged in a third world country.

A semi slowed my progress as it shifted through its gears, spilling noise into the slushy-gray city streets. Afternoon sunlight ratcheted down to dusk, and wind gusts swirled snow devils past vacant stores into alleyways. The homeless shelter was nestled between a pawn shop and a check-cashing joint.

I parked nearby at what appeared to be the intersection of a modern-day Sodom and Gomorrah. Hope was as dim here as the waning December light. A neon Budweiser sign blinked at me from a tavern across the street, enticing those who were short on cash but long on time.

A young Asian woman stepped out of the bar, a come-hither smile painted on her lips. A working girl providing curbside service in the dead of winter. She flashed a bare thigh at me, returned the merchandise to the warmth of her coat, and retreated back indoors. One hell of a way to make a living—or to live.

I locked my Ford Focus and wondered if it would be here when I came back. Although the bishop had temporarily allowed me to keep my medical income, between paying off my debts and raising my nephew I had little money left over. In desperate need of a car, I had purchased one that had been pre-owned. Driving one of the ego-mobiles that littered the doctors' parking lot was not only out of my price range, but would send the wrong message for a man-of-the-cloth. As unimpressive as my vehicle was next to the Cadillacs and BMWs at the hospital, on this street it screamed "steal me."

The sidewalk had not been shoveled and I trudged slowly toward the shelter's door, leaning into an angry wind that slapped my face. A bell tinkled as I entered a large, drab lobby where Juan Santana was engaged in an animated discussion with two men.

The man nearest the door was enormous. He shucked his coat off and threw it over a metal folding chair, revealing a mountain of muscle. His huge biceps threatened to burst through the sleeves of his black t-shirt, and he looked as if he belonged on the set of a gladiator movie. His body language read, *I pick my teeth with the bones of Christians.* His head was shaven, and the letters A and B were tattooed on his neck in jagged blue ink.

As I closed the door, Mr. Muscle aimed his pointy butt-kicker boots in my direction and approached with a wise-guy swagger, his movement fluid and full of threat. He glared at me, as menacing as a sharply honed blade. I leaned against the wall and tried to blend in with the pealing, gray-green paint as I waited for Santana's conversation to end.

The other man was short and paunchy, his gut draped over his belt. A thick Fu Manchu mustache hung from his upper lip like a furry horseshoe. He was all attitude and did most of the talking. From the way Tubby mangled the English language, I doubted that he was the brains of this outfit, or *any* outfit, but Muscle probably didn't provide much competition in the intelligence department.

Finally aware of my presence, Tubby spun around, pointed to the reception desk at the far side of the room, and commanded, "Sit." I pushed off the wall and complied. The fat man lowered his voice and turned back to Santana, revealing the gold fleur-de-lis of the New Orleans Saints football team emblazoned on the back of his black leather jacket.

After a few minutes of vigorous debate, Tubby lost his temper, poked Santana in the chest, and said in a loud voice, "I'm just gonna ask nice one more time, so listen up!" He stroked his mustache and stared at Juan, a hungry lion eying a gazelle. "Where the fuck is he?"

Muscle, equal parts brawn and testosterone, grunted his approval, which so far was his sole contribution to the conversation.

Santana took a step back. Fear glazed his face with a veneer of perspiration. His hands trembled as he lit a cigarette, took a drag, and studied the glowing tip as if it held the answer.

"I told you, I don't know him. He doesn't work here, doesn't stay here." His eyes darted to me, then back to Tubby. "What do you want with this Jacob Austin guy anyway?"

The fat man's lips twisted into a sneer. "We got us a business proposal for Jacob."

My mind reeled. I had never seen either of these men before, and neither of them recognized me. I gazed at the New Orleans Saints jacket again and suddenly the entire bizarre scene made sense. Alarm bells jangled inside my head.

Santana's forehead glistened with sweat and naked terror danced in his eyes, but he had delivered his warning.

Tubby advanced, backing Santana to the wall. "Gimme that." He snatched the cigarette from Santana and flicked it into an old metal wastebasket. A wisp of smoke drifted up and something caught fire. "Those things'll kill ya—and so will *lying* to me."

Muscle's venomous snicker was more hiss than laugh. He cracked his knuckles, which sounded like tree limbs snapping.

The fat man poked Santana in the chest again. "Stop jacking us around. Two winos here said *you* picked him up at some train yard. They ID'ed Austin's picture. Now, *where ... is ... he?*"

I wanted to sprint out of the front door, but had to take the heat off of Santana. I stood, walked over, and held up my hands in a gesture of reconciliation, wishing I had worn my clerical collar.

"Okay, gentlemen, let's all take a deep breath and calm down."

"Fuck off, douche bag, 'fore I lose my temper," Tubby said, his voice a low growl. "Dis ain't none of your damn business."

Muscle stepped close to me and worked his jaw, the tendons in his thick neck taut as suspension bridge cables. He smelled of garlic and sweat. His dark eyes fixed on me, hungry for a chance to shed blood.

I had been in enough brawls and bar fights in the Army to recognize that I was out-matched. I backed up to the reception desk in search of a weapon. My hand found a long, metal three-hole paper punch. I considered parting Muscle's hair with it to improve our odds. My years in the seminary, however, had dulled my aggressive edge, and replaced my penchant to rumble with a preference for reason.

"This is my business. I'm Austin. What's this about?"

"The hell you are! We know the ol' bastard and you ain't him. Get gone, if you don't wanna get dead."

Tubby nodded, and Muscle grabbed my shirt with a hand the size of a tennis racket and hoisted me a foot into the air with one arm. His eyes were a murky wasteland, his breath rank with decay.

While the two thugs were busy with me, Santana took out his cellphone. Before he could finish dialing 911, Tubby noticed and landed a right hook to his belly. Juan doubled over, dropped to his knees, and flopped facedown, the phone clattering across the tile. Tubby kicked him in the side, snarled, and kicked him again.

Muscle's attention shifted to the melee and he relaxed his grip on me. I knew I would only get one shot, so I swung the paper punch with all the strength I had.

The sound of Muscle's nose and teeth shattering was surprisingly loud. He let go of my shirt, tumbled, and slammed the back of his head against the floor. After a few seconds, he roared and staggered to his feet, spitting chunks of enamel. His teeth resembled broken pottery, his dazed, toothless expression reminiscent of the banjo-picking boy from the movie, *Deliverance*. He took a step forward, teetered momentarily, then charged.

To hell with turning the other cheek!

I hit him again, this time in the forehead. A deep gash gushed blood, which streamed down into one eye. Muscle stumbled backward, wobbled, and grabbed a chair for balance.

Tubby looked over and shook his head. "Bad fuckin' move, asshole." He stepped forward and a switchblade snapped open in his nicotine-stained fingers. A sneer spread across the fat man's lips. "Better tell me where Austin is, 'fore I slice and dice both you clowns."

He slashed the air as he edged toward me. I stepped back, waving the paper punch. Muscle's warm blood oozed down it onto my hand.

I desperately wanted to run, but Muscle blocked the front door. Although he was stunned and woozy, I did not want to try him. The other exit was at the far side of the room. Santana, however, was defenseless, crawling slowly toward the desk, and I could not desert him.

Time slowed. I backed up to the wall, my eyes locked on the knife, lamplight twinkling on its blade. I glimpsed motion to my right. Santana reached into the pocket of a sport coat draped over the desk chair. His hand came out brandishing a small silver revolver. He stumbled to his feet.

"That's enough," he bellowed. "Get out."

Santana appeared more scared than angry, but fear had no doubt pulled more triggers than anger. I stepped out of the line of fire.

"Jake," he said, "call the cops."

At the mention of my first name, Tubby's eyes narrowed and his lips curled into a smirk. He watched Santana's quivering hand, thought about making a move, and decided he did not like his odds. He lowered his knife.

"You dickheads done bought yourselves a shitload of trouble—especially you, *Mr. Austin.*"

"Out!" Santana took a cautious step forward. "Now!"

I dialed my cell with trembling hands, nearly dropping the phone from my bloody fingers.

Muscle glared at me. "You ain't seen the last of me, cocksucker. Got me a world of hurt with your name on it. You gonna *wish* you was dead!" He tottered out into the freezing December night, his coat still draped over the folding chair. Tubby grabbed it and followed, leaving behind an absurdly cheerful, sleigh bell tinkle as the door slammed shut.

A calm soprano voice sang in my ear. "911. What is your emergency?"

I told her as I followed a trail of blood out the door and into the snow. With the approaching winter solstice and the cloud cover, the sun was a fading memory. Wandering around this part of town after dark armed with only a phone and a paper punch was dangerous and downright stupid, but I desperately wanted to get their license plate number. I was too far away when a black or navy-blue Hummer peeled away from the curb, drove under a streetlight, and vanished.

The operator came back on the line and said a cruiser was on its way. Sweating in the frigid night air, I stepped back inside the shelter and closed the door. Exhaustion descended on me and I slumped against the wall.

Santana was holding his revolver, a tiny, snub-nose that looked like a toy.

"The cops are coming, Juan. Is that thing registered?"

"Yeah—though I'm not sure I could hit the saloon across the street with this pea-shooter." Santana stared at the gun and added, "I suppose I should carry a damn machine gun in this neighborhood."

Shaking violently, he slipped on his sport coat and shoved the pistol back into his pocket. Smoke poured from the wastebasket, flames peeking over the top. Santana grabbed a bottle of water off the desk, doused the fire, and sagged onto the chair.

"Holy shit!" he said, his voice unsteady. He glanced around the room, then back at me. "What the fuck just happened here?"

My eyes drifted to the blood spatter on my clothes, and I wilted. "I'm afraid I know *exactly* what that was all about."

I prayed to God I was wrong.

"Doesn't make any sense to me, Jake." Santana hung a Marlboro from his lips and lit it. "They came in here asking for you by name, and showed me a photo—"

"Yeah, a photo of the old man from the train yard." My past reached up, grabbed me by the throat, and dragged me under. "It's time he and I had a little chat."

CHAPTER TEN

Tuesday, December 3, 2002, 6:30 p.m.

I called Colleen and told her I would be home late, without giving her any details. She was used to my erratic hours and never failed to stay and care for RJ, but she often used her colorful Irish idioms as shillelaghs, never missing the opportunity to knock me down a peg.

"Don't you mind us, Father. An important man like yourself has far too much to be doing to get home at a decent hour." She released a contemptuous snort. "Ah well, RJ has a grand photograph of yourself that he can talk to if he gets lonely."

We Catholics are masters of the guilt game, and no one played the shame-on-you card better than Colleen. I swallowed the lump in my throat, apologized again, and hung up.

Santana led me into the living quarters at the homeless shelter. A couple of men with empty eyes were idling in the hallway. They scattered when they saw us. Salsa music dueled with a rap song opining the hard life in the hood and berating "bitches an' hoes." I had seen this particular hip-hop artist interviewed on television at his palatial home in Beverly Hills as he sat by his Olympic-sized swimming pool sipping champagne from a bottle of Dom Pérignon, suffering through another day in the neighbor-*hood*.

We walked down a dingy hall, empty except for one plastic chair. Next to it, an ancient payphone hung from a dung-colored wall decorated with decades of scribbled messages.

The smell of tobacco mingled with that of locker room sweat and something akin to the inside of a dumpster. My lungs recoiled with each breath and my stomach lurched.

Santana saw my reaction and misinterpreted my expression as disgust.

"It's not what you think, Jake. This place is worlds better than living on the streets. And these guys aren't a bunch of slackers and scumbags. Most are decent folks who've fallen far and hard." He pointed to a closed door on our left. "That man was once a professor of literature, and one of the guys in the next room was a prominent lawyer."

"No, I get it, Juan. Really."

Which was true. I completely understood. Santana did not know my background. He had no idea that at one point in my life I had struggled with substance abuse, stumbled close to the edge, and had peered into the abyss. If I had not found the Lord, this shelter might have been *my* home.

Ten feet down the hall, Santana stopped, knocked on a battered door, and said, "Open up." A dirt-brown paint chip fluttered to the floor. "It's Juan. We gotta talk."

No reply.

Santana turned the knob and we entered a room so small that there was nowhere for hope to hide. I had seen prison cells that were less depressing. Two unmatched dressers and four cots filled the tiny space. Only one cot was occupied.

The old man had undoubtedly heard the ruckus out front and was frightened. He shoved something under his unmade bed, came up with a metal pipe in his hand, tried to stand, then flopped down waving the pipe at us.

A southern drawl oozed from his lips, as slow and thick as Gomer Pyle strung out on downers.

"What y'all want?" Fear raised the pitch of his voice an octave. "I ain't done nothin'. Git out!"

His appearance was as ashen and weary as the gray walls in the room. At first, I was not sure it was him, but his eyes confirmed it. I hadn't seen him in decades and would never have recognized him if we had bumped into each other on the street.

My mind burped up sour, undigested memories, and I became queasy.

Although in his sixties, he looked much older. His face and arms were bruised as if he'd tripped and fallen—most likely after a bottle of cheap wine. What little remained of his hair was long, stringy, and the color of greasy dishwater. His nose was bulbous and road-mapped with capillaries. White stubble tufted his chin and cheeks. He wore filthy dungarees and was in desperate need of a bath. The ratty t-shirt that hung from his narrow shoulders could not conceal the hollow in the center of his chest. His eyes were the only hint of the man I once knew—silver-blue, same as RJ's and mine.

I gestured toward him.

"Juan, allow me to introduce …." A string of vulgar epithets danced on the back of my tongue, words I had tried not to utter since my ordination. "The other Jacob Austin. He's my …."

No matter what word I chose, the same dark history lurked in the syllables. *Role model* was closest to the truth, for he had taught me by example how to numb my life with booze and drugs. The word *Father* implied someone who had raised me. *Dad* suggested a caring relationship. *Pop* sounded too kind, too loving.

"This, Juan … is my old man."

Santana's eyes darted between us.

Recognition finally lit my father's face. He began to rise like a ghost from the grave but sagged back onto the cot, his gaze as blank as the wall. His expression could not have been more pained if I had kicked him in his gut. He dropped the metal pipe and it clanged against the concrete floor and rolled to my feet. His lips moved; no sound escaped.

When I was a boy and my dad was drunk, he had been quick to use his belt, leaving welts as his signature. Decades later, the memory still stung. I had spent years developing less destructive coping skills than the drinking and drugging he had taught me, distancing myself from the kind of man he was.

Now as a priest, I dispensed absolution for a living, and frequently ministered to all kinds of lowlifes, offering forgiveness for even the most grievous sins. It was my job. I prayed that God could forgive my father, because I sure-as-hell could not—though Lord knows, I had tried.

I bent down, picked up the pipe, and pointed it at my old man.

"This sad excuse for a human being walked out on my mother and me when I was a child. Blowing jazz and cocaine in New Orleans was more important to him than his family."

I remembered the day when I was five, not much older than RJ, and he locked me in a closet for three hours because I had been making too much noise while he watched football. The angry little boy inside me rose up, filling me with sorrow and rage. I hurled the pipe, taking a chunk out of one of the dressers.

I forced a smile. "How'd that gig work out for you?" I surveyed the shabby room. "I see you made it to the big-time."

"You're wrong, boy! Things ain't always been this way. I *did* make it big … for a spell. Hell, I even jammed with Albert King in Indianola, Mississippi a couple times. When we played *Bad Sign* together, we damn-near set Club Ebony on fire. Weren't no one better than Albert. Once that crazy left-handed bastard borrowed some guy's right-handed guitar, flipped it upside down, low E string on the bottom, and played it like he owned it. That man sure could sing life's own blue truth. That's a fact. All three Kings could—B.B. and Freddie too. Those cats could make God hisself cry—and I was *one* of 'em for a spell."

"Well, *that* explains everything and makes it all worthwhile. Glad you made the right decision about leaving us."

My old man peered up at me for a long moment. When he finally spoke, he choked the words out.

"I … I'm real sorry, Jake." He focused on his grimy socks. "Ah shoulda done right by you, shoulda …." He went mute.

The bell over the shelter's front door tinkled and I jumped. Santana reached into the pocket of his sport coat and pulled out his revolver.

A voice boomed from the other room.

"Police." My father's head jerked up. The salsa and raunchy rap music evaporated from the hallway, and a door slammed shut. "Mr. Santana, you here? We got a 911 call."

I nodded toward the door. "Go ahead, Juan. Holler if the cops want to talk with me. I have a lot of questions for my old man, and I don't want him slithering out the backdoor."

Santana left, and I turned back to the man I had never expected or wanted to see again.

CHAPTER ELEVEN

Tuesday, December 3, 2002, 6:45 p.m.

For decades, I had wondered what I would say to my old man if we ever met. Johnny Cash's ballad, "A Boy Named Sue," played in my head. In the song, his daddy deserts him and all he leaves behind are booze bottles and an old guitar. Besides empty gin bottles, my sole inheritance was a family gone to dust, and a mother who had to work two jobs to make ends meet—until it killed her. My theme song was titled "A Boyhood Squandered."

He had walked out on us when I was nine. Any reminder of my father had unleashed a torrent of my tears, so my mother removed all traces of him from our home and burned his photographs. A few months later, I found one from our trip to the Cedar Point Amusement Park. I stashed it in my closet. In the picture, we were three grinning idiots standing in line at the Blue Streak, waiting to board the old wooden roller coaster. It had been taken two weeks before he abandoned us, before the real roller coaster ride started for Mom and me.

My cauldron of anger and hurt had been simmering for years. As I stared at my namesake, it boiled over and my fists clenched. Like the boy in Cash's song, I wanted to hit him hard between the eyes and cut off a chunk of his ear.

"Jake, listen up. I gotta tell ya—"

I showed him the palms of my hands and silenced him with a shake of my head. My pulse was galloping, and the top of my skull threatened to blow off.

As a teenager, I had yearned for a chance to beat the crap out of him. After my discharge from the army, I actually scoured New Orleans looking for him. A merciful God had kept me from finding him. When I finally gave up the search, I tore his image from the right side of that photo, tossed it into the Mississippi River, and watched the muddy water carry it away.

Since that time, I had tried repeatedly to let go of my anger. We'd had some good times together as a family before he let the rising tide of drugs and booze carry him out of our lives, but the pain he had caused my mother always relit the fire of my rage. At first, I buried his memory under empty liquor bottles, later in medical tomes, and finally in pages of scripture. In the end, I accepted the fact that although I might someday be able to forgive him, I could never forget the hurt he had caused. I thought I had laid his memory to rest for good, but nothing stays buried forever in the cemetery of the mind. Eventually, a hand reaches up from the grave.

I did not know why the shriveled sack of human garbage before me had come back to town or what he wanted from me, but I was certain from experience that the mere presence of this man threatened to unravel my world. I gazed at the genetically-linked stranger who had once been the center of my childhood universe and wanted to spit. There would be no reunion hug. I let the expanding silence fill the room.

He picked at the bed sheet and finally looked up.

"Son, I—"

"Don't you dare call me *son*! You pissed away that right."

"Jake, don't nobody want to change the past more 'an me."

"You mean like when I was six years old, and you were babysitting and took me to your gig at the Hideout Lounge, then got so stoned after the last set that you drove home without me?"

He hung his head. "You got every right to hate my guts—"

"Oh, I'm well past hate. You're not worth the time and energy."

And yet, I could not walk away. The small crucifix I wore on a chain around my neck grew heavy, choking me.

"Why'd you come back, after all these years? What the hell do you want?"

"Got nowhere else to go." Moisture filled his red-rimmed eyes. "Bought me a peck of troubles."

"Yeah, I met two of your friends in the lobby. They were ... damned upset with you."

He tried to stand, did not have the strength or the will, and plopped down onto the cot.

"You gotta help me, boy. Them two, they're gonna fillet me like a flounder!"

A tear rolled from his bloodshot eyes down his cheek. I waited for the next installment of his melodrama.

"I ripped off my boss, Jake, and he sent his guys after me. Snorted a line or two of his product every now'n again, just enough to get feeling right, you know. I ain't shooting up or nothing, never used no needles." He lowered his head. "And I ... took some of his money, not much, a few bucks.

It was unlikely those two goons had chased him all the way to Ohio over a few dollars.

"And?"

"An' I … saw things. Bad things. Shoulda bailed out sooner, left Louisiana and that life behind years ago."

"And?"

"I, uh … took a little of their blow an' sold it on the side."

Stole from a drug dealer? The old fool had lived longer than most, but had not learned a thing. He had never had an ounce of self-control or common sense, and now he was a walking billboard advertising the ravages of substance abuse.

He sniffed and wiped his nose on his sleeve. I suspected he had snorted as much product as he had sold.

I knew he was playing me, just not to what end. I remained silent, waiting for the bottom line.

"I need a place to lie low, Jake. Whatcha say? Ain't got no friends here no more, and I'm a dead man back in N'awlins. *Please*, boy. Help me!"

How ironic. He had left Mom and me in the lurch, and now he wanted me to save his sorry ass! Screw him.

Without a word, I walked to the door, but froze when he began sobbing.

"Jakey, Jakey, I'm begging ya, son!"

I had seen firsthand what Tubby and Muscle were capable of, and knew what they would do to a drunken old man. I turned around, but what options did I have? He had already put Santana and the homeless shelter in jeopardy, and I sure as hell did not want him anywhere near RJ and the people I cared about.

There was a soft knock at the door. Santana stepped in.

"The police want to take your statement, Jake."

My father launched up from the cot. "Don't give me up to the cops!" His eyes widened. "There's some … warrants and such. Don't let 'em send me back home. Please, boy. We're kin."

"You kissed *kin* goodbye years ago. Sit back down."

The image of my old man in handcuffs being shoved into the back of a cruiser had a strong appeal and would solve Santana's problem. Unfortunately, it would not solve mine. Muscle had forgotten a lot of things over the years but he wouldn't forget my face, not after what I had done to his.

In for a penny, in for a pounding.

"All right, I won't turn you over to the police. We'll figure something out after I get back." I said to Santana, "Don't let him bolt. We're not done with our family reunion."

CHAPTER TWELVE

Tuesday, December 3, 2002, 7:00 p.m.

I sat in Santana's desk chair in the shelter's drab lobby and gave my statement to a policewoman along with a description of the two thugs. She furiously scribbled my responses down in a spiral notebook. The memory of Muscle, goliath-big and pit-bull nasty, made me tremble all over again. When I mentioned the large A and B letters tattooed on Muscle's neck, she stopped writing.

"AB? That helps a lot. Describe it."

"Blue ink, jagged letters. What's it mean?"

"'AB' stands for Aryan Brotherhood. Probably a prison tat. Anything else?"

"The guy has a shaved head, and the paper punch I hit him with left a mouth full of broken teeth and a large gash on his forehead that will probably require stitches."

"Good. I'll check the local emergency rooms and dentists. Maybe we'll get lucky. What about the fat man?"

I described Tubby's Fu Manchu mustache, his New Orleans Saints football jacket, and the ivory-handled switchblade, which thirty minutes earlier I would have sworn was a sword. If we ever met again, I suspected that both men would be armed with more than knives.

"That'll do for now, Dr. Austin." The policewoman took my contact information and pointed at a compact, gray-haired man in his fifties. "Go talk with our sketch artist. Mr. Santana already gave him a description of these guys. See if you can add anything."

I could not. The artist's renderings looked like photographs of Tubby and Muscle. The police department had evidently hired a direct descendent of Rembrandt.

Back in the shelter's living quarters, rap music again boomed from one of the rooms, the driving bass beat amplifying my throbbing headache.

My father sat on his cot, his saxophone case and duffel bag at his feet. Santana was perched on a folding chair near the door.

"Your dad can't stay here, Jake. I got no choice. Those goons will be back. I'm going to tell them he stole my money and disappeared. Sorry. I can't put the shelter at risk. He has to leave."

I nodded. No way could he stay at my apartment. I refused to endanger my nephew and Colleen, and the thought of RJ calling this dirt-bag *Grandpa* tied my stomach in a knot. I considered calling Tree for help, but couldn't ask the Sheriff to protect a drug dealer and fugitive. Besides, my old man would freak-out at the very mention of law enforcement.

Maybe Santana's solution was best. Get Daddy the hell away from all of us. I pulled out my wallet, emptied it, and shoved the cash toward him.

"Here. Take it and go. Do what Santana said—disappear. And don't come back. Ever."

My father whimpered like a lost puppy and stared at the money as if he had no idea what it was.

Santana's expression hardened.

"For the love of God, Jake! What're you thinking? You know damn well if you give him cash, he'll drink it or snort it, and he won't get farther than a back alley in Cleveland."

Santana was right. Even more compelling was the solemn voice that echoed in my mind: *Vengeance is mine, saith the Lord.* Abandoning my father into the arms of Tubby and Muscle would be nothing less than an act of revenge.

I believe that God tests us, and life is pass-fail—and on Judgment Day, I wanted to stand with the righteous. I stared at the battered shell of the man who had shattered my childhood, now brought low, humbled at my feet—and for the first time felt a twinge of pity.

I sighed and pocketed the cash. "Okay. I'll help you, old man—on one condition."

His eyes lit with hope. "What's that?"

"You get clean. No booze. No drugs."

Panic flashed in his eyes as if he was staring into a very real Hell and his gaze fell. The answer was a long time coming.

"Aw-right, whatever you say."

Not very convincing, but I am a man of faith and believe in miracles.

"Come on. Let's get you something to eat and a place to stay."

I apologized to Santana for the danger we had caused him and the shelter, then walked to my car, my father tottering after me.

Wanting him out of sight as soon as possible, I bought him a couple burgers at a McDonald's drive-through and parked at the Diplomat, a flea-bag hotel not far from the hospital. The once stately front porch was sagging and the exterior had not seen a paint brush in decades. The locals called it the Wiltin' Hilton, and my father's appearance would blend in nicely with the clientele.

Our approach interrupted the literary pursuits of the skin-head working the front desk. He took a moment to memorize the centerfold, grumbled, and closed his *Penthouse* magazine. Three clocks on the wall above him were labeled London, Tokyo, and Bombay, as if the patrons here required up-to-the-minute information on world events. None of the clocks worked. Their hands had probably frozen in time well before Bombay was renamed Mumbai.

I requested two keys and signed my father into the hotel register as "Kenny Babcock," my best friend during the war, hoping their fates wouldn't be the same. Kenny had died in my arms.

"You want the room for an hour or a day?"

I paid in cash for a week. The skin-head studied us from under his droopy eyelids, massaged the swastika tattoo on his neck, and threw the keys onto the counter. As we walked away, he mumbled, "Fuckin' fags."

The elevator was out of order, no surprise in this dump. I took my father's duffel bag and saxophone case, and he began a slow, unsteady climb up the stairs, clinging to the railing. I walked behind him, expecting him to topple over.

When I opened the door to his room, dust bunnies scampered across filthy shag carpet. The flowery, water-stained wallpaper had begun surrendering to gravity in several places. The double bed sagged like the back of a horse headed to the glue-factory, and the room smelled the way it looked. Raunchy.

I stepped into the bathroom and a chunk of plaster that had fallen from the ceiling crunched on the yellowed linoleum under my shoe. When I flipped the light switch, only one of the two bulbs above the sink lit.

Returning to my old man's room, I saw him slip a pint of whiskey back into his coat pocket. Although I am a man of faith, I am also a believer in *trust, but verify*. So much for keeping his end of our bargain.

I stomped over intending to confiscate the booze, then stopped. The Wiltin' Hilton was the last place I wanted him to go into DT's. After decades of abuse, he needed to be in detox. I let the whiskey slide, told my father to take a shower, and said I would be back in the morning with groceries and clean clothes. I did not leave him any money.

Anxious to get home in time to read a bedtime story to RJ, I sprinted down the stairs. As I passed the front desk, the clerk glanced up from his girly mag and said, "Shit man, that's gotta be the world's quickest quickie."

CHAPTER THIRTEEN

Wednesday, December 4, 2002 7:15 a.m.

The next day, I got up early, made pancakes, and enjoyed an unhurried breakfast with RJ. He was giving me a sales pitch for a new toy he had seen advertised on television when Colleen arrived. I apologized to her again for coming home late the night before, placed the dirty plates and utensils in the dishwasher, and kissed my nephew goodbye.

Before driving to the hospital, I stopped in my study and booted up my computer. The state of my office made me groan. I had been so busy over the past few months that a fine layer of dust had collected on a stack of unread medical journals on my desk. Between the hospital, the church, and my nephew, it was time to ask God to add a few more hours to each day.

I went online and downloaded my emails. In addition to a reminder about the upcoming Ethics Committee meeting and the AMA newsletter, I received spam for an "all-natural testosterone supplement guaranteed to enhance my sex life"—the perfect gift for your favorite Catholic priest.

After shutting down the computer, I ventured outside and scraped snow and ice from my windshield, then drove to the hospital through a white-out of blowing flurries—the kind of winter weather that made northerners long for the sweltering heat and humidity of August.

My parking angel somehow found a vacant space near the hospital entrance for me. I shut off the ignition and hopped out. The life-sized statue of St. Joseph near the front door wore a fluffy cap of snow and wept icicles.

When I heard my name, I turned. Harvey Winer trudged toward me.

"Morning, Harvey. I didn't think administrators came to work this early."

"Have to keep my eye on all you slackers." He stopped, pointed at my car, and released a hearty laugh.

"What's so funny?"

"Your bumper sticker."

It read, *Catholicism: Under the same management for over 2000 years.*

Harvey removed his old fedora, touched his yarmulke, and replied, "I think, Yaakov, that makes you Christians the new kids on the block." He laughed again, and we entered the hospital's main reception area, which already thrummed with the heartbeat of humanity. A large, blue-green Douglas fir tree had been erected overnight and lavishly decorated with tinsel, ornaments, and lights, filling the foyer with the scent of pine.

Winer veered left into the administrative wing. I continued straight to the doctors' lounge, hung my overcoat in my locker, and walked to the chapel. As I finished dressing for eight o'clock Mass, my cellphone filled the sacristy with the strains of Handel's "Messiah," my chosen Christmas ringtone.

I recognized the caller's number. "Hey, big guy. Top of the morning."

"Hey yourself. We gotta talk."

I hated those words. The last time Tree Macon had used that phrase, I had been a suspect in the murder of one of our high school classmates.

"Where are you, Jake?"

"In the hospital chapel, starting Mass."

"Good. I'm down in the Emergency Room, taking a victim's statement. I'll be there shortly." He chuckled. "You allow Baptists in the door, right?"

"Only if you belt out the hymns. Most Catholics sing as if they're afraid to disturb the Lord."

I exited the sacristy, approached the altar, and nodded to my Three Owls in the front pew. Adorned in the usual black finery of nuns, their eyeglasses glinted in the morning light like three pairs of binoculars. All three smiled at me, and it took a moment to realize why. They had set up a small ceramic nativity scene in the sanctuary, complete with wise men, animals, and shepherds—everyone, of course, except for the baby Jesus figurine in the manger, which would not appear until Christmas day.

Weekday attendance at morning Mass was often poor, but the pews were so empty that the service felt more like meditation. No sign of Emily and her father. Joey Childs waved from the back row. He gazed at the vacant alcove as if the broken statue of St. Joseph might somehow miraculously reappear, reminding me that I had forgotten all about it in the trunk of my car and needed to get it repaired. The empty alcove had the look of a missing tooth in the chapel's once radiant smile.

I cast aside my disappointment at the low turnout and focused on my hour with the Lord. When Mass ended, I blessed the faithful, reentered the sacristy, and removed my chasuble and linen alb. Putting on my dress shirt and tie, I transformed from mild-mannered priest to hard-charging physician like some bizarre comic book character. Such was my life.

Tree barged in and leaned against the wall. A slow, easy grin unfurled on his lips. "Well, that was weird, Jake."

"What was?"

"Watching my delinquent high school teammate say Mass."

I had seen him standing at the back of the chapel. His six-foot six-inch, two-hundred-fifty pound body was impossible to miss.

Tree went silent. His smile inverted, and his sudden change in demeanor gave me the willies.

"What's the matter, Sheriff? Did someone steal your hubcaps?"

"I just interviewed a friend of yours in the ER. Juan Santana was attacked this morning outside the homeless shelter."

"Dear Lord! How bad is he?"

"Cuts and bruises. Could've been a lot worse. Two scumbags broke fingers on both of his hands, as a warning. They threatened to torch the shelter if he didn't tell them where Jake Austin was hiding. Santana said these same guys hassled you both last night. He also told me that you rearranged the big thug's face."

Tree folded his over-sized frame into a brown leather chair the color of his skin.

"Why the hell didn't you call me, Jake? I could have gotten DNA on the blood and run it through the system for an ID before Santana cleaned it up." He tilted his head to the side. "And why am I not surprised you're involved in this mess?"

"It's complicated."

"The way you and Emily are *complicated*? Everything you do is complicated. Spill it."

"I'm not hiding, and they're not after me."

My old man had told me that there were warrants for his arrest back in Louisiana. I hung my vestments in the closet and slipped into my white coat, searching for a way to tell the truth without getting my father shipped off to jail. Tree and I went back a long way but not far enough for me to expect him to break the law, and I sure-as-heck could not ask him to put his career at risk for my father.

"Let's say *theoretically* that these goons are drug dealers, Tree, and they've confused me with a certain Mr. X."

"You mean like theoretically you don't know a drug dealer named Jimmy Sole, yet your name is on his contact list."

"That again? Cripe! Come on, buddy. Are you serious?"

"Serious as a heart attack. And don't *buddy* me, not when I got a body in a dumpster." Tree's cell vibrated. He checked the number and silenced it. "Tell me about Mr. X."

"He, uh ... double crossed the mob, and they want to skin him alive."

Tree's usual animation evaporated and his features grew immobile, as if his face was carved from mahogany.

"In that case, I'd say *theoretically* Jake, your ass is in a sling and you'd better give up Mr. X to me or them, before you bring down a shit-storm on yourself, the homeless shelter, and everyone around you. You said it—you're not hiding and pretty damn easy to find."

I shook my head. "I can't. The man is old and frail and won't survive a prison sentence."

"And he won't survive on the street, and neither will you. For Christ's sake, what're you thinking? This guy must be really special for you to …." Tree jumped up. "Son of a bitch! Jake Austin *senior*?" He slumped back onto the chair. "Santana left your father out of his story." His dark eyes lit up. "Well, that explains your name on Jimmy Sole's list."

I sat at the desk and cradled my head in my hands.

"You don't have a choice, Jake. If you get your father out of town, you're all these clowns have. They'll come after you and Santana. At least I can protect him, and take the heat off you."

"My dad's a bag of bones, maybe a hundred pounds, and he's addicted to booze and God-knows what else. I don't want him, or anyone, going cold turkey in jail."

"We got detox programs."

"Come on, I've seen jail detox. Guys convulsing in drunk tanks. Jailers who won't even give them Tylenol for withdrawal pain. Addicts wide awake for days, sitting stark-naked on metal toilets."

"Not in my damn jail!"

"You have no control over Louisiana jails, Tree. That's where he'll end up. My old man may be a total dirt-bag, but I can't put him through that. He should be in a hospital—or God help me, I'll detox him myself."

"Be realistic. You already got too much on your plate between the hospital, the Church, and RJ."

Tree's radio hissed, spitting out code numbers. He ignored it.

"As a friend, Jake, I'll do what I can. Maybe we find enough to charge your dad with a misdemeanor and keep him in Ohio, and maybe the judge'll be willing to count his rehab toward jail time. Maybe we get lucky and bust the two hoods from Louisiana, and your world gets a lot brighter."

"That's a truckload of *maybes*. Hell, what if they send more goons after him."

"I don't see a lot of alternatives here. If your father goes into the hospital voluntarily, I'll station a guard outside his door for protection. If he has any info we can use against the gang and he turns state's evidence, we'll have more options. That's the best I can do."

I deliberated for a minute. I could see only one way out of the dark cave that was my father's life.

"Okay, Tree. Let me stop in the ER first to check on Santana, then we'll go visit dear old Daddy."

I called Nurse Ochs in the Urgent Care Center, told her I had a family emergency, and asked her to get coverage for me. She was not pleased.

When we walked in, the Emergency Room was a circus, not the entertaining Ringling Brothers kind, just the usual three-ring on-going chaos. Tree stepped away from the bedlam to make a telephone call. Like hospital expenses and regulations, the patient load always increased beyond our ability to handle it, and the overflow crowd ended up lining the walls of the hallway. These patients often felt forgotten and ignored, and most were scared, angry, or frustrated. I stopped to speak with them whenever I had the time, but I was on a mission.

As I wandered among wheelchairs and stretchers of "hall people," I found Santana lying on a gurney next to a portable x-ray machine. His shirt was torn and bloody. A crescent moon of stitches held the skin of his left cheek together below a plum-colored eye, which was swollen shut. Aluminum splints immobilized fractures of both pinky fingers.

"Juan?"

He didn't respond. I put a gentle hand on his arm and he startled, opening the one eye that functioned.

"I didn't tell them anything, Jake. They threatened to fire-bomb the shelter unless I told them where your dad was hiding. If my assistant hadn't shown up, I don't know what those two would've done. Rocky shouted and called the cops, and they took off. Thought I was gonna die." Santana's voice was thin and shaky. "I'm scared. Not just for me, but for the folks at the shelter too."

"Sorry you got dragged into this. I'm putting my father in police custody to get him some protection—and take the heat off you and the shelter."

He nodded.

"Anything I can do to help, Juan?"

He closed his good eye and turned toward the wall.

CHAPTER FOURTEEN

Wednesday, December 4, 2002, 9:45 a.m.

When Tree and I entered the lobby of the Diplomat Hotel, the neo-Nazi punk working the front desk gawked for a second at Tree's skin color and uniform before whirling around and busying himself with a wall of empty mail slots. He massaged his neck to cover up the swastika tattoo with his hand.

The elevator still wore an "Out of Order" sign, so we climbed the stairs. I removed the spare room key from my pocket. I didn't need it. My father's door stood ajar.

I reached out to open it, but Tree placed a hand on my arm and pointed to gouges in the doorframe. "Been jimmied," he whispered.

Motioning me away, he pulled out his service pistol. Tree was SWAT-trained, and I had seen him in action. I stepped back. The last time he had fired his nine millimeter, he'd saved my life, but only missed my head by an inch or two.

Tree rapped his knuckles on the door jamb. "Mr. Austin, you all right?"

Silence. He knocked again.

"It's the police. I'm coming in."

No reply.

Standing off to the side, Tree swung the door open with the toe of his boot and followed his gun into the room.

It looked as if a hand grenade had exploded in a Goodwill store. The contents of my father's duffel bag littered the floor. The closet had been emptied and dresser drawers yanked out. The pillows and mattress hemorrhaged stuffing where they had been slashed.

Alarm bells clanged in my head. All this for stealing a few bucks and a couple ounces of dope? No, they had to be after something more important—and I hoped to God they had found it.

Tree pointed to the bathroom door and assumed a shooter's crouch.

I flashed back to my Army days and flattened against the wall. With just my right hand exposed, I twisted the knob and shoved the door.

The rusty hinges moaned as the door opened into an unoccupied bathroom. Tree entered and threw back the shower curtain. I half-expected a bloody scene from *Psycho*, but saw only a hair-clogged drain and a dead cockroach.

Tree punched the button on his radio, reported the break-in, and requested a patrol car. Petty larceny was well below the Sheriff's pay grade. If this had not been my father's room, he probably would have wheeled around and headed for his car without a word.

The radio squawked, and Tree said, "Wait a sec." He turned to me. "Your dad got a gun, Jake?"

I did not have a clue who my father had become over the years and was not sure how to answer. I didn't want to put the police in danger, nor did I want him gunned down. When frightened at the homeless shelter, my old man had brandished a metal pipe.

"No, I don't think he's armed."

Tree told the dispatcher that my father was a "person of interest" to be brought in for questioning, emphasizing that he was elderly and in poor health. He handed the radio to me, and as I finished describing my father's appearance, we heard footsteps in the hall. Tree shoved me toward the bathroom, darted behind the dresser, and aimed his weapon at the doorway.

An off-key, raspy tenor grew louder with every footfall. I recognized the old radio jingle.

What's the word? Thunderbird.
How's it sold? Good and cold.
What's the reason? 'Cause it's pleasin'.

The hallway serenade was interrupted by a loud thud, followed by a litany of curses.

My father stumbled into the room, his saxophone case in one hand, the top of an open bottle peeking from a brown paper bag in the other. I could almost hear the time bomb ticking in his liver.

His eyes widened as he took in the chaos, then fixed on me.

"Dang it, Jake! Why'd ya toss my room?"

"It wasn't my doing."

"Whadda fuck happened here?"

"You tell me."

"Don't know." He raised the bottle with a sheepish grin. "Got a might thirsty and moseyed out for a sip."

"At ten o'clock in the morning?"

"Now, don't you go raisin' no dust over a little nip." He gave me the stink-eye I had seen so many times as a boy. "You're all growed up now. You get how it is."

Alas, I knew exactly how it was. My boozing had led me to the edge of the precipice, and I understood the craving all too well.

My father ambled into the room, saw Tree's uniform, and tried to run but staggered into a chair and landed hard on his butt. Red wine splashed across the azure shag carpet adding a purple streak. Somehow he managed to hold on to the bottle and his saxophone case.

He glowered at me.

"You called the damn cops on me? You sonofabitch!"

My fists balled and I glared down at him. "I wouldn't talk about *my mother* like that if I were you, old man."

Tree helped him up and sat him on the bed.

"You may not remember me, Mr. Austin. I'm Tremont Macon. Jake and I went to school—"

"Yeah, I recollect who you are, boy." My father raised the paper bag, took a long draw from his bottle, and wiped his lips on his sleeve. "You two always was a burr under my saddle."

Tree let the "boy" comment pass and summarized the assault on Juan Santana and the arson threat against the homeless shelter.

When he had finished, I took over and explained that his return to town had placed me, and possibly the hospital, in danger. I did not mention RJ.

He took it all in, stood with a sudden burst of energy, and wobbled toward me.

"It's always been about *you*, Jake, ain't it?" Slurred words oozed molasses-slow past yellowed teeth. "Rat out your own pappy? You selfish prick!"

He shoved his crimson face at me like a red-hot poker. His breath reeked, and he clearly hadn't noticed the bathtub yet.

"We're done talkin'. I'm gone." He used the Lord's name without quoting scriptures, then spit a wad of pink saliva on the rug. "You ain't no son of mine."

I could not have said it better. *In vino veritas*—in wine there is truth. He sure-as-hell had been no father.

Tree gently sat him back down on the bed. "Leaving's not an option, sir."

Tree laid out our plan, suggesting that my old man could swap rehab days for jail time. My father scoffed when Tree promised police protection.

"Protect me from them hombres? You and what army? Y'all are nuttier than squirrel shit. I'm outta here."

Tree took out his handcuffs and waved them slowly. "Here's the deal, sir. If you leave, all these thugs got left are Jake and his boy, and they'll come after them both."

My father's eyes widened at the mention of my nephew. He began to speak but Tree continued.

"I'm not about to let you put them in danger. You can either go to detox in the hospital or to jail—with or without these bracelets." He waved the handcuffs again. "Your choice."

"Jail? 'Fraid not. On what charge? I ain't done nothin'."

Tree eyeballed him and said, "Vagrancy, drunkenness, public nuisance, disturbing the peace—we'll find something. I'm a very creative guy. If you want, I can ship you back to Louisiana. Up to you, sir."

My father stared at me. When I said nothing, his eyes darted around the room, finally landing on the saxophone case.

"Okay, okay, y'all win. But what about my sax? Don't give a shit about this other stuff." He pointed at his scattered clothing, lifted the case and offered it to me. "This here's my baby. Take care of her till I get out, Jake. She's all I got left."

So sad, and so true.

Tree stroked his chin. "Maybe, after I examine it."

My father handed the case over, and Tree opened it. Two tattered photographs were taped inside—my old man's version of a family scrapbook. One was of my half-sister at Mardi Gras, the other of me on a Lake Erie beach, both taken around age eight. I'd often wondered if I had any other half-siblings scattered around the country. By the look of his photo collection, we apparently were the only two lucky winners of the paternal booby prize—at least as far as my tomcat-of-a-father knew.

Tree carefully removed the saxophone and gave it to my old man. "Run the cleaning cloth through it, Mr. Austin."

When I was a child, my dad would guide a silk swab through his sax with the deftness of a magician pulling an endless chain of colorful scarves from the palm of his hand. Now a confirmed drunk, his hands trembled violently as he removed the mouthpiece and used a filthy rag tied by a string to a metal nut. The rag got stuck halfway, and he had to yank it hard to drag it through.

Tree refocused on the case, rummaging through cough drops, a few dollar bills, loose change, a couple keys, and a pack of cigarettes. He ripped the top off the pack and sniffed it, searching for marijuana in hopes of finding another reason to hold my old man in Ohio rather than ship him to Louisiana. Finally, he handed the smokes to my father. The side compartment contained cork wax, reeds, and an extra mouthpiece. After Tree was satisfied, he returned the saxophone to the case, snapped it shut, and handed it to me.

Two deputies knocked at the open door. Tree waved them in. One said, "Hey boss, you really going all CSI over a burglary at the damn Diplomat Hotel? We're supposed to be—"

Tree delivered a glare that silenced the deputy and scared the hell out of me.

Dad scratched his stubbled chin and belched loudly. "You boys always was a pain in my ass. Still are."

He raised the wine bottle, drained it, tossed it on the bed, then scanned the room and snickered.

"Hell, takes four of y'all to bring in one ol' desperado. Pitiful!" He pointed at Tree's handcuffs. "Won't need no shackles, gents. I promise I won't hurt you none. Aw-right, Ossifer Macon, let's get this here show on the road."

CHAPTER FIFTEEN

Wednesday, December 4, 2002, 11:30 a.m.

While my father was being interviewed at the police station, Tree dropped me off at the hospital. I stored my father's saxophone case in my locker in the doctors' lounge and finished my shift at Urgent Care. As I completed my charting for the day, Tree phoned me.

"Your dad's been admitted to the rehab unit at St. Joseph's. I'm on my way there. Think you should join us. He confessed to buying grass from Jimmy Sole years ago, but denied any current knowledge or recent contact. We did, however, find a dime bag of weed in a side pocket of his duffel bag and a small amount of cocaine stashed in a chewing tobacco tin."

"It just gets better and better with that old fool."

"On the bright side, Jake, it's enough to keep him in custody, detox, and out of a Louisiana prison—at least for now."

St. Joe's, an inner-city hospital, devoted its entire fourth floor to drug rehabilitation. I entered an elevator filled with white coats talking shop. My mind was elsewhere. When the doors opened on four, I saw Tree and a deputy huddled outside my father's room.

"Thanks for getting my old man police protection," I said to Tree, then nodded to a young officer who looked more like a Boy Scout than a cop. A florid case of acne was ravaging the young man's face, and I suspected his five-o'clock shadow would not appear until well after midnight.

"That's my job. Making the world a safer place. I live to protect and serve." Tree uncorked a hearty laugh. "Worked out well. Officer Kearney here is doing double duty. He was already guarding a drug mule." He hooked a thumb toward the adjacent room. "Guy got off a plane from South America and collapsed when the cargo in his gut leaked. Instant OD. Some surgeon with a quick scalpel saved his ass."

I bit my lip and let Dr. Glade collect all of the accolades.

Tree continued, "Our mule thinks he's Houdini and keeps trying to escape. Bolted for the exit the moment he woke up in the Recovery Room—stitches, tubes, and all." Tree ran a hand over his bowling-ball scalp. "Funny, though. He's originally from Baton Rouge."

"So?"

"So … your dad's being hounded by Louisiana drug dealers."

"Probably a coincidence, Tree. That's a big city."

"I don't believe in coincidences … or unicorns, or the Tooth Fairy. Coincidences are just unexplained connections. Problem is, your father won't tell me shit about his life in New Orleans. Maybe you can get him to open up."

"I doubt it, but I'll give it a try."

As Tree and I approached my father's room, Dr. Woisnet exited. He ran the detox/rehab facility and, unfortunately, Lorain County kept him and his staff extremely busy.

"Glad you're here, Jake. I ran a tox-screen on your father to see what's floating around in his system. He's in a bit of a mood and has some rough days ahead. Don't worry, we'll get him through this."

"Thanks."

Woisnet patted me on the back and walked down the hall.

When Tree and I entered my father's room, he popped out of bed. The cheery buzz from his morning bottle of wine had worn off and his greeting was less than warm.

"You got some nerve, Jake, selling me out, and waltzing in here as if nothin' done happened. God-damn, two-faced Judas!" He shook his head. "Cops got all pissy about a lousy half-gram of blow." He pointed a finger at me. "You been a big help, boy, so fuck-you-very-much. Don't nobody need a son like you. Get out and don't come back! I'm done with ya."

If he was trying to hurt my feelings, it didn't work. He had done that years ago. And agitation and labile emotions were early signs of withdrawal and completely expected. Besides, the animosity was mutual. A family reunion with this dirt-bag every forty years was *too often* for me. I wanted to spin around on my heels and go home to RJ, but I had promised my friend I would help.

"Come on, tell Tree what you know about the drug operation. Give him something. Anything."

I wondered if telling him I was a priest would soften his resistance. Unlikely. My old man couldn't name the Holy Trinity if I spotted him the Father and the Son.

"Level with Tree." I sighed. "You can't live this way. It's for your own good."

"It ain't about me! *You're* the one who's scared shitless. Hell, you run across two bad-ass Louisiana boys and you piss your pants. Well, I cain't abide no pussy!"

He paced the room twice, stopped, and his razor-sharp eyes slashed at me.

"You ain't got the guts God gave a rabbit, Jake. Couldn't find your balls if you tied a string to 'em!"

Heat ignited in my cheeks. The priest in me suggested a tolerant, measured approach and a gentle line of questioning. The angry boy inside told him to sit down and shut up. I'd had enough and pulled out the big guns.

"No, you old fool. This is not about me. I'm trying to protect *your grandchild.*"

We locked gazes. His mouth opened. No sound emerged.

"I met my half-sister for the first time in July. Turned out Justine and I had a lot in common." I waited for my old man to take the bait. He sucked air through his teeth but remained mute. "You walked out on her as a kid too! Some father you were. She hated your guts almost as much as I do."

He winced, made a false start, and finally said, "How's my little girl?"

"Why do you care?"

He flopped on the bed and the bottom of his hospital gown rode up, exposing thin, hairless legs. He covered himself with the bed sheets, picked at them, and took his time before answering, his delivery slow and very cold.

"Y'all never was the sharpest tool in the shed. She may be your half-sister, but I ain't got no *half-daughters* ... or half-sons. So, how's Justine and where's she at?"

Fury pounded inside my chest like a fist. My priest persona grappled with the rampaging boy inside me. The kid grabbed his cassock, threw him down, and pinned his tired ass to the ground.

I wanted to dropkick my father into next week. Instead, I launched the plastic wastebasket across the room. It bounced off the wall, spewing its contents.

"She's in a grave! That's where she is, damn it. Your little girl's dead ... just like my mother." My anger flared. "Everywhere you go, you leave a trail of bodies and heartache, you old bastard!"

"What?" He couldn't let go of the word and stretched it into two syllables.

It wasn't fair. My father was not really responsible for Justine's death, but my fire was raging and I didn't care. I was the hammer; he was the nail. Abandoning children was one sin for which I could find no absolution.

"How'd she ... pass, Jake?"

"Which one? Justine or Mom?" I moved toward him and shoved my finger in his face. He cowered against the headboard. "It's a bit late to give a damn now!"

I was out of control, a wildfire fueled by the kindling this man had made of my childhood and the people I had loved.

Tree came up behind me, wrapped his big hand around my arm, and dragged me backward. His voice came from somewhere cavernous. "Easy, Jake. Dial it down."

I had not begun to exhaust one tenth of the rage I had stored up over the decades and my pulse was galloping. I inhaled deeply and slowly let it out.

"Mom picked up a case of booze the day you left us, and she never stopped drinking. She passed out one night with a lit cigarette and torched the house and herself. Because of you, I came home from the Army to a closed casket. I couldn't even kiss her goodbye."

My old man nodded as if I had just given him the weather report.

"And Justine?"

"Leukemia. You were her best chance for a transplant match. We couldn't find you because you didn't want to be found, so I donated my bone marrow." I wriggled free of Tree's grasp and punched the wall. "It didn't work."

A nurse must have heard the noise, peeked in the door, stared at the hole I'd put in the drywall, and scurried away. My hand ached, but not as much as my heart.

My father refused to make eye contact. I allowed the memory of the two dead women I loved to hang in the air. That is where they always were for me—never far away, never close enough.

His sorrow surprised me. Surprised and disgusted. He had never cared when it counted.

"Justine had a son, old man. Randall James. RJ. *His* sperm donor deserted him too! I'm going to give my nephew the father I never had."

He sat up and took it all in. I had laid the harvest of dried weeds and brambles that my father's years of neglect had produced at his feet. A tear rolled down his cheek. He wiped it away with his hospital gown, blew his nose, and continued.

"The child have his mama's red hair?"

"Yes ... and the same blue eyes."

He leaned back, lost in a memory. "Justine was real pretty, always laughing." He wiped more tears. "Can I meet her boy?"

"No."

"That don't seem right. For Christ sake, he's my own flesh-n-blood. All I want is to see him ever' now'n again."

"No way! You have to be a father, before you can be a grandfather."

"Please. I ain't gonna be in this world for long and just wanna meet him." He looked away. "I'll get clean, do whatever you say."

I had been weaned from his lies and false promises years ago, but his tears began to douse my fire.

"How about this. You tell Tree everything you know about this drug operation and get through rehab, and *then* I'll consider letting you meet RJ."

"Okay. We got us a deal."

He reached out to shake on it. I did not take his hand.

"I promise I'll keep my end of the bargain." He dropped his hand into his lap. "Got any pictures of the boy?"

Even *that* was closer to my nephew than I wanted him to be. I kept silent.

"Please, Jake."

Taking out my cellphone, I showed him some photos, and asked, "What about the cocaine rap? Do you want a lawyer?"

Before he could answer, Tree said, "If you help our Drug Task Force, Mr. Austin, I can make the bust go away."

He thought for a while.

"Don't need no mouthpiece." His eyes darted from Tree to me. "I trust you boys. Y'all got yourself a snitch."

I didn't get my hopes up.

Tree patted me on the back. "Go home, Jake. Play with RJ. I got this. See you tomorrow."

As I walked from the warmth of the hospital into the icy indigo dusk, I wondered if turning my father over to the police had insured my nephew's safety and mine, or if I had inadvertently painted bullseyes on both of our backs.

CHAPTER SIXTEEN

Thursday, December 5, 2002, 7:30 a.m.

The next day before morning Mass, I stopped in the rehab unit. Tree was already there, leaning against the wall. He looked like hell. His eyes were bloodshot and baggy, and it appeared as if he had aged overnight.

"Morning, Sunshine." I smiled. "What're you doing up so early?"

Sheriff Sunshine's expression radiated no warmth.

"Someone killed my drug mule last night, Jake. Coroner says he was suffocated with a pillow."

The door behind him opened. Crime scene techs in hairnets, latex gloves, and paper booties swarmed the room.

My breath caught in my chest. I started toward my father's room. Tree pushed off the wall and stopped me.

"Your dad's okay."

"How could this happen with a guard on duty?"

"A man in a white coat said the kitchen sent up an extra meal and wondered if Officer Kearney wanted it." Tree dragged a big hand across his face. "Damn rookies! Food was laced with something. Gave him the trots. He was just coming back from the john when two guys walked out of the mule's room. Kearney pulled his piece and they bolted. He was too sick to chase them down. From his description, probably the same goons who attacked you and Santana."

"Do they know my father's here?"

"Not sure. We checked him in under an alias." Tree massaged his forehead. "My guess is they didn't, or they would have split up and hit both rooms. But I'm not taking any chances. We're moving him to the jail for protection."

"Wait. No. He has to be in rehab or he'll—"

"Dr. Woisnet came by this morning to check on your dad and I explained the situation. He's agreed to supervise your father's detox in lockup, as a favor to you."

I combed my fingers through my hair, trying to steady my trembling hands. "What a mess."

"Yeah, and your father stepped right in it. He's been working as a small-time delivery boy for Angelo Giordano in Louisiana. I've read Big Angie's rap-sheet. He's a real nasty S.O.B. His crew's been in a bloody turf war with the Russian mob in New Orleans—drive-by shootings, slit throats, maybe a horsehead in somebody's bed. Giordano's got the Ruskies on the ropes. He's been expanding his drug operation into their Midwest territory and wants to rename our state O-*High*-O."

Tree took a step toward me and lowered his voice. "Your father said he was delivering a little coke to a corner man in Shreveport when two of his pals got iced, gunned down in a coffee shop. Giordano retaliated by blowing up one of the Russians with the guy's kids in the back seat of the car, and your daddy decided it was time to retire. He took the dope he was supposed to deliver and detoured to Detroit, where he snorted some product and sold the rest for chump-change, pissing the money away on motel rooms and hookers."

"Sounds exactly like my old man. Mr. Instant Gratification."

"Gets worse. The heroin mule who collapsed at the airport was linked to Big Angie's South American suppliers. He knew too much and needed to be silenced. I suspect Giordano probably enlisted Tubby and Muscle to find and snuff both the mule and your father."

"My old man's a small-time player. Why would big-time drug smugglers go after him? Over a few lousy grams of coke? That makes no sense."

"Makes perfect sense. You cross the boss, you die. The code of the streets. Disloyalty is a death sentence, and a warning to any gang-banger thinking about freelancing. Burying Jimmy Sole's mutilated body under a pile of garbage in a dumpster was a *business memo* direct from Big Angie to his employees."

I groaned. Not even eight in the morning and already the little drummer boy was beating out a solo inside my head.

"My old man's not just using, he's dealing drugs too? Christ! So he's facing prison time?"

"Yup, unless he turns state's evidence against Giordano and testifies in court. That would buy him immunity from prosecution and witness protection. Otherwise, he'll spend the rest of his life glancing over his shoulder, if he's lucky enough to make it out of jail alive. All I can prove is possession of a small amount of cocaine, but your father already confessed to working for Big Angie and bragged about it. My hands are tied, Jake. The Feebies are all over this."

"Feebies?"

"FBI. One's in with your father right now. DEA's joined the party too. Interstate drug trafficking draws a crowd."

A tall woman wearing a black pantsuit with an American flag lapel pin exited my father's room and came toward us. She was in her mid-forties with dark hair, dark eyes, and a formidable athletic stride. Her face was handsome but stern.

"Jake, this is Special Agent Keri Novak." Tree gestured toward me. "Agent Novak, this is your suspect's son, the other Jake Austin. He's a physician at St. Joe's."

"Glad you're here." Her handshake was firm, almost vise-like. "You're a pain management doc, right?"

I nodded and my chest tightened. I knew what was coming.

"Then you understand that the majority of illegal prescription drugs are dispensed by members of your specialty." She skipped only a beat, her gaze steel-cold. "I took a peek at your background. You partied a lot back in the day and left an ugly trail of DUIs and bar brawls."

"What?" When I glared at him, Tree shook his head, denying any involvement. "Come on, Novak, that was years ago. I was a kid. Are you accusing me of something?"

"Not accusing. Assessing. Pills are pouring into this county, and as far as I'm concerned, *every* doctor here is guilty until proven innocent. The Sheriff said you can be trusted, but I've learned on the job that most tigers don't change their stripes. It would help me to believe that you're the exception if you cooperated."

"What do you want from me, Agent Novak?"

"We've been after Angelo Giordano for a long time. His operation's spreading up from the South like kudzu, leaving a path of destruction. Crank, crack, and pills, mostly narcotics." She placed a hand on her hip, and the butt of a gun peeked out from under her jacket. "Giordano's got an endless supply of prescription drugs flooding Ohio, probably courtesy of the local medical community." She set her jaw in grim determination and gave me a look that could have frozen warts. "You help me find out who the dirty doc is, and I'll make sure things go better for your dad."

I glanced around the hall and lowered my voice. "What are you implying? If I don't spy for you, you'll take it out on my father? Is this a threat?"

"Not a threat. A statement of fact. Let's say I want you to be vigilant—and to keep me informed."

I thought of the congested parking lot and the line of patients outside of Dr. Taylor's office. Agent Novak must have sensed my hesitation.

"What? Don't hold back. Tell me everything."

Tree said. "Spill it, Jake."

What did I really know about Taylor? Nothing.

Images of the dying child in Urgent Care came rushing back, and I remembered the light in his eyes flickering out and his mother's anguish. The memory pried my lips apart. I told Novak what I'd seen at Taylor's office.

"Now *that's* what I'm talking about, doctor." The corners of her lips turned up but never quite made it to a smile, an expression she had probably perfected at Quantico. "What else?"

"You might also want to speak with Gavin Glade. He's a surgeon here and has his finger on the pulse of the hospital and an opinion about everything. I'm fairly new here and haven't met many people."

"Even better. That'll keep you under the radar. Between the hospital and the church, you'll have the trusted ear of a lot of folks."

"The church? How'd you—"

"Already told you. Background check. Shoot," she said, the word whistling softly through the small gap between her front teeth, "the Bureau is so thorough, I probably have your shoe size and favorite color on file at the office. Glad to see you've been behaving since you entered seminary. Keep it up. And call me if you think of anything else." She handed me her business card and walked away.

"Great. Now I'm in the middle of this crap." I leaned toward Tree and whispered, "That's one ball-busting lady. Who the hell does she think she is?"

"Relax, Jake. All FBI are hard asses. Part of their job description. And if you're a Feebie born without a dick, sometimes you have to *be one* to survive. Novak figures the possibility of your father in prison will motivate you."

"She doesn't know me as well as she thinks. I couldn't care less about the old fart."

"Yeah, right." Tree rolled his eyes. "That's why you already put your ass on the line for him. And don't underestimate Novak. Word has it her son died of a prescription drug overdose. She's motivated as hell."

It wasn't Novak that I was afraid of. With the attacks at the homeless shelter and the murder in the hospital, I was *scared* to death, not just for Santana and myself, but for everyone around me. The forest fire of violence that my father's return had ignited had to be contained, and quickly.

"What about RJ, Colleen, and Emily? Are they at risk, Tree?"

"Nah, Giordano's after your dad. And with an organization like his, Big Angie will probably find out that your father's in custody before the sun goes down. But you and Santana aren't out of danger, so you both better be careful."

No need to worry about me. I had mastered both paranoia and vigilance during the war.

Tree heaved a sigh befitting his size. "Now, to further screw up my morning, I have to break the bad news to the drug mule's wife and three young kids. He was a friend-of-a-friend of mine, a laid-off steel worker whose unemployment ran out, and by all accounts a decent guy before the recession put him in the poorhouse. Shit. Some days I hate this job."

CHAPTER SEVENTEEN

Thursday, December 5, 2002, 8:00 a.m.

I spoke briefly with my father. His nose dripped like a leaky faucet, and I suspected he'd sampled more of the stolen cocaine than he had sold. Dear old Dad was strung out, and his emotional coin had flipped again. After enumerating the many ways in which I had disappointed him as a son, he reiterated his displeasure with our plan of moving him to jail for rehab and police protection. Somehow, he managed to spin his return to Ohio into a fable in which Tree and I were the villains and he was the innocent victim.

He had had a bath and no longer defiled the air in the room, but he was unshaven, sweating, and his hands trembled. I recalled coming off some horrendous benders in my youth, and it hurt to know that in addition to our eye color, he and I shared a penchant for self-destruction. All parents inadvertently pass on a few undesirable traits to their children. In the genetic lottery, I had inherited a predisposition toward alcohol abuse and addiction, and had nearly plummeted into the abyss as a young man. I hoped that wasn't true for RJ, but owed it to my sister to keep a close eye on him as he grew older.

Pain crept from my temples to the back of my eyes and lodged there. When my old man finished his tirade, he began complaining of abdominal cramps and seeing rats in the room. I informed the nurse so they could medicate him and prevent a full-blown episode of DTs. I had witnessed too many cases in the past and made my exit.

Dazed by the morning's events, I set off in quest of serenity at the chapel. Over the past four days, Juan Santana and I had been attacked at the homeless shelter, a police officer's food had been laced with a laxative, a patient was murdered in the hospital, drug dealers were flooding the county with pills, the DEA and FBI were preparing for war—and my father had placed Santana, Tree Macon, and me squarely at the center of Armageddon.

Two disheveled interns exited the elevator as I entered, and I rode down alone as my once serene world unraveled. The Muzak version of "I Shot the Sheriff" floated from the elevator speakers, filling my mind with unshakable dread and images of my best friend in a coffin.

Ten minutes late for Mass, I rushed through the service, unable to concentrate on the sacraments or my treasured time with the Lord. The nuns in the front pew sensed my lack of focus and avoided eye contact. When the service was over, my Three Owls took flight without stopping to say their usual good morning.

My day was off to an exponentially crappy start. As I removed my vestments, it got worse. "Onward, Christian Soldiers" marched from my cellphone and Bishop Lucci's office number appeared on the screen. I knew exactly what my commander-in-chief would say. It had been nearly three months since I had begun my leave of absence from my duties at Sacred Heart Church and he considered my *spiritual retreat* over. Lucci wanted Emily out of my life or my "indult of laicization"—my signed resignation from the priesthood. "Poop or get off the pot," as Tree had so elegantly put it.

I let the call go to voicemail, sat on the desk chair, leaned back, and closed my eyes. Lucci and Tree were both right; I had to choose. Since my return to town, I had prayed long and hard for guidance about my relationship with Emily. The choice was finally obvious.

After my troubled youth, medicine and the priesthood had provided the joy and inner peace I had been searching for. I *couldn't* give that up. Emily and I had settled into a blossoming friendship over the past few months that I cherished and never wanted to lose again. The problem was the lingering shadow of our youth. I needed to set aside the missing letters and all of the mistakes we had both made, and stop living in the past.

Time to move forward. Emily's relationship with Todd indicated that she already had. Bottom line: I loved her—loved her *too much* to jeopardize her chance at a future with Todd and a real happy ending. That left me with the Church and our friendship, and that was enough. It would *have to be* enough.

My cellphone awakened, jangling me back to reality. I answered.

"Dr. Austin?"

"Yes."

"This is Rudolph VonKamp, the hospital attorney."

"What can I do for you, counselor?"

"The administration and the board of directors have been reviewing physician privileges and we see that you have training in pain management. Of all the subspecialties, *yours* poses the greatest legal risk to the hospital. Given our recent discussion at the Ethics Committee meeting about prescription drug abuse, we want to go on record strongly encouraging you to stop dispensing Schedule Two drugs."

This man and his governing board had no concept of what my job entailed. Successful pain management at times necessitated the judicious dispensing of narcotics.

And Dr. Glade was right. VonKamp used a lot of syllables to say very little, probably at three hundred dollars an hour.

I hesitated, and he filled the void.

"Dr. Guo, among others, has acknowledged the importance of our effort to minimize hospital liability, and she has already pledged her support in this regard."

Which, of course, was not a problem for Dr. Guo, as an herbalist practicing acupuncture and alternative medicine.

"Your concern is duly noted, counselor. I'll do what I can, but narcotics and other Schedule Two drugs are a necessary part of my practice."

"I see," he said with an inflection that suggested he was not happy with what he had seen. "Nevertheless, I hope you'll proceed with restraint and caution in this regard. We on the board of trustees are quite concerned about this issue and its legal ramifications. We wish to avoid any adverse outcome for St. Joseph's and would prefer not to be forced to suspend anyone's hospital privileges. Thank you for your time, Doctor Austin."

Click.

What? Suspend hospital privileges? That sounded a lot like a threat. Not only was my practice in the FBI and DEA crosshairs, now the hospital shyster had me under the microscope.

On my way to Urgent Care, I turned my attention to my father's ongoing disaster. In the doctors' lounge, I booted up the desktop computer, googled Angelo Giordano, and found a string of allegations and arrests but no convictions. Several of his foot soldiers were dead or in prison, and one article alleged that he was behind the car bombing of a competitor and his kids—yet there he was on the front page of the New Orleans Times-Picayune, beaming at the camera during a fundraiser for sick children. Giordano was clearly a very dangerous dude and slick as Teflon.

I shut down the computer, threw on my white coat, and walked into a packed waiting room in Urgent Care. Nurse Ochs summed up the situation in her usual succinct manner.

"Freezing rain. Rush hour. Time's a wasting and you're out-numbered."

She handed me a patient chart, pointed to exam room four, and we were off and running. Fortunately, my resident "du jour" was competent and we managed to clear out the waiting room before lunch.

I sauntered toward the cafeteria to meet Emily, searching for a way to tell her that all we could ever be was friends, nothing more, without making it sound like a rejection. The last thing I wanted was to cause her more anguish. On the way, I passed Agent Novak and Dr. Glade near the auditorium. I could not hear their animated conversation, but knew they were talking about illegal prescription drugs.

When I entered the cafeteria, Handel struck up the "Messiah" on my cell.

"Jake, it's Tree. I wanted to let you know your dad's been safely moved to our lovely correctional resort. He's currently enjoying our fine cuisine and accommodations at tax-payer expense."

"Did he give you a hard time?"

"Nothing I couldn't handle—just added to another fun-filled day in the life of a public servant. Listen, gotta run. Talk to you later."

CHAPTER EIGHTEEN

Thursday, December 5, 2002, 11:30 a.m.

After Tree hung up, I noticed I had missed a call from Emily and clicked on my voicemail.

"Jake, P.T. had a cancellation, and I can swim at ten-thirty. I'll try not to be late for lunch. See you in the cafeteria around noon."

The hospital allowed medical staff to use the Physical Therapy pool whenever there were no patients scheduled. Emily had been a tennis player and an avid runner, but had taken up swimming for exercise after she had lost her vision.

I had some free time and decided to watch. I hopped on an elevator and rode down to the heated pool in the basement. I'd seen her in action twice before and was dazzled each time. No tentativeness, no crashing into walls. Counting strokes and listening to the reflected sound under water, she streaked like a torpedo from one end of the pool to the other, straight as a laser. It was a thing of beauty—and so was she.

In the dead of winter, the heated pool was an unexpected perk and the warm, moist air inviting. I had begun using the facility for exercise whenever I could, and Emily and I had even started to teach RJ to swim.

The smell of chlorine tickled my nostrils, and the clack of my loafers echoed off tile as I approached. Emily was doing the crawl in lane one, well-toned arms snaking into the water, her head rolling out on the beat for air, her legs a blur. A yard from impact at the far end, she glided into a perfect flip turn that propelled her a third of the way back underwater, where she resumed her effortless stroke. She completed a dozen laps, climbed up the ladder, snapped off her swim cap, and toweled her hair dry.

Freckles dusted the skin on her upper chest, and her blue one-piece suit drew out the color of her eyes. I stared for a moment before I could break the spell she had cast over me. Finally I said, "Hey, Em. I had a few minutes, so I decided to watch Aquawoman in action. Very impressive."

"Thanks." Her smile was luminous, and my heart sped up. "Be with you in a minute, Jake."

Emily finished drying her long legs, straightened, and took a deep breath that expanded the top of her swimsuit. My resolve about only being friends wavered, and I forced my eyes away. I should never have come down to the pool and placed temptation in my path.

She tossed the towel to me. "Please drop that in the basket while I get changed."

Grabbing her collapsible red and white cane from a table, she snapped it to full extension and tapped her way toward the women's locker room.

A full head of blond hair popped up from lane four. Todd. He called out to her and she twirled around.

"Emily, my dear, you haven't forgotten the concert this evening, have you?" His East Coast accent smacked of Ivy League schools, private clubs, and trust funds. "I'm looking forward to the pleasure of your company. Pick you up at seven?"

"Can't wait, Todd. See you tonight."

Emily walked into the locker room and Todd glanced over at me, then butterflied his way to the far side of the pool.

I wanted to know more about their relationship but had already crossed that line once with Emily. The answer had been succinct and veiled. *A good friend and fellow poet.* I didn't believe one word of it. Yet, who was I to judge? I had no right. None.

CHAPTER NINETEEN

Thursday, December 5, 2002, 12:10 p.m.

Emily exited the locker room wearing a green blouse and slim-cut chino pants, her auburn hair blow-dried and combed. We walked to the cafeteria, grabbed soup and sandwiches, and settled into a corner table.

My waffling resolve to end the Neverland relationship we were currently living and my old man's return to town had left me distracted and my thoughts jumbled. I gazed out of the window at the drifting snow.

"You're awfully quiet, Jake. Problems?"

"Sorry." I told her about my father's sudden reappearance on Monday and the violence that had followed him here.

"Good Lord, an attack at the homeless shelter?" Emily trembled. "I'd heard about the patient murdered in the hospital, but didn't know your dad was involved."

She went quiet and I changed the subject.

"How'd your poetry therapy workshop go yesterday?"

"Glad you asked. I wanted to show you something." She pulled a sheet of paper from her purse. "This mother's child was admitted to the fifth floor unit with a brain tumor. I cried when she read her poem to our group."

She took off her sunglasses. In contrast to her father's rheumy eyes, Emily's were clear and cobalt blue.

"Honestly, Jake, I have no idea how these parents do it. Every time I work with families in the pediatric cancer unit, I'm reminded what a minor inconvenience my blindness is, and how blessed most of us truly are." She tilted her head and a curtain of hair fell across one eye as she handed me the poem. "This child is RJ's age. As you doctors say, 'This may hurt a bit.'"

I unfolded the paper and read:

My Universe

There is no crystal staircase,
just a trek on tired feet
to the Fifth Floor, nearer to Heaven,
as far as I can go.

It's a shelter for my shifting life, this place
of misery, kindness, endings, beginnings --
where a poem is a prayer,
a down payment on faith.

Every day I learn
about *holding on*
and *letting go* -- here
at the center of the universe.

"Wow!" My mind wandered from the gloom of the oncology unit to my nephew playing with building blocks on my living room rug, and a chill shivered me. I blinked moisture from my eyes. "What strength. I can't even imagine."

"This mother was so despondent, Jake, her psychiatrist couldn't get her to open up. He asked her to attend my workshop. She sat silently in my class for two weeks listening to the others and didn't say a word … until the dam broke and that poem poured out."

"Better than a handful of pills. You should be proud, Em."

"Thanks. I do what I can. What's the little guy been up to?"

Emily often referred to the two most important people in my life as the big guy and the little guy, Tree Macon and RJ.

I filled her in on my nephew's most recent antics, and she chuckled.

"Speaking of my favorite young man, I checked my schedule and I can babysit for him tomorrow, so you and Tree can go to the football game."

Emily had begun filling in whenever Colleen was unavailable. She had memorized the necessary step counts and become comfortable maneuvering around my apartment.

She shifted her sunglasses to the top of her head. I preferred it when she didn't wear them so I could see her eyes, but knew that her blindness sometimes made her sensitive to light.

"How about a deal?" She slid her tongue over the curve of her lips. "I stay with RJ Friday evening, and you get us tickets to hear the Cleveland Orchestra."

Emily leaned forward, and her scent enveloped me with the sweet fragrance of wild berries and the promise of springtime. She flashed a killer smile and I felt like I had won the lottery.

"You drive a hard bargain, Emily Beale. Let me find out when Colleen is available to babysit RJ, and I'll call you with possible dates."

Our conversation remained pleasant. We were laughing about something Tree Macon had said when my Three Owls walked past our table. They scowled and avoided eye contact. The unfounded rumors of our supposedly lurid relationship had apparently pierced the seclusion of the convent.

I told Emily about the nuns' reaction, adding, "The tall one reminds me of Sister Very Nasty. I wonder if her frown is painted on."

Emily and I had attended Parish School of Religion classes together as kids, what many call Sunday school. Sister Mary Nancy, our PSR teacher, had acquired her nickname the old-fashioned way—she had earned it. We used to quake at the swish of her habit, the clack of rosary beads, or the sight of a ruler in her hand.

When I mentioned that Bishop Lucci had called again, Emily's mood darkened. She knew His Excellency wanted her out of my life, or me out of the priesthood. I had tried for months to read her thoughts about our renewed feelings for each other, and I suspected she had been trying to gage mine as well.

"What did you tell him, Jake?"

I shoved my unfinished meal away and pushed back from the table.

"Nothing. I didn't answer the phone."

"You know, Jake, if you tread water long enough," she said, her voice hard-edged, "eventually you will drown."

She let stillness expand between us.

Since my return to town, we had grown closer, but our relationship was stuck in neutral. I did not want to jeopardize our friendship, yet one question, *the question*, haunted me as it had for years. I had hesitated to ask it because I couldn't predict how she would respond. She was part Emily Dickinson, part Emily Post, and part Hurricane Emily.

The question buzzed like an angry hornet inside my head, demanding an answer.

I could not contain it any longer and it flew from my lips.

"Em, why didn't you write to me during the war? I was in a damn bloodbath over there, alone and scared. After your first three letters, I got … nothing. Not even a damn *Dear John* letter. Next thing I heard, you were engaged to Everett! Why'd you stop writing?"

My long-shackled words poured out, sounding more and more like an accusation than a question. Doubt rumbled in the back of my mind. I was not sure I wanted to hear her answer, but I had pulled the pin on the hand grenade and couldn't put it back.

Emily's head jerked in my direction and her eyebrows stitched together. Her blue eyes flared from pilot lights to flames. She slowly covered the blaze with her sunglasses, opened her mouth once, twice. No sound came out. The seconds ticked by as her expression hardened. Nothing worried me more than when Em went quiet. But the question of the letters had required an answer for decades, so I waited her out. I had to hear the truth from her lips.

Across the table, one hundred and twenty pounds of plutonium emitted radioactive rage. Emily's jaw jutted forward and her lips were a thin bloodless gash.

"Why didn't I keep writing?" Five simple words, taut with meaning. "Are you serious? You broke my heart!"

I threw my napkin on the table. "Right back at you, Em! You broke mine too."

"I didn't keep writing," she hissed at me, slamming a small fist on the table, "because *you* never wrote back to me, damn it!"

Each syllable shattered like glass inside my head, the sharp-edges slashing into me.

"What? That's crap! Not true."

The cafeteria grew unnervingly silent, and dozens of heads swiveled in our direction. I lowered my voice.

"I wrote you all the time, Em, even sent some poems. I asked you to *marry me* in my last letter. That letter is chiseled into my brain! I never heard back from you. Not so much as a postcard. Nothing!"

"What? That's a crock! I sure as hell never got *that* letter. Haven't you heard a word I've said? You're not being fair, Jake!"

That comment stopped me cold. Fair? I wasn't sure of many things, but I was certain that the heart *never* played fair. What the heck was going on here?

A post-apocalyptic hush enveloped our table. We sat motionless, searching for the right words, trying to gauge each other's temperature. I was simmering; she was boiling.

Slowly her heated appearance faded and her voice became icy. "I never got *any damn letters* from you!"

Her words hit me like stones, and the hollow feeling in the pit of my stomach grew to the size of a sinkhole. I searched for the hint of a lie but couldn't find it. Having been raised on a diet of my father's lies as a child, however, I sometimes lacked confidence in my ability to recognize the truth.

Doubt drifted across Emily's face. For a moment, we were complete strangers, marooned in a fog of turbulent memories and confusion.

"I ... I don't understand." She shook her head. "Could your letters have gone to the wrong address, or been lost in the mail?"

"Not a chance. Not all of them."

"None of this makes sense. There has to be an explanation ... and by God, I will find it!"

Her cellphone rang and she answered.

"Hi, Todd. What?" She ran a finger over her watch. "Christ, I lost track of time. I'll be right there." She hung up and stood. "This is insane, Jake. I can't deal with this. We're done!" she said, edging past me as if I were poison ivy.

Done? I opened my mouth, but by the time I managed to say, "Em, stop!" the rhythmic tapping of her cane had vanished through the cafeteria door.

I felt lost and empty, and my aloneness echoed inside me.

CHAPTER TWENTY

Friday, December 6, 2002, 7:30 a.m.

On my way to the hospital chapel the next day, I called Tree for a status update. He told me that Dr. Woisnet had stopped by the jail and he had my father's DTs under control. Although my old man continued to bitch and moan about his incarceration, at least he was alive and in good hands.

Fragments of what Emily had said rattled around inside my head all morning, and I fumbled through Mass for the second day in a row. I had intended to set up a small, understated Christmas tree in the chapel sanctuary after the service, but I was no longer in a holiday mood.

While dressing in the sacristy for my shift in Urgent Care, I realized Emily had left me a voicemail during Mass. I hesitated, then hit play. Her message was short and not so sweet: *I promised RJ I'd see him tonight, so I'll come by cab and babysit. Forget about buying the orchestra tickets.*

I listened again. There was no misinterpreting her message or her mood.

I had spent the prior evening picking at the knot that the missing letters represented and mulling over Emily's denial that she had received them. I had dialed her phone number twice, gotten her answering machine, and was told to leave a message. I didn't. We needed to meet again face-to-face and talk things through, but her voicemail indicated that she was nowhere near ready.

My mother had been the only person who had written to me during the war, on the few days when she was sober enough to scribble a note. Electronic communication was not much of an option in those days, and telephone calls overseas to the front lines were nearly impossible. The abrupt loss of Emily's letters was like the amputation of one of my legs, leaving me off balance, vulnerable, and without hope.

I arrived in Urgent Care fifteen minutes late for my shift. Between yesterday's confrontation with Emily and my old man's on-going disaster,

I could not untangle my thoughts. I was distracted and unable to focus on my patients. Nurse Ochs didn't say anything to me, but she commandeered an additional resident to help with the workload.

Lost in a dense, swirling fog of questions and roiled emotions, I picked up a chart, refocused on medicine, and walked into the next examination room. I stopped near the doorway.

A man about my age wearing bloody camouflage fatigues sat on the exam table, his hospital gown still hanging from a hook on the wall. He ran a hand over his crew cut and rolled up his sleeves, revealing a dragon tattoo, similar to the one inked on my forearm—a souvenir from the war. It was my mark of Cain, a daily reminder that I had killed my brother—a man with a different skin color, uniform, and language, but my brother nonetheless. My mind leaped back in time.

Although my patient's face was bruised, slightly swollen, and marred by several minor lacerations that no longer bled, he looked vaguely familiar. I checked the chart for his name. Shane Gingrich.

Once, half-a-lifetime ago, we had been buddies during basic training. That kind of hell can form strong bonds between soldiers. I was sent off to learn how to be a medic, he was assigned to the mortuary affairs office, and we parted ways until we were reunited again overseas.

Back then, everyone called him "Shades" because he always wore reflecting sunglasses, even indoors. Of course, he was stoned most of the time. We all were in those days.

Shades ended up as a "Logistics Warrior" with the Army Quartermaster Corps, an M.A.S.—Mortuary Affairs Specialist. He had collected and transported our dead and their personal effects back to the States. His nickname stuck with me because in mythology a "shade" was a spirit in the underworld, a ghost. His job was much like that of the fabled Greek boatman who ferried bodies across the River Styx to the afterlife—or in our case, from our earthly Hell back home to grieving friends and family.

But the nickname, Shades, also derived from his sideline job. As in *shady*. Early on, he saw a niche and filled it, becoming a "procurer." In the chaos of every war, an underground black market always developed. With his connections at the Tactical Field Exchange, a mobile PX, he could get a soldier anything he wanted—for the right price. He had been a handy friend to have and had always been kind to me.

I walked into the room and closed the door. "Shades?"

He turned his head slowly and stared as if from miles away before a smile parted his lips.

"Jake?"

I nodded.

"Well, I'll be a sumbitch. Just my luck." He chuckled. "I spinout on the ice, take out a telephone pole, catch an airbag in the kisser, and all they send me is a damn medic! Can't even get an honest-to-god doctor."

I flashed the hospital staff ID badge on my white coat. "I'm the real-deal now, Shades. What in the world are *you* doing around here?"

"Grew up in Youngstown."

St. Joseph's Hospital was a hundred miles west of Youngstown, and I waited for him to elaborate. A long silence passed, and I wondered about a concussion. He finally snapped back.

"I flew in a few days ago … to see a lady friend." He grinned.

"Some things never change." I laughed. "Flew in? Where?"

"Lorain County Airport. I was on my way there today so I could fly back to the base when I spun out." He hesitated. "Learned to fly choppers a few years ago. Got me a little bird of my own."

The county airport was not much more than a field with a concrete runway and would not have been my first choice for air transportation in a raging snowstorm.

"Must be a special lady."

He shrugged. "They're all special."

He wore a Battle Dress Uniform in various hues of brown and beige with scattered patches of green. I wanted to check his mental status with more chitchat, so I pointed to his tri-color desert camouflage fatigues.

"Why are you wearing B.D.U.s? Don't tell me you're still in the service, Shades. I always assumed you'd parlay your experience into a job in forensic medicine or the funeral business and make some real money."

His eyes narrowed. "Hell yeah, I'm a lifer, and proud of it! I *volunteered* for overseas duty right after the attacks on the Twin Towers." He gave me a look that made me feel like a coward and a deserter. "Been a 92M all my life, Jake. It's not about the money. Those kids, their folks, they mean something to me. It's an important job and gotta be done right. I'm a honcho now, overseeing part of Afghanistan, directing search and recovery, training MAS recruits, that sort of thing."

His gaze drifted from the black aviator's jacket hung from a hook on the back of the door to the white-out frosting the window pane, then to his expensive titanium watch, the kind worn by Army Rangers and Special Ops guys.

"Shit, I gotta get going."

"Are you serious?" I pointed at the blizzard outside. "You're not taking off in that, are you?"

"No choice. Got to catch a transport back overseas at 0800 hours tomorrow." He wobbled when he stood and put a hand on the table to steady himself.

"Let me run a quick CT scan of your head and a few tests to make sure you're okay, Shades." I reviewed his chart. "EMTs said you were disoriented at the scene."

"Hell, Jake, you know me. Been a bit loopy all my life." He grabbed his flight jacket. "Got things to do, buddy."

True enough. Shades had been *loopy* back in the day, even when he was not stoned—but his eccentric behavior had been harmless and was always good for a laugh with the other guys in our battalion.

"All right, all right, no x-rays. Let me perform a quick exam before you take off. Do it as a favor to me, for old-times' sake."

He shrugged and sat down again. I performed a neurological examination, which was normal, but even a careful exam had its limitations. Not wanting him flying with a brain injury, I made another pitch for a CT scan. Shades was having none of it.

"What I could use, Jake, is something for my backache. Damn things been a bitch for months. Flared up again after I slid into that telephone pole." He threw on his flight jacket. "Roxanol worked good last time."

What the hell? Roxanol was a liquid form of morphine used to treat severe, chronic pain, not a backache. Shades did not appear uncomfortable when he moved, and I wondered if he had become a user. Was he playing me, trading on our bond as brothers-in-arms to score narcotics?

I decided to prescribe something less potent, particularly in light of the hospital lawyer's phone call advising caution. The prescription pad that we kept in the bottom left desk drawer of each exam room, however, was missing. I made a mental note to suggest to our administrator that leaving them there was an unnecessary risk. I was certain Counselor VonKamp would agree. If a patient stole a pad, once he had a legitimate prescription from his physician, he could prescribe any drug he wanted simply by forging the doctor's signature and DEA number.

I grabbed a prescription pad from the nurses' station, reentered the room, and paused. There was no doubt he had been in an accident and his injuries were real. I was deciding on my next move, when a nurse poked her head into the room and told me I had an important telephone call, so I handed him a script for Tylenol with codeine instead of morphine. No refills.

"Here. Don't take it till you land. Now, go save the world."

"Roger that." Shades examined the prescription and shoved it in his pocket. "Yeah, thanks. Call you next time I'm in town, buddy. You can buy a poor grunt some lunch, doctor."

We exchanged cellphone numbers, and he slipped on his mirrored sunglasses.

"Take care, Jake." He gave me a half-assed salute. "Over and out."

Shades zipped up his jacket, shaped his hand into a pistol, fired an imaginary shot in my direction, and vanished out the door.

I shook my head. Déjà vu all over again.

My *important* phone call turned out to be the record room reminding me to complete two charts. For the rest of the day, I could not stop thinking about my blowup with Emily. As questions about the missing letters spun through my mind, Marcus Taylor charged into the room with the fury of a hailstorm.

CHAPTER TWENTY-ONE

Friday, December 6, 2002, 1:30 p.m.

Dr. Taylor had the look of a snowman with his roly-poly build, pale skin, white hair, and coal-black eyes, but the fire in his cheeks gave Frosty a psychotic edge. He rumbled toward me swearing like a sailor on a bad drunk.

"Marcus, what's wrong?"

He pounded the desk, and the chart I was working on jumped.

"Who the hell do you think you are, telling the FBI I'm a drug dealer?" Taylor's belly and jowls quivered. He cursed me with venomous fervor using language I had not heard since my army days. Flecks of spittle flew from his lips. "I'm going to sue your ass for slander and defamation, you arrogant son of a bitch! You think you know me? You don't know shit!"

Nurse Ochs popped up from her desk, grabbed a chart, and scampered from the nursing station. DeQuan Kwame, our orderly, however, leaned against the wall with a smug expression, listening to every word and enjoying my discomfort.

"I never called you a drug dealer, Marcus. What I said was—"

"Don't lie to me! One of my residents overheard you on the rehab floor."

"All I said was that I saw a crowd of patients outside your office early one morning, and Agent Novak—"

"A crowd? That's why you set the hounds on me? Christ! I know you haven't been in town long, but damn it!" His eyebrows knitted together and his eyes nearly vanished in a mesh of fleshy skin folds. "That *crowd*, as you call it, is the result of the trickle-down misery from the shaky economy."

He waved a plump finger in my face. "I don't owe you an explanation, but I'll tell you this. My father founded Taylor Industries, and I never had to work a day in my life, let alone bust my ass in med school. You think I'm selling drugs to get rich? You couldn't be more wrong. I've practiced here for thirty years and made a good living, so I'm giving back to the community. I run a *free clinic* three mornings a week at my office. So yeah, the patients line up at my door!"

An intern peeked out from an exam room as Taylor thundered on, then quickly closed the door. DeQuan chuckled softly.

I began my mea culpa. "Sorry, Marcus. I had no idea. Wish I could—"

"Too late for that! And don't bother attending any more Ethics Committee meetings. You don't have the ethics of a damn Washington lobbyist." He turned his great bulk toward the door and added, "Judge not, Father, lest ye be judged!"

And he was gone.

I placed my head in my hands and sighed. If I had felt any smaller, I would have completely vanished.

DeQuan sauntered over, sat next to me, and patted me on the back. "Very smooth, Doc. Very smooth!"

Hospital orderlies normally are not comfortable harassing physicians, and I was sure DeQuan never spoke this way to any other doctors, but he and I had a unique relationship. On my first day of work at the hospital, I had been required to provide a random urine sample because of my history of substance abuse and a prior DUI. He had been instructed to watch me urinate into a specimen jar so I could not cheat the test, and he owned my discomfort like a debt. Whenever I needed my ego deflated, he was always there to oblige.

"Thanks, DeQuan. Your opinion means so much to me. There's a stool sample container on the counter. Why don't you take it with you when you leave?"

He was laughing as he left Urgent Care.

After regaining my composure, I muddled my way to the end of my shift. As I walked to my car, Handel played "Messiah" again on my cellphone.

"Two things, Jake." Tree's voice sounded strained. "Your father's cooperating, but unfortunately he doesn't know the identity of Tubby or Muscle. I'll pump our street snitches for info and pass around the artist sketches of those two, but till we get them locked up, you better be careful."

"My middle name is *careful.*"

"Funny, I would have bet money it was *trouble.*" He paused. "Also, I wanted to make sure you hadn't forgotten about the game tonight."

"Of course not! I wouldn't miss your big day."

Somehow, I had allowed myself to be cajoled into volunteering as the physician for the high school football team. Tonight, however, was special. Tree was scheduled to be honored at the game and inducted into the Athletic Hall of Fame. He had been chosen as first-team all-Ohio defensive lineman for four straight years in high school and impressed the pro-scouts when he played at Ohio State. If not for a devastating injury, he undoubtedly would have had a career in the National Football League.

"Emily's babysitting RJ," I said, neglecting to mention that at the moment she would rather spend time with *anyone* other than me. "So I'll definitely be at the game."

"Great. Give her a hug for me."

"Will do." Though I doubted that was likely to happen. "I'd wear my old football jacket tonight—but the darn thing must have shrunk over the years."

"Yeah, mine's a little tight now too. See you at the game, buddy."

CHAPTER TWENTY-TWO

Friday, December 6, 2002, 7:00 p.m.

The Alberta Clipper that had roared across Lake Erie and buried the county in snow had finally sailed away. Nevertheless, a bitter wind continued to howl, whipping in from the northwest. Most of the snow had been cleared from the Oberlin High School football field, although the east end looked icy and treacherous during warm-ups. I braced myself for a slew of injuries.

As team physician, I sat on the end of the Oberlin bench with my black bag, hoping it wouldn't be required. That was not why I was jumpy. Since the assault on Santana and me at the homeless shelter, I had reverted to the hyper-vigilant mindset of a soldier on patrol. Two of my squad had been gunned down in the open countryside during the war. Sitting on the team bench left me exposed on all sides and an easy target.

I had good reason to be edgy. When Tree took my old man into protective custody at the jail, it was only a matter of time before Tubby and Muscle came after me. They were not the brightest of bulbs, but at some point, even they would figure out that I was their target's son. I had even been foolish enough to tell them my name. And as Tree had pointed out, I was not very hard to locate.

I scanned the crowd for a giant man missing his front teeth and his nasty mustachioed sidekick. The problem was that they could easily blend in with the other fans, making them difficult to spot. I felt a slight tremor in my hands as my nervous system amped up—or maybe it was merely numbness as frostbite nibbled on my fingers through my Gore-Tex gloves.

Inclement weather is a part of the game of football, but unfortunately the recent blizzard had limited attendance for Tree Macon's induction ceremony. When he finally stepped onto the podium before kickoff and the school retired his jersey number, I clapped and hooted enough for ten fans, until my voice flagged and my hands ached.

The marching band fired up the National Anthem. I removed my watch cap and placed my hand over my heart—and immediately grew saddened. Dozens of fans, both young and old, stayed seated, laughing and talking on cellphones. Discouraged, I focused on the sacrifice of my friends and fallen comrades until the song ended, then returned to my seat.

Next to me on the bench, the team's kicker appeared more nervous than I was. He had a round, Charlie Brown-shaped head, and his face was pale and full of worry, as if Lucy might suddenly yank the football away when he tried to kick it. He sat mumbling to himself, probably praying that the outcome of the game would not hinge on an extra point or field goal attempt through the swirling arctic gusts.

Tree plunked down on the bench next to me.

"Colder than a witch's … ah, breastplate, Father. You got any pull with the Great Weatherman in the sky?" He handed me a steaming thermos. "Just coffee, no Irish."

"If I had any influence, there'd be palm trees in Ohio." I poured a cup of warmth and started sipping before the coffee transformed into cold, black slush. "I was worried you'd be late for your own induction ceremony."

"Yeah, me too." He took the thermos and reloaded his cup. "Some punk confused a local Stop and Shop convenience store with a Stop and Rob. Must have thought the place was an ATM machine because he'd made a cash withdrawal as I was walking to the door. Fifteen years old with a kitchen knife. Can you believe that crap?"

"And?"

"He wouldn't drop his weapon, so … ah, he fell on the ice a couple times before the squad car arrived to escort him to lockup. I explained to the little shit that waving a knife at an officer carrying a Glock always pisses us off and could be hazardous to his health. After that, I read him his rights."

I had once seen Tree blur legal lines in order to arrest a murderer. It had diminished him forever in my eyes, and he knew how disappointed I had been.

"He slipped on the ice, huh? Come on Tree. Reminds me of the game you ran on the Hernandez woman."

"Hey man, this was a righteous bust. I just wanted to get the kid's attention and give him a valuable life lesson."

"You do love playing the tough guy, don't you?"

"Yeah, it gives me a woody."

I smiled. Some people might consider what Tree had done as "police brutality." I knew him well enough to suspect his description was partly bravado and partly his adrenaline rush wearing off. I suspected that his own life had been in danger, or he had tried to scare the boy straight. Either way, resisting arrest was always unwise, particularly when the arresting officer had arms the size of I-beams.

Elyria High won the coin toss and elected to receive. The crowd roared as our kickoff team took the field. I envied the players and wanted to be out there. Not for the "glory" and certainly not to take the hits. Been there, done that, hurt like hell. But sitting quietly in the cold was freezing my tail off. The marching band in the stands resembled a box of cherry popsicles. At least the players could run around to stay warm.

Tree's cellphone rang and he answered. "I don't give a damn. You keep sweeping through the crowd, and have Raymond keep an eye on the parking lot and refreshment stand. I want these bastards in steel bracelets tonight!"

"What's going on, Tree?"

"Saw a black Hummer in the parking lot and ran the plates. It's a rental. I got two deputies scouring the stadium, looking for those Louisiana scumbags. Not to worry. I'm your personal bodyguard."

Not to worry, my frozen ass! Easy for him to say. The tremor in my hands returned.

My neighbor on the bench, the kicker, made his debut. He uncorked a short, dying quail that fluttered into the hands of an Elyria receiver at the thirty-yard line. The first two would-be Oberlin tacklers missed him, the next two face-planted on the ice, and within ten seconds, we were down by a touchdown.

Things only got worse. I benched Oberlin's best wide receiver early in the first quarter because the young man was dazed and his routes were so erratic that he undoubtedly had a concussion. With his game plan unraveling, the Oberlin coach frantically paced the sideline, probably in search of job security. As the visiting team ran the score up, the one player who was completely relaxed was the kicker because his team needed touchdowns, not field goals. I suspected, however, that his leg was getting tired from punting so often. As the first half wound down, the score was twenty eight to zip.

Tree emptied the thermos and shook his head. "Damn. I'm supposed to give the team a pep talk at halftime. This feels like a funeral. A eulogy would be more appropriate."

His beeper screeched. He checked the number and made a call. His expression wilted and he stood up.

"Jake, the homeless shelter just burned to the ground. Probable arson. There's at least one DB inside."

My heart flip-flopped in my chest. "Please tell me the 'D' doesn't stand for dead."

"Wish I could."

I jumped to my feet. "Oh God. It's not Juan Santana, is it?"

"Don't know yet. The body's … too crispy."

My fear mutated into anger. I stepped toward him, poked him in the chest, and yelled, "Damn it, you guys promised to protect the shelter!"

"Easy Jake. I upped the number of neighborhood patrols. That's all I could do. I have a small force, not an army. We do the best we can with what we have." He put a hand on my shoulder. "Sorry, gotta run. I'll call you soon as I find out about Santana. Stay vigilant, buddy … and give my pep talk for me."

He began to leave, then turned back. "This is a public school, Father, so please don't call upon the Lord for any miracles," he added before fading into the night.

Juan Santana did not answer when I called, so I left a message asking if he was okay. I was not about to leave my name or any information in case Tubby and Muscle had his phone. All I said was that I hoped to see him in church on Sunday and hung up.

I shuffled my frozen feet past a six-foot high mound of shoveled snow. I had lost my personal bodyguard when Tree left, and the fifty yards to the locker room felt like a mile. My legs and heart shut down when a black leather football jacket pushed through the crowd and charged in my direction. I scanned the area, looking for a place to run. My pulse finally jump-started again when I recognized the Pittsburgh Stealers logo on the front of the jacket instead of the New Orleans Saints.

The locker room walls were papered with macho quotes and Cleveland Browns posters, the lockers painted in the school colors of red and blue. The room was silent as a morgue and reeked of liniment, decades of sweat, and utter defeat. Every eye except mine was glued to the floor.

St. Jude is the patron saint of lost causes, but I was not about to bother him with an impossible request. From what I had seen in the first half, this game was well beyond his expertise.

I set my worries about Santana and the homeless at the shelter aside, and gave the team my best Knute Rockne, sans Notre Dame and Jesus. *Football is a tough game played by tough guys. You don't need to see a hard tackle, you hear it. Greatness springs from adversity.* Yada yada.

It didn't help. Oberlin was hopelessly behind late in the fourth quarter when Tree finally called.

"Got an ID on the victim at the shelter fire, Jake. The good news is it's not Santana—it's his assistant, Rocky Smith."

Tree was wrong. The news was not good. I had met Rocky. He was Santana's right hand and a fine young man.

"Appears there was only one death, Jake, so the homeless must have all made it out, far as we know. Bad news is we can't locate Santana. I sent uniforms to his house. The door was unlocked. Nobody there. His stuff was scattered everywhere. No car in the garage."

I hung up and whispered a prayer for Santana, Rocky, and all of the homeless folks who were now back on the streets in this brutal Ohio winter. My father's return had literally brought a firestorm down on my friends. Muscle and Tubby had gone from angry to desperate and upped the ante. God-only-knew what they would do next?

The final gun sounded, and I called Emily. She told me that she and RJ were fine. I explained the situation, asked her to lock the door, grabbed my medical bag, and drove to my apartment as fast as the icy roads permitted. If Santana was tortured, who knew what information he would divulge?

When I arrived at home, RJ was sound asleep in his bed. Emily threw on her coat, and I grabbed a metal poker from my fireplace and escorted her to a waiting cab. We didn't speak.

I usually loved the aroma of chimney smoke, but as I watched the taxi's taillights fade in the distance, the night air smelled like a crematorium. I sprinted back inside, threw the deadbolt, set my security alarm, and did not relax until Emily phoned me from her place.

After checking on RJ again, I poured two fingers of Johnnie Walker Gold Label, which I usually reserved for celebrations, and called Santana's cell again. No answer.

Tired and hungry, I shoveled a large scoop of crunchy peanut butter onto a tablespoon. Childhood comfort foods died hard. I plopped onto my recliner, leaned back, and nibbled away as I watched the late night news.

I awoke two hours later as an infomercial man was shouting about an incredible advancement in laundry detergent. The half-eaten spoonful of peanut butter lay on my lap, and a long brown streak stretched like a skid mark from my shirt collar to my belt.

Changing into pajamas, I said my evening prayers and collapsed into bed, but could not get back to sleep. I didn't want to take a sleeping pill in case I had an uninvited visit from Tubby and Muscle, so I read Laura Lippman's most recent novel late into the night. My mind was in turmoil, however, and I had trouble focusing on the plot. The ex-soldier in me wanted to buy a handgun for self-defense, and the priest wanted nothing to do with weapons. The outcome of the debate was too close to call when sleep finally slithered in and coiled around me.

CHAPTER TWENTY-THREE

Saturday, December 7, 2002, 6:45 a.m.

The flickering light of prayer candles danced across a dozen flag-draped coffins. Body-bags were piled high, the scent of death thick and pungent. "Shades" Gingrich stood off to the side, his camouflage fatigues spattered with blood, his expression solemn. He saluted. A small boat floated on the River Styx behind him as Juan Santana played "Taps" on a bugle, then segued to Handel's "Messiah."

* * * * *

My cellphone yanked me from the first nightmare I'd had in months. I shook the dream from my head and answered with one eye still closed.

"Hello?"

"Jake? It's Juan Santana."

My eyelids popped up and I clawed my way back to consciousness.

"You okay? Where the heck are you?"

"I'm all right, but I won't tell you where I am. What you don't know … can't hurt me."

He was right. My father and I had delivered this disaster to his doorstep just as surely as if we had struck the match that burned the shelter down. I heard traffic noise in the background and hoped he was far away.

"What happened last night, Juan?"

"Rocky called from the shelter, said someone was snooping around outside, peeping in windows. I came in the back door and found the place on fire. I pounded on doors to get folks out. When I heard gun shots, I took off. Jumped in my car, grabbed some stuff from my house, and started driving." Santana went silent for so long I was certain I had lost his call. Finally he said, "I don't have the stones for this, Jake. I shoulda made sure everyone got out safe. What a damn coward I am!"

"You're no coward, Juan. Running into a burning building, banging on doors and warning folks? That takes guts. You saved a lot of lives. Listen, you did the right thing. Stay clear until I call you. The shelter's a total loss, but the homeless are all safe."

"God, I hope Rocky's okay. He's not answering his cell."

I didn't have the heart to tell him over the phone, so I changed the topic. "It turns out my old man stole some drugs, and those goons are desperate to find him. I'm so sorry we dragged you into this mess."

"Yeah, me too. Call if you hear anything about Rocky."

"You should speak with Sheriff Macon. He's in charge." I gave him Tree's phone number. "Take care of yourself, Juan," I said and hung up.

What a gutless-wonder I was.

I phoned Tree, told him Santana was alive and would be calling, and asked him to break the news about Rocky. Somehow, I had migrated into the living room and was pacing in my pajamas when the doorbell rang. I peered through the peephole at a dress as green as clover. Colleen, my personal shamrock, right on time as always.

"Are you not well, Father?" My disgruntled Leprechaun stared at my pajamas and scowled before carrying a bag of groceries into the kitchen. "Would you prefer I ring you as a warning before I arrive, so you can make yourself presentable?"

I apologized, retreated into my room, and recited Lauds, the prayers said at dawn to remind us that Jesus, the light of the world, came to dispel spiritual darkness. That morning, though, the world seemed poorly lit and very gloomy. I added a prayer for the repose of Rocky's soul and thanked God for Santana's safety, not only because he was my friend, but because he had not given up information about RJ and me to Tubby and Muscle.

I skipped my morning calisthenics, walked into the bathroom, and began shaving. My reflection in the mirror appeared frightened and unhappy to see me. I showered and splashed on some cologne. I usually met Emily for lunch on Saturdays and hoped she would show up after our quarrel.

Father Vargas, who covered Sacred Heart Church during my leave of absence, also said morning Mass at the hospital on Saturdays, which gave me an extra hour with my boy. When I heard him stirring and entered his room, he was sitting up in bed with a bad case of morning hair that made him look like a sleepy elf wearing a red gnome hat. I grabbed a comb and noticed he was wiping his eyes on his pajama sleeve.

"What's wrong, RJ? Are you crying?"

"Nah." He wiped them again. "Got some sleep boogers in my eyes."

A weight lifted off me when he grinned. No matter what crap was raining down on my world, he was my umbrella.

After I got him dressed, he crawled onto my lap with *Goodnight Moon* and we read about the bunny in his great green room until Colleen called us to breakfast.

Christmas was approaching, and RJ had the secular concept down pat. I smiled as he chatted about Santa, reindeer, and his wish list, which included a talking Sesame Street doll and a train set.

He stopped talking and glanced into the living room. "Oh no, Santa!" Words gushed from his lips. "Don't light the fireplace anymore! Promise? Please, Daddy. Santa won't come down the chimney!"

I was a fireplace junky in winter, but for my boy's sake, I would go cold turkey until after Christmas.

"You got it, RJ." I held out my little finger and he grabbed it with his. "Pinky promise. No more fires. Santa will be fine."

Colleen, however, did not share my amusement. "Father, the lad needs to understand the true meaning of Christmas. Surely you, of all people, should appreciate that." She turned to my nephew. "Christmas is not about toys and sweet treats. That part is in remembrance of the wise men and their gifts to our Lord."

RJ stared blankly at her. She refocused on me.

"Beggin' your pardon, Father. Do you teach the child nothing?"

My boy appeared bewildered for a number of reasons. First, this gray-haired lady kept referring to me as her "father." Second, for any four-year-old, Christmas was *definitely* about presents.

"She means baby Jesus, RJ."

He raised his silver-blue eyes to mine. "Like in the picture book?"

Of the small library of religious books for children that Colleen had purchased for him, only one had made his top-ten list.

"That's right. We'll read it again tonight after I get home, okay?"

RJ nodded. I collected a hug and kiss from him, wished Colleen a good day, and headed to the hospital.

Another blast of winter had arrived in the morning with renewed high winds and heavy snow, making the drive a nail-biter. When I arrived in Urgent Care, Dr. Glade was pacing near the nurse's station. His white coat was rumpled and stained.

"Nice hours you got, Jake."

"And good morning to you too. What can I do for you?"

"What you can do is a percutaneous biliary drainage procedure on the Grabowski girl, so I don't have to take her back to the O.R. this morning."

This was not how I wanted to begin my day. I hesitated.

Having referred a child with appendicitis to Glade and having helped diagnose a drug mule with a belly full of heroin-filled condoms, apparently he now considered me his new best friend. To me he was the same old jackass.

"Come on, Jake, her bilirubin is sky-high, and she's literally ripping her skin off with her fingernails."

Anna Grabowski was a ten-year-old with non-Hodgkin's lymphoma. Viewing her x-rays was like staring at a firing squad. A large tumor blocked her bile ducts. I had been able to minimize her pain, but bile was backing into her bloodstream causing jaundice and unrelenting itching, which could be worse than pain. Glade did not want to subject her to more surgery because she was weak from chemotherapy and her prognosis was poor.

"Call the interventional radiologist. That's his job."

"Not anymore, Jake. He resigned last week. Moved from the Rust Belt to the Sun Belt for more money and a golden tan. Until the Radiology Department replaces him, you're the only guy around with interventional training and hospital privileges."

Although I had learned how to place needles and tubes under x-ray guidance during my fellowship in pain management, I had been in a turf war with Radiology since my arrival.

"The radiologists won't let me use their fluoroscope."

"They will now." Glade smiled. "Our illustrious administrator finally grew a pair of cojones and told them that if they can't provide the service, they get no say over St. Joe's equipment. When they objected, Winer had VonKamp threaten legal action and the Rads folded like a house of cards."

"I don't know. My training was on adults. I've never done a drainage on a child. Why don't you fly her to Rainbow Babies and Children's Hospital in Cleveland? They have pediatric interventional specialists there."

"Are you kidding me? Fly her through that blizzard? No way!" Glade pointed at the elevator. "Go. The girl's in agony. Room 505. I'll cover Urgent Care till you get back."

I rode the elevator up to the fifth floor. Every time I entered the pediatric oncology unit, I thought of RJ and trembled. It always broke my heart to work on kids.

Anna was asleep under a pile of blankets. Her mother dozed in a chair, snoring softly. Mrs. Grabowski was far too young for the haggard face she wore, which grew more drawn every time I saw her. I wondered if she ever made it home. A poem she had written in Emily's poetry therapy class hung on the bulletin board. Its heart-shape drew my eyes to it:

The Children's Ward

I'm tired, not sure I can
do what must be done, yet
I am as faithful as sunrise
where endless days begin,
where every dawn I rise
from this lonely chair
to find the courage
in me to share
suffering
again.

Moisture filled my eyes. I firmly believed in a loving God, but sometimes His all-knowing silence frustrated the hell out of me. Though I had learned to make do with unanswered prayers, I was not happy with the arrangement.

As I approached Anna's bed, the tap of my loafers woke mother and daughter. Anna sat up. Her skin and eyes were pumpkin-colored. She immediately began scratching. Red train-track lines were visible where her fingernails had drawn blood. My heart ached for both of them.

Anna was a bright girl, and her mom had involved her in all medical decisions. This, however, made obtaining informed consent more difficult. Full disclosure of risks and complications terrified many adult patients, let alone a ten-year-old child. I told her the procedure was intended to relieve itching and prevent infection and would make her feel better, ignoring the fact that it would do nothing to cure her cancer.

Anna hunched over, hugged her ragged teddy bear, and rocked silently. I kept the details of how I would gain access to her liver to a bare minimum, but when I mentioned the use of a thin needle, she rocked faster.

I asked if they had any questions. They both shook their heads solemnly, no fight left in either of them. Mom signed the consent form.

Soon Anna lay on a cold, hard x-ray table with enough IV sedation floating through her tiny body to droop her eyelids and temporarily stop her from scratching.

Gowned and gloved, I whispered a prayer for all children, and asked God to guide my hand and judgment. That was how I approached medicine. I prayed as if everything depended on God, and worked as if everything depended on me.

I numbed the right side of Anna's abdomen with Lidocaine while visions of the past few days kept replaying in my mind. My father's hotel room in shambles, the homeless shelter in flames, a mutilated drug dealer in a dumpster, crime scene techs swarming over the corpse of the drug mule murdered in the hospital.

Enough! Time to get my shit together. I banished the images, took a deep breath, and refocused on the child whose life was in my hands.

"I'm going to start now, Anna."

Her droopy eyelids popped up. "I'm scared."

"I know, sweetie, but I need you to be brave. Though this may hurt for a second, I want you to hold very still."

She nodded and closed her eyes again, and I glided a thin needle through her skin, deep into her liver. Although Anna winced, she did not move. She was a tough little girl.

Attaching a syringe, I applied gentle suction and pulled the needle back slowly. As soon as a flash of dark yellow bile appeared, I knew the tip was in a bile duct. I held the needle motionless and injected x-ray dye. Anna's ducts lit up white on the fluoroscope like the branches of a birch tree. Holding everything steady, I slipped a floppy-tipped guide wire through the needle and maneuvered it all the way down to the "trunk" of her biliary tree, but it wouldn't pass through the tumor. Damn it!

I removed the needle and slid a thin catheter over the wire and tried several times with different wires to maneuver past the tumor. Nothing worked. Under the lead apron I wore to protect me from scattered radiation, my scrubs were damp with sweat. I was walking a fine and very dangerous line. If I was too aggressive, I risked forcing bacteria into her blood stream, potentially producing a life-threatening infection. Rather than submit Anna to more radiation and cause her more pain, I slid a larger plastic catheter with multiple side holes over the guide wire down to the blockage, and removed the wire. A large amount of bile poured immediately from the catheter into a drainage bag next to her. I affixed the tube and bag to her skin.

After thirty minutes that felt like hours, we were finished. Her blood pressure and pulse were stable. I snapped off my gloves, said a silent prayer thanking the Lord for His guidance, and accompanied her back to her room.

I explained that her itching would stop, and I might be able to eliminate the tube and bag in a week or two by placing an internal drainage catheter through the blockage. I did not want to complete the thought: *but only if chemotherapy shrinks the tumor.*

Anna's mother wept for joy.

I teared up too.

CHAPTER TWENTY-FOUR

Saturday, December 7, 2002, 12:30 p.m.

I returned to Urgent Care and relieved Dr. Glade. The rest of my morning was routine. Colds, flu, bone-vs-ice fractures, and sprained ankles. But on my way to the cafeteria for lunch, it felt as if I was walking through Jell-O. Only two days since my blowup with Emily, and already I felt lost and disoriented. I hoped she would join me so that we could talk things through, although I had no idea what I could say to calm the waters.

I set a plate of beef stew on my tray and sat at a two-top table sipping industrial-strength coffee. I barely had the energy to lift the cup. With eyes fixed on the entrance and my meal getting cold, my mind kept boomeranging back and forth between the past and the present. For the first time in decades, I would have killed for a cigarette.

My Three Owls greeted me on the way to their table. Even Sister Very Nasty's doppelgänger grinned. They must have approved of my solitude.

From the corner of my eye, I watched Emily enter the cafeteria. She grabbed a sandwich, spoke with the cashier who gestured in my direction, and came toward me. I stood and pulled out her chair. She hesitated for a moment, then Todd called out to her and she walked over and sat with him.

I sank back into my chair and took a bite of my meal. I was no longer hungry and was thinking about leaving when Father Vargas waved and came over.

I was glad for the distraction. Short, with chestnut-brown skin and dark eyes, he wore his cassock and ever-present smile.

Before my sister died, Sacred Heart had been my parish. Vargas had been assigned to fill in temporarily while I cared for my nephew and guided him through the traumatic loss of his mother. When Child Services granted me guardianship of RJ and the bishop extended my leave of absence, the added workload had fallen on Father Vargas. Never once had this kind and gentle man complained.

I said, "Thank you for covering Mass this morning."

"No problem, my friend. Will you be at tonight's vigil service?"

"I'll be there. What brings you back to the hospital?"

"Visiting sick parishioners. I have many to see and better get going." He slapped his forehead with the palm of his hand. "Ah, I almost forgot. Someone asked about you this morning after Mass, Jake. Didn't give me his name."

"What'd he want?"

"Said he was a funeral director, and needed you to officiate. Strange man. Pushy, not dressed for church. Wore an old football jacket and dirty cowboy boots. There was something *muy ... loco* about this man. Kept smiling when he mentioned the funeral. I told him you weren't available. He said he could convince you to do it. Asked for your address. I told him I didn't have it." Vargas shrugged. "Anyway, the guy wouldn't take *no* for an answer, so I said you'd be celebrating morning Mass here tomorrow."

"What did his jacket look like?"

"Black leather, some kind of flower on the back. I do not follow American football, but I could root for this team. The Saints."

Crap.

"Was there anyone with him?"

"I do not think so."

"Describe him."

"Middle-aged. Short and stocky. Thick southern accent."

I dropped my fork on the tray. "Fu Manchu mustache? Belly hanging over his belt?"

"Most definitely. You know this man?"

"I'm afraid so." I stood. "He's one of the guys who torched the homeless shelter in town. Call the cops if you see him again, and lock the rectory doors at night."

"*Madre de Dios!* I don't understand. Why in the world—"

"It's a long story. Just destroy my card in that old office Rolodex and any contact info you have on me at the rectory. Today."

Father Vargas scurried from the cafeteria, leaving me alone, my fears strung together like rosary beads.

CHAPTER TWENTY-FIVE

Saturday, December 7, 2002, 1:30 p.m.

Tubby and Muscle had tracked me to the hospital and knew I was a priest. Not only was I in danger, but so were my friends and family.

I called Colleen and told her to lock the door, put on my security system, and stay inside until I arrived.

"But Father, that alarm machine is demented! Twice this month I've set the infernal contraption off just by looking at it. I'll not be touching that thing. There, I locked the deadbolt." When I failed to respond, she said, "Dear Lord, Father! What is it that's happened?"

I promised to fill her in after I got home. She was not pleased and sprinkled a few colorful Irish idioms into her goodbye.

Next, I phoned Bishop Lucci's office. His secretary said he was in an important meeting and refused to disturb him. I called his private number and left a message requesting that my contact information not be released under any circumstance, adding that lives were at stake. I knew he would comply—if he got my message in time.

I tried Tree's cellphone, got voicemail, and dialed the Sheriff's office. I finessed my way past his secretary, who functioned as a goalie blocking incoming calls. When I finally skated past her, I told Tree about the fat man's visit to the chapel. He said he did not have the manpower to station a guard outside my door, but promised to put out another BOLO on a dark Hummer and have a cruiser patrol my street. His efforts would have been more reassuring if I didn't suspect that Tubby and Muscle had probably rented or stolen a different vehicle by now.

After lunch, Urgent Care was a zoo. I did not have a clue what my next move should be, only that I wanted to get home to RJ. Unfortunately, the intern assisting me didn't know which end of the stethoscope to put in his ears and could not be left unsupervised.

I beeped Harvey Winer in administration and explained that I had a family emergency and needed to be relieved. He said it would take time to find coverage on a weekend. The wait was excruciating. I called home every thirty minutes, sending Colleen into a panic.

My replacement finally arrived in Urgent Care three hours later. I grabbed my coat from the doctors' lounge and was entering the parking garage when my cell played Handel's "Messiah" and Tree's phone number lit up. That ringtone had become the theme song for bad tidings.

"Shit, I hate to have to tell you this, Jake. Your father's been admitted to St. Joe's again. An inmate at the jail made a shiv from a toothbrush and stabbed him in the belly. I suspect this is the work of those Louisiana thugs. You'd better go see him in ICU. There was … a lot of blood. Sorry, buddy."

Christ! They'd gotten to my old man in the jail! How was that possible? These guys were everywhere!

Officer Kearney was guarding the door to ICU. The drug mule had been killed on his watch, and he stepped aside when he saw me charging down the hall.

"Great job of protection you guys do, Kearney!" I shouted.

He flushed bright red and lowered his eyes. He had not been guarding my dad in the jail and my outburst was unfair, but I didn't care. Pissed off and scared are a volatile combination.

My father was in bed six, near the window. He spewed a string of obscenities at me as I approached—a good sign. At least he was feisty. He finished his tirade with a flourish, emphasizing my stupidity and the ineptness of the damn po-lice.

While he ranted, I glanced at his chart. No vital structures had been damaged. He had been admitted for observation and IV antibiotics. So far, so good. The extra hole near his belly button had been sutured and would scar into a nice memento of his prison stay but most likely cause no long-term complications. For a stabbing victim, he had been darn lucky.

I, however, was not feeling the least bit lucky, and doubted that my old man had the mettle to protect my boy and me when his own life was in danger. I placed a hand on his arm.

"What did they want? What'd you tell them?"

"Din't tell the guy nothin'." He shrugged my hand away. "That's why he shanked me."

"Did you say anything about RJ and me? Tell me the truth, old man!"

He gazed down at his abdomen, then back at me, his eyes as dark and dangerous as gun barrels. "What kinda guy do you think I am?" He used the electronic controls to raise the head of the bed and his expression hardened. "You don't know shit about me. I'd just as soon let that sumbitch shove that shiv in my eye as give up my own kin."

I hoped that was true—but truth and my old man were not well acquainted. As we used to say in seminary, *Falsus in uno, falsus in omnibus.* False in one thing, false in all.

All I wanted was to hold RJ in my arms. "I have to get home to my boy."

"Good, the sun's set on this here conversation anyway. You done enough already. Thanks a bunch for asking the cops to protect me." His eyes wandered to the wall. "Been swell talkin' to you."

I was not going to let him lay a guilt-trip on me. He had brought this catastrophe on himself—and on us. In minutes, I was out the door, in my car, and on my way home.

Ohio sunlight is scarce in winter and was fading fast. Ebony clouds drifted across a rising bone-white moon. The streets were an ice rink, and it was all I could do to keep my car on the road.

I had parked at my apartment and was locking the driver's door when I saw an SUV with its turn signal on, about to enter the lot. A dark Hummer. Under the streetlight, I could see that Tubby was driving and Muscle riding shotgun, with a third person silhouetted in the back seat. A police cruiser drove onto my street and spooked them. The Hummer revved its engine and took off west.

Fear swept over me and cold air lodged in my lungs. These bastards had tracked me to my home and put RJ at risk! My anger came alive. I jumped back into my car, racked the transmission into drive, and raced out of the lot, tucking in between a taxi and a delivery truck. Heavy traffic and icy roads had slowed the Hummer, and I followed three car-lengths behind it as I speed-dialed Colleen.

She said everything was fine. I told her not to open the door for anyone except me, hung up, and called Tree.

"I'm on it, Jake. Stay out of it!"

"I want to get their license number."

"Forget it! The car's probably stolen anyway."

"Doesn't matter. I'll follow them to wherever their staying."

"No friggin' way."

"I'll be damned if I'm going to let them drive off, Tree! Besides, there's a third guy in the back seat that I want to ID, so I can be on the lookout for him."

"Crap. Okay, I'll send a uniform to your apartment to protect RJ till you get home. Where are you now?"

I told him and listened as he shouted orders, then returned to the phone. "Two patrol cars are on the way to rendezvous with you. They'll call you to get an update on your location. *Follow* these goons, Jake, nothing more until my guys arrive. And don't get too close. No hero shit, okay?"

"Fine, I'll be careful." The back end of my car fishtailed for an instant and I white-knuckled the steering wheel. "Tell your troops not to shoot the guy in the blue Ford Focus."

I didn't really give a rat's ass about getting their license number. These thugs had threatened my boy. This was personal! I wanted them all in jail, or in the ground. There would be no turning the other cheek today. The fury I had felt in battle long ago lifted its head like a cobra. I was an angry man and wished to God I owned an Uzi!

The taxi ahead of me skated across a patch of ice and slowed to a crawl. I could barely see the Hummer's taillights in the distance. I sped up and passed the cab. The driver gave me the finger. Telephone poles flew by. I slid on the ice past a second car, and he laid on his horn.

The sun had dipped below the horizon, and when the moon disappeared behind a cloud, my headlights carved through inky blackness. A railroad crossing signal blinked at me like the Devil's red eyes winking. Tubby and Muscle flew across the tracks just before the crossing gates swung down.

I could see a locomotive's headlight to my left but could not gauge distance in the darkness. My heart clawed at my chest as I swerved around the gates. The train horn screeched and the engine roared. I felt my tires lose traction, the back of my car drifting to the right. The locomotive's headlight grew huge and its beam lit the inside of my car. The horn again shrieked its warning. I couldn't breathe as I skated over the crossing, barely clearing the tracks before the train roared past me, its draft shaking my little Ford as if it were a matchbox car.

Trying to make up lost ground, I floored the accelerator and was edging closer when the Hummer made a hard right onto Cleveland Street and accelerated. I stayed as close as I dared. When the moon reappeared, the Hummer's license plate was almost visible in the half-light. Another ten yards and I would have the number, but that was not enough. I would follow these guys to the gates of Hell if that's what it took! I wanted to be there when Tree and his troops took them down.

Brake lights flared again and the Hummer swerved left onto Lorain Road.

I took the curve too fast. My car fishtailed into the berm and the trunk took out a mailbox, burying the back end in a snowdrift. I punched the gas and the tires whirred and whined, but the car refused to move.

As the blush of the Hummer's taillights faded into the distance, I beat my fists on the steering wheel, inhaled the icy air, and screamed it back out, "I'll get you, you bastards!"

When I had regained my composure, I called Tree and told him where I'd last seen Muscle and Tubby.

Using the shovel I carry in the trunk during winter, I dug my way out of the drift. Two police cruisers flew by me in pursuit. My right rear fender had a large dent that leaned against the tire, and my car groaned mournfully all the way to my apartment. By the time I arrived, my adrenaline had worn off and I barely had the strength to unfasten my seatbelt.

CHAPTER TWENTY-SIX

Saturday, December 7, 2002, 6:30 p.m.

I showed my ID to a policewoman outside my apartment, unlocked the door, and called out to Colleen. The door swung open and she jumped to her feet. She held rosary beads in one hand and my old Louisville slugger in the other. RJ clung to a handful of her skirt, his eyes as big and wide as a Margaret Keane oil painting, only my little doe-eyed waif was wearing an Elmo t-shirt.

"Sorry, Father. I tried to shield the lad from my distress, but after your phone calls …." Colleen dropped my baseball bat and made the Sign of the Cross three times. She was shaking. "Put God between us and all harm!"

I dropped to my knees, extended my arms, and caught my boy as he leaped into them. He whispered, "I'm scared, Daddy." I was too. We clung to each other. His tears streamed down my neck.

"What is going on, Father?" She studied her prayer beads. "I've been storming Heaven with prayers and have almost worn out my rosary."

I didn't want RJ to hear the details. "Later."

"No!" She stamped a foot. "I've been terrified since your call. Tell me this very minute."

My boy was not about to release his hold on my neck any time soon, and Colleen was definitely not going to let go of the question. I related a sanitized version of the story, leaving in enough detail so she would understand the severity of the situation.

RJ listened intently, shuddered, and tightened his grip on me. I kissed his forehead.

As in Exodus, the sins of the father were again being visited on the children and grandchildren. No way could I let that happen! The sins of *this* father would fall solely on my old man, and if need be on me. I wanted my nephew out of danger. The trouble was, with the exception of my dad, I had no family to ask for help.

"What a fierce, terrible thing this is, Father!" Colleen placed a hand on her chest and slumped onto the couch. "The hounds of Hell are baying at our door."

In a way, she was right. My father had unleashed a pack of wild dogs on everyone I knew. Having recently moved to my apartment, my new address and landline weren't listed in the local phonebook yet. Though Tweedledumb and Tweedledumber were clearly not members of Mensa, even those two yokels had added two plus two and ciphered that I was their target's son. It would only be a matter of time until they found my boy.

I thought about asking Colleen to take RJ to her house for safe keeping, but Oberlin was a small town where nothing remained secret for long and virtually everyone knew her. Too risky. Instead I said, "You have a sister in Toledo, right?"

"I do indeed."

"Please call her. See if you and RJ can stay there for a few days."

She eyed me for a time, then scowled.

"Would you listen to yourself? Do you not realize what you're asking? I can't put my sister and her family in harm's way. How would she feel if I brought misfortune down on her head with this? I love the boy dearly, Father, but ... blood is thicker than water."

My nephew trembled in my arms. "I have no one else to ask, Colleen. Please help me! I'm begging you."

"Dear God in Heaven, 'tis the Wisdom of Solomon I'd need to do the right thing here, Father. Look at the poor scrap! He's frightened out of his wits."

She walked over and gently rubbed RJ's back. Her expression softened.

"Breaks your heart, it does." RJ gazed up at her and she paused. The two of them *were* my family, and I knew Colleen loved him. "Sure, 'tis a dark day—dark as the inside of Lucifer's pocket."

She sighed. "Jesus, Mary, and Joseph. Fine, Father, I'll take the lad." She made a phone call to her sister and hung up. "I don't fancy driving in this weather, so we'd best be off. My sister's married name is—"

I held up my hand to stop her. I didn't think Tubby and Muscle could beat the information from me but did not want to take the chance.

"Better I don't know. I'll call you on your cell when it's safe to come home."

Colleen packed some of RJ's clothes and toys, while I explained to him that everything would be fine and he was going on a short vacation. It would be special and fun. I lied shamelessly to the person I loved most in this world, watching his face morph from fear to excitement.

Guilt washed over me. As hard as I tried to be nothing like my old man, I sounded exactly like he had years ago when he would twist reality to suit his own purposes.

I set my home security alarm, locked the door, strapped my nephew into the car seat in Colleen's old Chevy, and handed her all the cash in my wallet.

"Thanks. I owe you big time for this."

"That you do, Father." She managed a weak smile. "So when I go to my reward and join my dear departed husband, I expect to skip Purgatory and go straight through the Pearly Gates."

She started her engine and edged onto the icy street. I jumped into my car and followed her. No Hummers were visible. My dented rear fender moaned pathetically against the tire. Colleen drove onto the entrance ramp to Route 2. A car-length behind her, I put on my hazard lights and slowed to a crawl, ignoring the angry chorus of honking horns as I blocked traffic onto the freeway. When Colleen and RJ were well on their way, I picked up speed and headed home.

CHAPTER TWENTY-SEVEN

Saturday, December 7, 2002, 7:30 p.m.

After guiding Colleen and RJ safely on their way to Toledo, the drive back to my apartment seemed endless. I considered leaving town too, but that might simply send these thugs after the vulnerable people in my life: Emily and her father, both sightless, and Father Vargas, alone at the rectory. And I sure as hell did not want Tree to risk his life to save mine as he had done once in the past. No, better to keep Tubby and Muscle focused on me.

The more I reflect on the past few days, the less things made sense. If these guys were hired to kill my old man, how did coming after me help them? They had somehow managed to get to him in jail. They probably knew he was in ICU under police guard. What danger did I pose to a Louisiana drug lord and his minions? Maybe I was merely a pawn in the game, a form of familial leverage intended to help them get to my old man.

As I pulled onto my street, the strains of Handel's "Messiah" filled the car. I was beginning to detest that ringtone.

"Jake, it's Tree. The bad news is my troops lost the scent and those Louisiana punks are back in the wind. But I put out an APB on the Hummer and every cop-shop in Ohio now has artist sketches of Tubby and Muscle. Unless they're holed up in a cave, somebody's gonna spot them."

"God, I hope so." Knowing Tree was as relentless as a hunting dog after a jackrabbit eased my worries somewhat. "Any good news?"

"Yeah. I remembered what you said about these clowns stalking you at the hospital."

"So?"

"So, guess what? There's a video camera in the hallway outside the chapel. I'm in the hospital security office about to watch home movies. Bring popcorn."

Fifteen minutes later, Tree and I were staring at video that was washed-out and grainy.

"Hell, Jake, this equipment is older than I am."

The camera was positioned ten yards from the chapel door. Dozens of people appeared on the screen and then disappeared. Worshipers filed in for Mass, their backs to the camera. Colors blurred as if seen through the spinning cylinder of a kaleidoscope.

More images rolled by. My eyes burned and my head throbbed. When the service was over, two dozen people, including my Three Owls, exited and we were able to see their faces. No sign of Tubby or Muscle.

"Is there another entrance to the chapel, Jake?"

"No."

"Well, it was worth a shot." Tree swiveled his chair toward the security guard and ran his finger across his throat. "Kill it. We're done."

"Not yet. We haven't seen Father Vargas come out."

We watched and waited. When the time signature read 9:29 a.m., I recognized Vargas.

"Here we go." I sat forward on my chair. "That's him, carrying the Bible."

Vargas turned toward the camera and a heavy-set man with a jacket slung over his shoulder joined him. The guy spoke briefly with Vargas and walked away. As he was about to vanish from view, he slipped on his coat, revealing the black and gold New Orleans Saints' fleur-de-lis.

"That's Tubby! Can you run it again in slow motion?"

The fat man had his back to the camera and wasn't on the video for long. We only had a brief glimpse of his face.

"You sure that's the guy, Jake?"

"Positive. That's him."

"I'll have the lab geeks enhance the image and run it through the system, see if we can get an ID from mug shots or facial recognition software. If we get his name, maybe we can put a trace on his credit cards or ping his cellphone for a location. His known associates might also give us Muscle's identity. Let's hope we get lucky, 'cause right now I got bupkis. Sorry to drag you here, buddy, but this could be the break we're after."

"No problem. I should check on my old man and visit a couple of my patients anyway."

As Tree pocketed the video and left the hospital security office, Handel struck up the band. I stopped in the hallway and took the call.

"Dr. Austin, this is Home Guardian Security. Your house alarm just went off."

CHAPTER TWENTY-EIGHT

Saturday, December 7, 2002, 9:00 p.m.

I doubted that Colleen had returned and set off the alarm, so I told the security company to send the police to my apartment and ran through the halls. I caught up with Tree and told him about the break-in at my apartment.

"Christ, Jake! What about Colleen and RJ?"

"I sent them out of town. They're safe in Toledo."

"Good, let's go. Hop in."

Tree's unmarked Crown Vic was parked near the hospital's front entrance in a "No Parking" zone. A pair of handcuffs draped the steering wheel, indicating that the vehicle belonged to a cop. I slid into the passenger seat, glad not to be driving on the treacherous roads.

Tree pulled a magnetized emergency strobe beacon from the back seat and affixed it to the roof. He lit it up and climbed in. Blue and red lights danced across the snow.

He grinned as he eased into traffic. "Every time I slap that gumball machine up there, I feel like I'm on one of those TV cop shows."

He called in the burglary at my address, punched the accelerator, and we slid along ice-covered streets. I fastened my seatbelt and placed one hand on the dashboard. I wasn't afraid of dying, but I was not in any hurry either.

"I hate playing Robin to your Batman, Tree."

"What's-a-matter, are the tights chafing your crotch? Lighten up. At least you sent Colleen and RJ away. We'll deal with this." He glanced over, saw me bracing for impact, and chuckled. "Come on, Jake, you're an Ohio boy. Did you forget how to drive in winter?"

"I'm just not anxious to meet my Maker anytime soon."

"What about the night you drove home from that wild party after the Amherst game?" He smiled. "Hope you didn't forget what you hollered when we went into a spin on Route 58."

"What'd I say?"

" 'Hold my beer, this should be fun!' Your exact words. You were one crazy mother back then." Tree chortled, cleared the intersection with his siren, gunned the engine, and yelled, "Hang on!"

Ever since I had known him, Tree had been calm under pressure and quick to laugh when things were darkest. In football, they say the action slows down for the great players and the mayhem moves frame by frame. In the big games, he had been like that. No doubt, being cool and collected were real assets in his current profession.

We roared into the parking lot at my apartment as two uniforms arrived. Tree led the way, gun drawn. I followed them up the stairs.

My door had been kicked in. The alarm was silent.

Tree put a hand on my chest. "Wait here." He nodded to the two cops, called out "Police!" and entered.

From the hall I heard, "kitchen clear," "bedroom clear," and "study clear."

Tree filled the doorframe. "They're gone. Had to be pros. Disabled your bargain-basement security system. Probably took them five seconds."

I remembered the third guy I had seen in the Hummer and wondered if he was their security alarm expert.

"They tossed the place, Jake. Come in and tell us what's missing." Tree handed me a pair of latex gloves.

My living room was a mess, the couch and recliner overturned, cushions slashed. Same for RJ's bed and mine. The contents of my dresser drawers and closet were scattered across the bedroom floor.

It felt as if gravity had doubled. I could barely move.

Tree was shouting on the phone. "I want techs here *now*! This isn't a routine burglary. I got one family member knifed in ICU and the other threatened by out-of-town talent. I need fingerprints or DNA on these perps, something I can run through IAFIS or CODIS!" Tree listened and hung up. He sent an officer to interview my neighbors and told another to secure the premises, then he turned to me. "Anything missing?"

"It's hard to tell with this mess." I swept my hand around the room. "I don't get it, Tree. This doesn't make sense. There's not much worth stealing here. I can't believe they'd go through this much trouble or take the risk."

"They tossed your father's room at the Diplomat Hotel too. They're after something, and it sure as hell ain't the dime bag of weed or the few hits of coke I found in his duffel bag, or the forty bucks in his wallet. Whatever it is, they figure your dad gave it to you, and you stashed it here. Any ideas?"

I shrugged and wandered amid the pile of rubble that had been my home. I tried to shake off the sense of violation, failed, and forced myself to make a more thorough examination of my apartment. My watch was on top of the dresser, however my computer and camera were missing. The old TV in the living room was untouched and not worth hauling away. Then it hit me.

"Hell, Tree, they took two photos! One of Emily and me at a hospital party, and one of RJ."

"Shit. What the hell do these bastards want? I don't like this, buddy. We're missing a piece of the puzzle. Your father's been holding out on us. Let's go have a chat with him."

CHAPTER TWENTY-NINE

Saturday, December 7, 2002, 10:30 p.m.

Before abandoning the remnants of my home, I threw some clothes into a small suitcase, grabbed my shaving kit, and decided that my replacement door would be made of steel and my new alarm system top-of-the-line. Maybe I would ask Santa for a Glock and a gun safe for Christmas.

Tree and I ducked under crime scene tape into the hallway and walked over to a black policewoman knocking on my neighbors' doors.

"Must have been one hell of a racket," Tree said to her. "Get a description?"

"Most folks claim to have been sound asleep. Who the hell goes to bed that early? You gotta love this *I ain't seen nothing, don't wanna get involved* shit. Course they don't say that when they get robbed or vandalized." She hooked a thumb down the hallway. "But the old fella over there ID'ed two escapees from the laundry. Said one guy was a stuffed pillowcase. The other was a king-sized sheet, maybe six and a half feet tall, and two hundred eighty pounds. I already called for the sketch artist."

Tree gave her further instructions and we headed downstairs.

"Huh? Laundry? Sheets and pillowcases? What the hell'd she just say?"

"Oh, sorry, Jake. Ghetto-lingo." He gave me a sheepish grin. "Shorthand for two gentlemen of the Caucasian persuasion. One short and fat, the other a big dude. Sound familiar?"

I had no doubt Tubby and Muscle had ransacked my place, and I suspected that those two red-necks probably wore their sheets to Klan meetings.

Tree opened the driver's door of his car. "Let's go see your daddy."

On the way, I called Emily. She did not answer. I was probably the last person she wanted to talk to and delivering bad news was not going to improve things. I left a message, explaining that the thugs from Louisiana had taken a photo of the two of us at a hospital fundraiser and that she needed to be careful. I asked her to return my call but doubted that she would.

When we arrived at the hospital, I stopped in the doctors' lounge and stowed my suitcase and shaving kit in my locker, then we rode the elevator up to ICU. Officer Kearney was back on duty guarding the door. He greeted Tree, avoiding eye contact with me.

My father was asleep and not pleased to be awakened. His doctor had reduced his pain medication, and he clearly was less comfortable but more lucid. Also, more irritable. I preferred being around him when he was sedated.

Tree started by asking open-ended questions about Giordano's drug operation, which set my old man off like a Roman candle.

"I already done told y'all! We was takin' turf from the Ruskies and all hell broke loose. A couple of our corner men got hit on Bourbon Street, and Giordano blew up one of their guys in his car. The boss gets like that. I plumb-near shit myself." His nasal twang sounded like an out-of-tune A-string. "I'm too friggin' old to go to war. I wanted out, so I took a few hundred bucks and hightailed it to Ohio." His eyes flashed from Tree to me. "Hoping my son would *help* me. Y'all are both useless."

Amazing. Now Tree and I were the problem. With each retelling of his story, my father became more of a victim. The guy constructed lies and excuses to keep the truth at bay the way the Dutch built dikes to hold back the sea.

"You left out the part about stealing Giordano's coke, old man."

"T'wernt that much." He gave me a shrug and an *aw-shucks* expression. "Sold a little, partied some with friends in Detroit, blew through it in a week. No big deal."

Definitely a big deal to me, Santana, and everyone I knew. It had turned our lives upside down.

"Giordano obviously thought it was pretty damn important. He had his guys chase you across half the country. And partying with friends? What a joke." The man was an aging tomcat, probably popping handfuls of Viagra. "I'm betting your *friends* weren't wearing any panties and charged by the hour."

I glowered at him.

"Don't you be judging me, son," he said, shooing my disgust away like a pesky horsefly. "We done here? Y'all can leave now."

Tree commandeered the conversation. "I know you're holding out on us, sir." He told my father about Tubby's visit to the hospital and the break-in at my apartment. "Those guys are after something besides you. What else did you take from Giordano? Come on, spill it."

"Didn't take nothing else. Just a couple of snorts of blow and a few bucks. Honest. The boss cain't abide no turncoats. When he loses his temper, he's meaner than a diamondback with poison ivy."

As Tree's account of recent events sank in, anger drained from my father's face, replaced by fear.

"And the boy, Jake? Is RJ okay?"

"He's safe … for now."

He looked away. "Sorry I dragged you and him into this. Never meant for you two to get hurt. Think it's time I skedaddle." He pointed at his IV. "Yank this crap outta my arm and I'm gone."

"You're not ready to leave yet …." I was about to call him "old man" again, but apparently he was not going to be out of my life anytime soon, and I couldn't call him that forever. I considered my options and chose the least onerous. "Be reasonable, Pop, you've just been stabbed."

"This?" He pointed to his belly. "Oh hell, this little scratch ain't nothin'."

"You ought to be on antibiotics for at least a week," I said, thinking more about detox and rehab.

"So gimme some pills. You're a doctor, ain't you? What's the big deal?"

"The problem is, Mr. Austin," Tree leaned forward, "there's the matter of the drugs. Yours, and the dope flooding our streets. I can't let you go. The FBI needs your help nailing Giordano and so do I. These bastards are selling to kids. Help us and we'll make all your charges go away."

"Fuck Giordano and fuck the Feds. I'm knee-deep in shit already. I done told you everthin'." He slid his feet over the side of the bed and sat up. "Gimme a few bucks, Jake, and I'll get on Amtrak. Got me a friend in the Big Apple. Let 'em try and find me in *that* zoo. Where's my stuff anyway?"

"Leaving's not an option, sir," Tree said. "There's a patrolman guarding the door. Your duffel bag, minus your stash of weed and coke, came with you from jail to the ICU. It's stored around here somewhere."

"And my sax, Jake?"

"It's safe in my locker in the doctors' lounge."

I'd had enough of my old man, his attempts at manipulation, and his smart-ass attitude. My watch said it had already been a long day and my body agreed. Fatigue draped my back like a wet overcoat, its pockets filled with rocks.

"Listen, Pop, if you help Tree and the FBI, you can get all of us out of this jam—you, your grandson, and me. Think about it. Besides, I don't have any money on me. I gave it all to the friend who took RJ out of town. Let's both get some rest, and we'll talk in the morning."

My father nodded, and Tree and I left ICU. As we walked down the hall, he said, "I'd feel a whole lot better if I could get my hands on Tubby and Muscle."

"Me too. And I want to know who the third guy in the Hummer was, so I can watch out for him."

"You saying Mass in the hospital tomorrow morning, Jake?"

"Yes, but I could ask Father Vargas to cover for me, if you think that's wise."

"Got a better idea. How about we stake out the chapel. I bet these jackals will be back, sniffing around. Wanna be the bait in the trap?"

I had fished a lot as a kid and knew one thing for certain—the bait usually died. I shook my head, then took RJ and Emily into account, along with the very real possibility that my new life could explode in a hailstorm of bullets at any time.

"Think about it, Jake. Between the FBI and my troops, they'll be surrounded like Custer at Little Bighorn. And if we get one of them to turn stool pigeon, we might wipe out Big Angie and his whole operation. I'm sick and tired of folks in the county overdosing on the shit they're peddling."

I must have hesitated because Sheriff Cool-Under-Pressure grinned and said, "All the color just drained from your cheeks. You ready to go on the warpath, Paleface?"

"You can't come riding in with guns blazing, Tree. What about my parishioners? There might be kids at the service."

"Okay, Custer was a bad example. This won't be an O.K. Corral shootout. These clowns are after something and want to scare and intimidate you, not kill you. They're probably not going to show up in the chapel armed to the teeth."

"Probably?"

"Look, normally I try to avoid crowded places for these kinds of operations, but I can't imagine a better opportunity. My guys will be in plain clothes surrounding the chapel and when Tubby and Muscle show, we'll scoop them up in the hall like fish in a net. No bloodshed. It's our best shot."

"I suppose I could ask Father Vargas to offer a special pre-Christmas service for the children and their parents in a classroom down the hall to get them out of harm's way." I tried to think of a better plan but came up empty. "All right, if it'll put an end to this nightmare, count me in. I'll be the guy in the vestments at the altar wearing the war paint."

"Good. Not to worry, we'll take these bastards down without firing a round. I'll call the FBI and put together a joint operation, and tell hospital security to keep the areas surrounding the chapel as free of patients and visitors as possible tomorrow."

As we arrived at the elevator, Tree said, "Tubby and Muscle know you're a priest here, so they may have figured out you're also a doctor. Be careful. And say a few extra prayers for all of us; we may need them. See you in the morning, buddy."

Tree joined a flock of white coats on the elevator and the doors closed. I walked away and made my evening rounds serenaded by the soft hum of fluorescent lights, the occasional patient moan, and the page operator's voice. The nearly empty hospital corridors felt eerie and surreal, the air thick with the scent of disinfectant and danger. From a distance, every orderly reminded me of Muscle.

By the time I arrived on the pediatric floor, a dizzying ache had crept from the base of my skull and lodged behind my eyes. I asked a nurse for three aspirin, swallowed them dry, and peeked into Anna Grabowski's room.

She and her mother both slept. Mom stirred briefly in her chair, then resumed snoring like a buzz saw. Anna's paintings hung on the wall. Some children drew dark and disturbing pictures when gravely ill. Anna's pastel colors, however, radiated hope and joy. I prayed that she would remain in this world long enough to become another Monet.

She had kicked the bedcovers off. The tube I had placed in her liver was draining buckets of bile and the dressing covering it was clean and dry. The nursing notes indicated stable vital signs and a reduction in her itching. So far, so good. Now, if the oncologist could poison the tumor and not the girl, Christmas would indeed be merry and we would all sleep a lot better.

Anna stirred, mumbled something, and snuggled with her tattered, old teddy bear. I pulled her covers back up and left the room. At least one thing had gone right today. I had learned over the years to celebrate even minor successes whenever possible, and I basked in my small victory all the way to the doctors' lounge.

Retrieving my shaving kit and suitcase from my locker, I contemplated hobbling my damaged car to a motel but found an empty on-call room instead. I set the alarm clock on the nightstand for 7:00 a.m. and left my beeper on. Because of Tree's warning, I did not tell the page operator I was in the hospital.

After reciting my evening prayers, I tossed for an hour, worried about celebrating morning Mass for a congregation of felons, cops, murderers, and FBI. Finally sleep wrapped its enormous, dark arms around me and carried me down a deep mine shaft. For the second night in a row, I dreamt of Shades Gingrich. He was guiding a small boat with a push-pole across the River Styx. RJ was his cargo, his skin ashen, lips blue. I awoke in a cold sweat at one in the morning, again at three, and finally plunged back into infinite blackness.

CHAPTER THIRTY

Sunday, December 8, 2002, 8:00 a.m.

I was dressing in my vestments for Mass when I heard a soft knock at the sacristy door. A fluffy red cloud of Orphan Annie curls peeked in. Kristin, my regular altar girl from Sacred Heart Church, smiled up at me.

"Surprise, Father! My mother and I came to visit my grandpa at the hospital, and I decided to stop in and help you offer Mass."

She was a wonderful child and *it was* a lovely surprise, but on the worst possible day. Before I could respond, she handed me a piece of paper. "A nun asked me to give this to you."

I unfolded the hand-written note and read: *Blessed are the lame, for they shall guard the temple gates. And blessed are the vigilant, for they shall not enter God's kingdom today. Pray, and we shall pray with you. K.N.*

The battle plan from Special Agent Keri Novak. I read the note again, peeked out from the sacristy, and surveyed the chapel. My Three Owls sat in the left front pew, near Kristin's mother, with a couple of other regulars directly behind. Another nun knelt across the center aisle from them. Novak looked up and nodded, then resumed her devotions. I suspected that she had more than a rosary stashed in the folds of her habit.

A middle-aged man in a wheelchair was positioned near the chapel door. He had muscular arms, and his stocky legs suggested that he had not been an invalid for very long. His eyes repeatedly swept over the room like a lighthouse beacon.

I was not surprised that Tree Macon was nowhere in sight. His photo was on the front page of every newspaper, and he was too large a man to be inconspicuous.

On the plus side, the number of worshipers was smaller than usual. Thank God it was not Easter or December twenty-fifth, when our wayward members were miraculously filled with their biannual allocation of the

Holy Spirit and the pews were chock-full of *CEO Catholics* who attended on Christmas and Easter only.

As I released a relieved sigh, a frazzled Hispanic woman entered and sat in the last pew with a brood of small children. Her baby fussed and cried loudly as she tried to calm it. Somehow she had bypassed the special service for children that Father Vargas was about to conduct at the far end of the hall.

I ducked back into the vestry and scribbled my reply: *Blessed are the innocent children and loving parents, for they shall be shielded from all harm. The Chosen shall guide them to a place of safety. J.A.*

Not wanting any child placed in harm's way in case all hell broke loose, I handed the note to Kristin and asked her to give my response to the nun. I explained that I appreciated her kind offer to help but preferred that she attend the Yuletide service for children with her mother, adding that there would be presents and cake afterward.

"Come on, Father," she replied, stomping her foot. "I'm not a little kid!"

"I know you're not, Kristin. I'll explain everything to you next Sunday. Promise. Please do as I ask. This is important." She continued to resist, so I switched to my authoritarian priest voice and said, "Now, no more debate, Kristin. Take your mother and leave the chapel." Her expression of hurt and confusion pained me as she left the sacristy.

I watched Sister Keri Novak read my note and escort Kristin, her mother, and the Hispanic family from the room. When she returned, I made my entrance as if trudging up the hill to Golgotha. I ordered my heart to stop pounding. It refused. Although I did not feel my usual joy as I walked to the altar, I managed a thin smile.

The hospital chapel was as serene as a monastery—or quiet as a tomb—until a tapping sound shattered the silence. Emily entered, using her cane to maneuver around the man in the wheelchair and into a back pew.

What had I been thinking? I should have warned her not to come! Now, I could not envision a way to get her to leave without spooking our prey.

I greeted my parishioners and opened the service by chanting the entrance antiphon, my mind running on auto-pilot, my eyes scanning the room. No sign of Tubby or Muscle, although several men appeared shifty and out of place. I had no clue who the third person in the back seat of the Hummer had been, and it occurred to me that in all likelihood I would be confronted in the chapel or ambushed outside it by a complete stranger.

The Kyrie and the Gloria passed uneventfully. Wanting no tongues of fire in my sermon, I kept my homily short, choosing hopeful words about the Lord as our shepherd and protector. Offering the bread and wine, I recited the Eucharistic Prayer, exhorting everyone to lift up their hearts— as mine fluttered in my chest.

During the Lord's Prayer I shifted my gaze from the crucifix to Sister Keri and said, "Deliver us from evil," meaning every word. The congregation responded with, "For the kingdom, power, and glory are Yours, now and forever"—reaffirming that my life, today as always, lay in His hands.

I stepped down from the altar to offer communion, the point in the service that left me most accessible and potentially most vulnerable. Sister Keri prayed softly, her head bowed close to her folded hands, communicating with her team.

More than half of the parishioners stood and lined up before me.

I held my breath as I placed the Host on the tongue of a disheveled man, partly because he reeked of smoke and booze, but mostly because he smelled like trouble. He had more tattoos than teeth, and craziness surged from him in waves. His vacant eyes suggested that he had little left in life to lose, and a chill shivered me. Not long ago, a serial killer had looked at me the same way when he was deciding whether or not to gun me down. So did the soldier I had killed in the war, just before I shot him in the head. My life had been divided forever into *before* and *after* the moment I pulled the trigger.

The disheveled man accepted the Host, however, and shuffled back to his seat. Sister Keri must have seen him as a potential threat too, for she had positioned herself behind him and was next in line.

"Anything?" she said softly.

I shook my head and whispered, "I'll make the Sign of the Cross backward if I see something."

She nodded, received communion, and returned to the front pew.

An old woman approached me. Age and osteoporosis had twisted her spine into the shape of a question mark. As she hobbled away, a caravan of seniors followed, all too feeble to be dangerous.

A burly young man stepped forward. Inked oriental letters climbed the side of his beefy neck, and iron-pumped biceps bulged the sleeves of his dress shirt. Moisture dampened my armpits, and blood roared in my ears. He took the Host and walked harmlessly away as my lungs began to function again.

My Three Owls preceded a bear of a man, nearly the size of Tree Macon, wearing a three-piece silk suit that probably cost more than my car. His face was cherub-like, his demeanor serene, so I was surprised when he stepped close, invading my space. I could not exhale until he received the Lord's precious body and walked away.

Emily was near the end of the communion line. I couldn't think of a way to warn her without sparking a discussion and compromising the surveillance, so I offered her communion and nervously watched as she tapped her way to the back of the chapel.

The last communicant was a skinny, young man wearing a thread-bare sport coat over a t-shirt imprinted with the image of Dr. Dre. I had seen him somewhere before but couldn't quite place him. His pants rested low on his hips, revealing the top of his jockey shorts. Below cornrows, his brown eyes focused on his Nikes and he seemed oblivious to my presence.

In a strange way, I felt disappointed that no one had made a move. I had hoped to end this nightmare today. Maybe Tubby intended to intercept me after Mass as he had with Father Vargas.

When I raised the Host to the young man's lips, he lifted his eyes to mine and grinned, revealing a grill of gold teeth.

"Virgin Mary's got somethin' for you, Father," he whispered, then snared the Host like a trout grabbing a fly, whirled around, and sauntered down the aisle toward the exit, his sneakers emitting squeaking sounds in the hushed chapel.

I looked directly at Sister Keri and made the Sign of the Cross the way Orthodox Catholics do, from the right shoulder to the left. My Three Owls regarded me quizzically. Keri's attention, however, was focused on the behemoth with the angelic expression who was slowly plodding back to his seat. She had missed the signal.

I stepped in her direction, tilted my head toward the young man, and said softly, "Sister, have a word with our *brother*, please."

She whispered something into her folded hands and the man in the wheelchair rolled out the door. Sister Keri stood and followed the teen down the aisle.

I expected commotion as they left the chapel but heard nothing. Bracing for chaos, the seconds slowly limped by. My palms were damp, my mouth dry. I was purifying the sacred vessels when the PA speaker sparked to life: *Condition Gray, One East. Condition Gray, One East*—the hospital code to evacuate patients and visitors near the auditorium.

My hands trembled violently and I vaguely heard myself say the prayer after communion. Omitting the announcements, I dismissed the congregation and hurried to the statue of the Virgin. A piece of paper peeked out from under Mary's foot.

I was reaching for it when Tree charged into the chapel.

"Jake, no. Wait." He pointed at the paper. "Is this a gift from the skinny black magi?"

"Yeah, though I doubt he left us any frankincense or myrrh."

Tree reached into the pocket of his suit coat, pulled out a pair of latex gloves, and slipped them on. He tilted the statue, removed the note, and unfolded it. After he had read it, he showed it to me.

Cascade Park. Two a.m. Bottom of the hill by the river. Bring the saxophone case—or the boy and pretty lady join the angels.

"Damn it, Tree, the sax! *That's* why they ransacked my apartment and my father's hotel room."

"Damn right, damn. Your father didn't take a *little product* for his personal use. He must have made off with one of Giordano's drug shipments. Crap, this doesn't make sense. I examined that saxophone case back at the Diplomat Hotel and there sure as hell weren't any drugs in it. Maybe he stashed the stuff somewhere near the hotel. Where's your dad's sax?"

"Inside my locker in the doctors' lounge. Let's go."

We heard a tapping sound and when we turned around, Emily smiled at us.

"Tree, is that you?"

"Yes, ma'am. You have good ears."

"I thought I heard your voice. Aren't you a Baptist? Don't tell me you've converted."

Perhaps recognizing the scent of my cologne, she added, "Oh, Jake. Remind me not to underestimate your powers of persuasion." Her icy voice thawed when she said to Tree, "Although I have to admit, I'd love to hear the story behind your conversion, Sheriff. That has to rank as a minor miracle."

She paused and laughed. "I just realized what the three of us must look like! A priest, a cop and a blind woman. If we walked into a bar, we'd be the first line of a joke." She chuckled again. "Wish I knew the punchline."

The punchline was that my old man's return had placed everyone I cared about at ground zero, and it was no joke.

When she got no response from either of us, she asked, "What?"

"Listen, Em. Didn't you get the voicemail I left you last night?"

"No."

"Those thugs broke into my apartment and tore it apart ... and took photos of you and RJ."

Tree read her the note and we watched her smile dissolve.

"My God!" She leaned unsteadily against me. "Is RJ safe?"

"Yes, I sent him out of town with Colleen last night. But you and I can't be seen together until this is over." Her shoulders slouched and she stepped away. "Em, this might be a good time to take a vacation, somewhere far away from here."

Tree cleared his throat. "I'd prefer you stay in town, where I can provide protection."

"No, I think Jake's right. Besides, I have my dad to consider. If I leave, they might come after him. He's always wanted to hear the Boston Symphony Orchestra live, and we have relatives there. I'll talk with him and try to convince him to leave. Maybe we can catch a flight out today."

"Okay, if that's what you want to do," Tree replied. "Let me know, and I'll have a uniform take you to the airport."

"Thanks, Tree." She turned toward me and some of the frost in her voice melted away. "Maybe you should go too."

"Soon. There's something I have to do first."

"No hero stuff, Jake. I don't want to be lighting prayer candles for you." She reached out, found my hand, and squeezed it. "Seriously. Take care of yourself, okay."

CHAPTER THIRTY-ONE

Sunday, December 8, 2002, 9:30 a.m.

Emily left the chapel to break the bad news to her father and arrange an impromptu trip to Boston.

The chaos of my father's return to town and the stress of the morning stakeout roared up on me like a bullet train and flattened me. I leaned against a pew, dazed.

While Tree spoke with Keri Novak and another FBI agent, I called Colleen to make sure that all was well, then listened to RJ expound on all the fun toys at Colleen's sister's house.

Tree strode over to me. "C'mon, buddy, we got work to do. I suspect I know the answer, but let's go see what's so important about your dad's saxophone."

On the walk to the doctors' lounge, I was lost in worry, my head hanging low.

Tree slapped me on the back and said, "Lighten up, or folks in the hall will think I arrested your sorry behind. And given your outrageous choice of clothing, I probably *should* bust you for disturbing the peace."

I glanced down and groaned. I was still wearing my vestments.

"Listen, this is a *good thing*, Jake. They want the sax case, and I want them. We'll surround the drop-site and swarm in. These bastards won't know what hit them. We'll shut 'em down for good. Already got someone in mind to take the sax case who could almost pass for your twin brother."

I stopped and fixed him with my gaze.

"No way, Tree. I'm going in with the case. If Tubby or Muscle is there, your guy's dead! They've *seen* me. And Muscle sure-as-hell won't forget my face after what I did to his. We're too close to screw this up with some snafu. I want RJ home safe and my life back."

"Sounds like a great plan, Jake … till it all goes sideways and turns to shit. Not a chance." He began walking again, then stopped. "I get what you're saying, buddy, but I can't—"

"No *buts*. I was military and can do this. I have to."

"Absolutely not."

"It *has to be* me, Tree. Just think about it." I didn't want to push Tree too hard and shifted gears. "Did you grab the kid who hid the note? The one with the gold-teeth."

"Oh yeah, we got him. Willy Warner, street name, Willy Wonka—a.k.a. *The Candy Man.* The guy's been dealing drugs for years, passing 'em out like bonbons ever since he could tie his sneakers. Busted his skinny ass selling a dime eight years ago. He's a revolving-door junky who's spent his life in and out of juvie. But he's no kid anymore. Didn't say bupkis in the hall. When his druggie-buzz cool wears off, I'm gonna crank up the heat and watch him snap, crackle, and pop.

We entered the doctors' lounge. Tree eyed the doughnuts on the counter, reached for one, but resisted the urge and walked past.

"Willy's a bug in search of a windshield. The bad news is he's only a low-level street punk. Good news is he has a long rap-sheet and two strikes as an adult, so a third strike buys him serious jail time. I don't think the skinny weasel wants to spend years sharing a shower with biker bubba or some skin-head. I'm betting we can turn him."

The PA speaker came to life. *Condition Walk, third floor, ICU. Condition Walk, third floor, ICU.*

I froze. "Oh no!"

"What? What's *Condition Walk*?"

"A wandering or missing patient—and that's my dad's floor. The sax! Come on."

We burst into the men's locker room. Dr. Glade was sitting on a bench, changing his shoes.

"Hey, nice duds, Father. Gold filigree over deep purple really works with your eyes." Glade smiled. "You just missed your dad. No worries. I told him which locker was yours, and he got his stuff."

I moaned.

"Your father looks a lot like you. He showed me a picture of you at the beach. You sure were a scrawny kid." Glade laughed. "He was in a big hurry but said he'll catch up with you later."

Yeah, maybe in forty years or so.

I threw open my locker. The sax was gone. I slammed the locker closed and pounded the door with my fist. At the sound, Glade stiffened, his eyes the size of half dollars.

Tree hit the button on his radio and growled, "What the hell'd you do, Kearney? What? You let him rabbit? Jeezus!" The big man drew a deep breath into the bellows of his lungs and used it to stoke the roaring furnace of his anger. "Yeah he's old, but he's got legs, and now he's in the wind. You better pray we find him! He can't get far dressed in a patient's gown."

Tree listened, massaging his forehead. "What? You let a damn x-ray tech watch him 'cause you had to piss? Sonofabitch, you gotta be shittin' me. Call every damn taxi company. I wanna know the second anyone with a southern drawl hails a cab. And Kearney, my office, nine a.m. tomorrow."

Tree turned to me. "Your father asked for his duffel bag this morning, said he wanted to read some scripture from the Good Book."

"Yeah, right. The only taste of religion my old man ever got was licking spilled beer off the family Bible."

"He must have grabbed some street clothes. Ten minutes later, he started complaining about belly pain. They sent him for x-rays. Kearney had to pee and left the x-ray tech watching him. When your dad got the chance, he bolted. He's slippery, very slippery." Tree pointed at my locker. "Really? You leave this thing unlocked?"

"I never keep anything of value in it. Didn't think anyone would steal a beaten-up old sax."

Tree dialed his phone, ordered his troops to set up a perimeter around the hospital, and put out an all-points-bulletin on my father. He collapsed onto the bench, his head in his hands.

Dr. Glade sat motionless, watching us. "Did I do something wrong, Jake?"

"No, I did." I joined Tree on the bench. "I underestimated how big a dirt-bag my old man actually is."

CHAPTER THIRTY-TWO

Sunday, December 8, 2002, 10:00 a.m.

Embarrassed about helping my father ransack my locker, Dr. Glade retreated sheepishly from the doctors' lounge. Tree and I remained seated on the bench.

"What do we do now, Tree?"

He didn't hesitate. "We find a saxophone case that looks like your father's, show up for the meet, and hope-to-God we get these bastards before they find out your dad and the drugs are gone."

"I'll take the case to the drop site. It has to be me. Those thugs *know* me."

"There you go again." Tree cupped a hand behind one ear. "Sorry, I can't hear you when you talk bullshit." His chin sank to his chest. "You can't make the drop, Jake. It's too damn dangerous. Not a chance! This is all on me."

Tree was shaken. I had never seen him lose his cool before. Sweat ran down his forehead and he massaged the back of his neck.

"Listen, buddy, this is my fault and my problem. I'm the one who screwed this up. I should have confiscated the sax at the Diplomat Hotel. That's procedure, and the reason police aren't supposed to give their friends special treatment. Being a cop is about judgment, and I lost mine. I let our friendship get in the way of my job."

"And that's exactly why *I should* make the drop. I'm your best chance to shut these guys down before they murder anyone else or overdose another kid. Heck, I've been a soldier, I can handle myself. Come on, Tree, my life's already in danger, and now they're after RJ and Emily. It's *my world* that's crashing down."

"I don't like it." He was silent for a long time, then pounded a meaty fist on the bench. "All right, Jake, you win. You go to the drop. But if you get hurt, I'm gonna kill you."

"Deal."

True, my world was crashing down, and I wanted Tubby, Muscle, and my father gone. Despite my bravado, however, I wondered if I had just made the worst decision of my life—and I had made some really bone-headed choices in the past.

"Tree, please get protection for Colleen and RJ in Toledo." I gave her cellphone number to him.

"I trained with a sergeant there. He'll make it happen."

"Thanks, buddy." I stood. "And the drugs?"

"If your father ripped off Angelo Giordano, he probably took uncut cocaine or heroin. That sax case isn't very big, but those could bring major bucks in small quantities. I'm guessing coke. That's what your dad had in the tobacco tin. A couple pounds of uncut nose candy could fetch thirty or forty grand in the Big Apple."

Tree paused. "And I'm sure your dad didn't sell it yet. If he had, he wouldn't be drinking that rotgut wine. He must have stashed it somewhere." He stood. "Think I'll go visit Willy Wonka and rattle the cat's cage, see if he'll cough up a hairball or some useful info."

"What about me?"

"You've seen your father's saxophone case. Go get one that looks like it, while I do my thing. Where's your car?"

"Second floor of the parking garage, but I don't think I can drive it very far with the rear fender rubbing against the tire."

"Give me the keys, Jake."

"What? Why?"

"We'll put a GPS bug in it so we can track you tonight. Drop sites usually change last minute. And I'll have my guys pound out your fender so you can haul-ass if you have to. Get yourself another ride for the afternoon."

I flipped him my car keys. Halfway to the door, he stopped. "Blue Ford Focus, right?"

I nodded.

"With Jimmy Sole in a cooler at the morgue, Jake, I suspect your old man is looking for another buyer. Any idea who that could be?"

"Not a clue."

'Where'd your father hang out, back in the day?"

"How many bars are there in the county? Pick one. Maybe Bogart's. My old man spent more time there than at home."

Tree pulled out a spiral notebook. "Bogart's went belly up years ago. Where else, Jake?"

"How about the Bent Elbow in Lorain? And the Train Station in Elyria. Maybe Wahoo's."

Tree scribbled away.

"Good. I'll call you when I get things set up for tonight," he said and disappeared out the door.

I returned to the sacristy, changed into my street clothes, and opened the phone book to a list of music stores. Most were closed on Sundays. The Driscol Music Company, however, opened at one p.m. I also wrote down the addresses of a few pawn shops, then sank onto a kneeler in the chapel and asked God for His guidance and protection.

After I had finished praying, I walked to the hospital ATM machine and extracted two hundred dollars from its metal mouth.

Gavin Glade turned the corner and came over. "Sorry, Jake. I didn't know your father was a problem. Wish I could make it up to you."

"There's one way you can." I stepped closer. "Lend me your car for a couple hours."

CHAPTER THIRTY-THREE

Sunday, December 8, 2002, 11:00 a.m.

I leaned back into the baby-soft leather of Gavin Glade's new Jaguar, listened to the engine purr, and tried to keep the beast under eighty miles per hour. The rich fresh-from-the-showroom aroma filled my senses, and I wondered why I had never considered becoming a surgeon in medical school. But even the exhilaration of driving this ego-mobile could not dislodge the anxiety about my rendezvous with drug dealers in the dead of night in a deserted city park.

The tires chirped as I slid into a parking space in front of Cold Cash Pawnbrokers, located near the edge of the urban sprawl that is Lorain, Ohio. Not a great part of town to leave a Jag parked for long, but I didn't need to. The store had no musical instruments or cases in stock. Neither did E-Z Money Pawn and Jewelry.

I had never owned a car with a navigation system and it took a while to obtain directions to the Driscol music store. At last, a perky female voice with a British accent suggested that I "follow the highlighted route."

Traffic was light and I was cruising along when a black Hummer took the corner at an intersection ahead of me and raced south. The road had been cleared of snow and salted, and I quickly closed the gap, asphalt flying under the Jaguar.

The Hummer had Florida plates and I memorized the license number. We took the ramp onto Route 2 toward Toledo, and I accelerated into the passing lane. The Jag's tires lost traction for a second, its tail wagged, and I nearly tapped a guard rail before I regained control. Visions of crumpled metal and Dr. Glade's fury danced in my head.

Cloud cover and the Hummer's darkly tinted windows precluded any chance of ID'ing the occupants from a distance. I was about to speed dial Tree when the sun popped from behind a cloud, spotlighting the front seat. I drew up parallel to the Hummer and got a clear view of the driver—an elderly woman on her cellphone.

Crap! Disappointment washed over me, and I backed off the accelerator and eased into the right lane. I was chasing rainbows, or as Tree called it, goosing ghosts.

An angry roar closed in on the Jag, and a Harley hog flashed chrome in my rearview mirror. The rider looked like he had come off the set of some outlaw biker movie. It appeared that I was not the only idiot testing the roads for black ice. He leaned hard left and flew by me, eager to donate his internal organs for Christmas. I, however, was not anxious to leave this world and had sold *my own* two-wheeled donor-cycle years earlier.

I exited the highway and headed toward the music store. A section of the road was closed for construction, and I followed a detour sign down a side street. The mechanical voice on the GPS said "Recalculating" in a tone that implied that the road block was my fault. I told her to shut-the-hell up and relaxed my white-knuckle grip on the steering wheel.

At 12:40, I parked on Broadway in front of the Driscol Music Company, the finest purveyor of instruments in the area. I would have preferred a less expensive retailer than Driscol, but none of the others were open on Sunday. The sign on the door confirmed that the shop opened at 1:00 p.m. With the tension of the morning churning inside me, a twenty minute wait seemed like an eternity.

I had missed lunch and my stomach rumbled with the ferocity of a subwoofer. Despite the adverse effects of a double cheeseburger and fries on my coronary arteries, I decided to get them anyway and was shifting into drive when my cellphone rang.

"Dr. Austin?"

"Yes."

"I'm a pharmacist at CVS in Amherst. Sorry to bother you. Mr. Matthew Burns' prescription for oxycodone has too many refills requested for a narcotic."

I shifted the car back into park as my pounding pulse missed a couple of beats. I had not prescribed any Oxy recently and certainly would have remembered the name "Matt Burns." I had been a wrestler in high school and had accumulated more than a few *mat burns* on my skin. The coach had even nicknamed me that my sophomore year.

"Does it have my signature and DEA number?"

"Yes doctor, and they match our file. The prescription has St. Joseph's Hospital printed across the top."

Damn it! "Can you describe the guy?"

"Skinny, white, mid-twenties, long brown hair. Pretty disheveled, and acting a bit squirrelly. No insurance. I got even more suspicious when he pulled out a wad of cash."

"It's bogus, don't fill it. I'm positive. Thanks for being diligent and notifying me. You should call the police." I doubted the cops would get there in time, because any hesitation from the pharmacist and the guy would probably dash for the door.

I hung up and sank into the soft embrace of the Jaguar's seat. Crap! The Drug Task Force was already suspicious of all pain management doctors who prescribed opiates on a regular basis. Forged prescriptions in the county with my signature and DEA number put me back in their crosshairs.

Recalling that a prescription pad had gone missing from Urgent Care a couple days earlier, I called Harvey Winer's number in the administration office, got his machine, and left a message suggesting that the hospital lock up all of their prescription pads.

The clock in the wood-grained dash glowed 12:45. Fifteen minutes before the music store opened. My appetite was gone. I shut the car off and listened to the engine tick in the cold before turning on the Bose stereo. The Hollies filled the car with "He Ain't Heavy, He's My Brother." I absently caressed the steering wheel's fine leather and pondered the mystery of peoples' priorities, Dr. Glade's in particular. The eighty grand or so that Glade had spent on this Jag could have stocked the Lorain County Food Bank for a year. I sighed. The Good Lord had given us two hands for a reason—one to help ourselves, and one to help others. I wished more folks would use both.

That thought made me feel very old and very tired, and I was about to close my eyes for a few minutes when a young man came bopping down the sidewalk. He wore earbuds and was lost in the music, his head swinging back and forth like a metronome. His fingers moved as if he was auditioning for air-guitarist in some imaginary band. He produced a set of keys from his coat pocket and unlocked the music store's door.

I jumped out of the car and trotted up to him.

"Excuse me. May I come in?"

He unplugged one ear.

"Sorry, sir. We don't open till one."

He began to slip inside, and I grabbed his arm. He spun, panic in his eyes.

"Wait," I said, releasing him. I took a twenty dollar bill from my wallet. "Sorry. I'm in a bit of a hurry."

He glanced from me, to the pricy Jaguar, back at the money in my hand, and his fear drained away.

"I'm sure we can make an exception, sir. Please come in." He pocketed the cash and locked the door behind us. "My name is Malcolm. How may I assist you today?"

"I'd like to buy a saxophone case. An old one would be best. I'd prefer if it looked a little … weathered and scruffy."

He stared at me as if I had gotten off a spaceship from Mars.

"We don't carry used cases. No instrument for you then?"

"No, just a case. Please show me whatever you have."

His enthusiasm waned. "Alto, tenor, baritone, or soprano?"

"Bring them all."

Perplexed, Malcolm entered a back room. He came out rolling a small pushcart holding eight different saxophone cases. None matched the style of my father's battered old case, though an oxblood one was fairly close in appearance and nearly as large in size.

"I'll take this one."

"Wonderful choice, sir." He didn't even try to hide the sarcasm in his voice. "Shall I fill it with a saxophone for you as well? We have an enormous selection of beautiful instruments ranging from two thousand to seven thousand dollars." His eyes twinkled at the possibility of a fat commission. I could almost hear my credit card whine.

When I hesitated, he added, "We do also offer a few ... pre-owned instruments for sale at bargain prices."

My life depended on realism tonight. My dad's sax was as old as his case, and I couldn't show up tonight with one right off the shelf. I nodded and his smile reemerged.

He returned with three saxophones, and I settled on a used one with "character" for $400.

"Would you care to try it out, sir?"

"No, thanks."

He pointed at the battered reed and the teeth marks on the mouthpiece. "I'm embarrassed. These should have been removed. Allow me to replace them for you."

I'd already spent too much money and authenticity tonight was critical. "That's okay. They're fine as is."

"Please sir. I can't allow you to leave the store with this type of substandard equipment."

When I shook my head, he shook his.

He put the sax into the case, swiped my VISA card, unlocked the shop door, and ushered me into the street. He didn't even say goodbye.

CHAPTER THIRTY-FOUR

Sunday, December 8, 2002, 2:30 p.m.

I grabbed a cheeseburger and coffee at a McDonald's, drove to the hospital, and returned Dr. Glade's car keys. In an unoccupied exam room in the Urgent Care Center, I removed the saxophone, cut several slashes in the beige lining of the case with a scalpel, and splashed coffee inside it. Using a surgical probe, I gouged and scarred the leather exterior, aging it twenty years.

Our orderly, DeQuan Kwame, must have heard the noise as I kicked the case around the room because he opened the door and peeked in. His lips spread into a wide grin.

"Have you been imbibing large quantities of adult beverages today, Doctor?" he asked, his British accent somehow adding gravitas to his wisecrack. "You are truly a puzzlement. Please do not do anything that will force me to witness your donation of more urine samples."

"Very funny, DeQuan." I kicked the case in his direction, and it skidded across the floor and bounced off the wall. "Don't let the door hit you in the butt on your way out."

He chuckled and left.

When the case finally looked as if it had spent the last decade in a series of honky-tonks, I put the used sax with the chewed up mouthpiece inside it, threw in two singles and some loose change, and called Tree. His mood was better.

"Just cranked up the heat on Willy 'the Candy Man' Warner, and he melted like a Hershey bar in the August sun. He would have given up his mother to save himself jail time. How soon can you get to my office, Jake?"

"I have to check on a couple of patients first. Half an hour?"

"Perfect. Any luck finding a matching case?"

"Got it. I think it'll pass inspection."

"It damn-well better. Bring it. Your car's ready, right where you left it. Keys are under the driver's seat."

I made my rounds, medical bag in one hand, saxophone case in the other, drawing a lot of quizzical stares from staff and patients.

As I entered the elevator, I glimpsed Shades Gingrich in a crowded hallway wearing his aviator's jacket and sunglasses. I called his name, but he turned the corner and was gone.

The elevator doors closed and I rode up to the pediatric oncology unit. Anna Grabowski was not in her room, and dark thoughts sprang up like mushrooms. A nurse assured me that she was fine and directed me to a lounge where Anna was playing cards with her mother. I could see the outline of the bile bag strapped to her side under her gown. She appeared comfortable and relaxed, although her skin and eyes remained a light lemon color.

Anna saw me and waved.

"The itching's like almost totally gone, Doctor. It's like, you know ... a miracle!" She lit up an enormous smile. "Thank you *soooo* much."

I wanted to steal the medicine man's line from the classic old movie *Little Big Man*—"Sometimes the magic works." Instead I said, "You're *soooo* welcome, sweetheart."

I had learned over the years to relish my medical victories, big or small, because I knew that sometimes the magic *didn't* work.

Anna's mom jumped up and hugged me. "I'll never forget you, Doctor!" She gave me another squeeze. "You're an angel. I'll be praying for you."

I would need all the prayers I could get if I was to avoid joining the angels tonight.

I thanked her and was leaving when the elevator door opened. Emily stepped out. Her lips were a tense pink gash, her clothes rumpled, her complexion parchment-pale, and her hair a bird's nest of disarray. I had never seen her this frazzled and disheveled. Never. Something inside me tightened. She looked as if she was about to shatter into a thousand pieces.

She must have heard the click of my loafers on the tile and caught the scent of my aftershave because she stopped and asked, "Jake, is that you?"

I didn't know what to expect. Were the last remnants of our tattered friendship about to disintegrate? The dress she wore was yellow, the color of caution on a stoplight. I took it as a warning.

"Em, are you okay?"

"Jake! Oh, thank God! Dr. Glade told me you were up here. We need to talk."

CHAPTER THIRTY-FIVE

Sunday, December 8, 2002, 3:30 p.m.

I guided her into the conference room, closed the door, and set the saxophone case and my medical bag on the table.

"Damn Em, I was hoping you'd be in Boston by now." I was not sure how real the threat to her was, but I had always believed that an ounce of paranoia was worth a pound of regret. "Don't blow this off. These guys are unpredictable and dangerous."

"I couldn't get a flight today. Dad and I leave first thing in the morning."

I focused on her agitation and disheveled appearance. My pulse pounded a drumbeat of dread in my ears.

"What the heck happened? What's wrong?"

Her expression crumbled and she trembled violently. I threw my arms around her and helped her into a chair. Through her muffled sobs, I made out, "Can't believe ... betrayed me ... so hurt ...."

"Talk to me, Em."

She turned away.

"What's going on? Tell me." I put my hand on hers. "Come on, spill it."

The first thing she spilled was tears. Lots of them. Shadows crossed her face and her chin dropped. I waited. Finally she regained her composure and spoke, her words small and frail.

"Why didn't you call me back this afternoon, Jake? I almost had the hospital operator page your beeper." Her breathing was ragged, and the pain in her voice raw. "I left two messages!"

I pulled out my phone. It had died after Tree's call. "Sorry, I forgot to recharge it. What's going on?"

"Dad and I ... had it out today. I told him what you said and confronted him. It got ugly." Her words sounded distant and jumbled. She removed her sunglasses, revealing red-rimmed eyes framed by dark bags that looked like twin bruises. "When you were overseas, my father had some vision left." She wiped tears away with the back of her hand. "Jake, he ... intercepted your letters. They never got to me."

"What?"

"Dad said he didn't want his daughter loving a man who might come home in a body bag. He was frightened by your drinking and drugging, and wanted to shield me from your influence." She paused, searching for the right words. "He knew that I would lose my vision someday, and he doubted that a man who could barely take care of himself would be *capable* of caring for his blind daughter. After my wedding, he couldn't tell me about your letters for fear of breaking up my already shaky marriage."

She cradled her head in her hands.

A fiery rage flared inside me. "Damn it! How could he do that, Em? I was just a kid, terrified and alone."

Deep inside, I knew the answer. Before joining the Army, I had been fueled by booze and testosterone, a teenage powder keg in search of a spark. Her father had been a kind and loving man, simply trying to safeguard his child. I might have done the same thing if I had been in his position. Without a doubt, I would do whatever it took to protect RJ.

Emily raised her head, closed her eyes, and spoke slowly, as if reading each phrase off the back of her eyelids.

"Jake, it's worse than that. Dad ... read your letters."

Embarrassment, hurt, and a sense of violation replaced my anger. I dropped onto a chair and said nothing. She opened her eyes and continued.

"I won't try to justify what he did. It was cruel and hurtful to both of us. When he told me today, I was furious with him. He said he had to do it because between you and my abusive ex-husband, I had ... a weakness for rogues and scoundrels. I threw a book at him, missed, and shattered a lamp. Then I called him names, terrible names—even though what he'd said was ... true. But," she added, "Dad really feels awful. He has for years. He knew you were in pain, but he was afraid you'd hurt me again. He still is."

Her expression softened. "Now that you're caring for a child, he hopes you'll understand and forgive him. Dad *likes* the man you've become. Please don't hate him, Jake."

"That damn war blew up my youth. I didn't ask to be there and wanted something, someone to hold on to. Your dad took that from me." With all the years that had passed, and all that had happened since my father's return, however, I no longer had the energy or the will to hold on to more anger. "This is a lot to process. Give me some time, Em. I'll try to forgive him."

"Thank you." She reached over, found my hand, and squeezed it gently. "All that time, I believed you didn't care enough to write, that you'd *forgotten* me."

Her words fell hard between us. We had *both* given up, both failed to trust the strength of our love. The letters had been the bricks that we had used to erect the wall between us.

Yet, this explained everything, answered all the questions, and dispelled the doubts that had separated us for decades. Our relationship had been crippled by a man who only wanted to protect his daughter, and by our failure to believe in each other.

As my emotions began to calm, they were replaced by the terror of my impending encounter with killers in a deserted park. I stood and was about to tell Emily that I had to leave for a meeting with Tree when she spoke again.

"Knowing what my dad did changes everything." Her mouth moved as if tasting the words before she spoke. "Half of me wants to … try to recover what we've lost."

"And the other half?"

"Is scared to death."

I knew the feeling well.

She bit her lower lip until it blanched. "Have you heard about those team-building exercises at corporate retreats, where they do 'trust-falls'? One person leans backward and depends on his partner to catch him before he hits the floor. That's what being sightless is like. Every day. It's about trust, confidence that you have people around who have your back."

I was stunned. Emily rarely spoke about her disability or displayed any sign of vulnerability.

"You can trust me, Em."

"Can I? Really? After you cheated on me in school?" She released a deep sigh. "I don't know what to think. My world's in shambles. Heck, I'm not sure I can even trust my own father!"

"I'm not that kid anymore."

"No. Now, you're a priest."

There was no rational response to that. She was right. What were we anyway? Friends. At most, a work-in-progress.

The silence dragged on until she finally placed her hand on mine, squeezed it, and stood. "I have to go pack for our trip and help Dad get ready." She extended her cane and began tapping her way to the conference room door, then turned. "I need time, Jake. We both do. There's a lot to work through and consider."

And she was gone.

CHAPTER THIRTY-SIX

Sunday, December 8, 2002, 5:15 p.m.

I walked to the parking garage replaying my encounter with Emily. A hodgepodge of emotions washed over me, as did a faint stirring of something unexpected and fragile … a distant hope.

But none of that mattered if I did not make it through my meeting in Cascade Park tonight. Tree's guys had done a nice job of repairing the dent in my car. I didn't know where they had hidden the GPS tracking device, but was quite happy to have Big Brother watching me. I placed the saxophone case on the passenger's seat, hopped in, and plugged my cellphone into the lighter to recharge it.

Already late, I hurried to my meeting with Tree. The serene hammered-tin sky slowly transformed to beaten-bronze as the sun surrendered its last rays. A fast approaching wall of purple and black clouds to the west gave the late afternoon a schizophrenic edge. And given the rollercoaster ride that Emily and I had just taken, and the shit-storm my father had rained down on me, that is exactly how the world felt—schizophrenic.

My tires hissed and spit through the slush, and the snowplow truck ahead of me scraped slowly along, hurling rock salt against my front bumper. I veered off and traded the tired city landscape for the countryside. The contrast was stark, like flipping over an oil painting from the brown paper backing to a lovely winter pastoral.

A few minutes later, I entered the parking lot of the Lorain County Sheriff's Department on Murray Ridge Road. The guard at the building's entrance called Tree and directed me to his office. On a Sunday, I had expected things to be quiet, but dozens of people hurried about.

Tree was sitting at his desk, talking on the telephone. His expression read *do not disturb*. He held up a hand in my direction and continued his conversation. "Yes, sir. That's very clear. I understand."

I knew that something was seriously wrong because he had cradled the phone between his ear and his shoulder and was unfolding a paperclip. That is what he would do in high school when he was under pressure in the classroom—straighten paperclips. As far as I knew, this was the only sign of nervousness that Mr. Cool-Cop ever exhibited. Ironically, he now earned his living trying to straighten out twisted lives and take the kinks out of society.

He flipped the new and improved pin-straight clip into the wastebasket, and said, "I agree, sir. That's right. Yes, sir." With each *Yes sir*, Tree slouched lower in his chair. "Count on it, Governor. We'll shut 'em down. Yes, sir. Thanks for your ... encouragement."

He hung up and waved me in.

"You look like hell, big guy. Ever get any time off?" I spoke with a lightness I didn't feel. "As your doctor, I'm prescribing a good night's sleep—but not tonight."

"There's no sleep when the political poop hits the fan."

"A friendly chat with the Governor? Boy, have you come a long way from Civics class."

"Not a chat. Marching orders. Let's just say His Honorableness is very concerned about our drug problem—and his reelection."

Tree swiveled his chair around and stared out of the window. I followed his gaze. Leafless trees, black and skeletal, cast dark shadows on sequined snow.

"I want to tell you what Willy Warner said about Angelo—*Big Angie*—Giordano's operation, and about your old man." He turned back to me. "Ever since we picked that weasel up and I explained the consequences of a third strike on his rap sheet, he's been very talkative. It's clear now why Giordano's sent an army after your father. It's not just the drugs he stole. The stakes are much higher than that." Tree let the silence underline his meaning. We locked eyes and I waited. "Grab a seat."

I sat across from his horseshoe-shaped desk. His office was decorated with an eclectic mixture of sports collectables, law enforcement awards, political photographs, and civil rights memorabilia. Tree had always been a complex guy.

He lifted a coffee mug with "World's Greatest Cop" printed on the front, took a drink, and continued.

"Willy Warner tells me most of Giordano's shit flies in from overseas, pills included. Agent Novak and the DEA were as surprised as I was."

"And my old man?"

"Remember what your dad said about Big Angie ordering the murder of a Russian bagman, and then blowing up the guy's car with his kids in the back seat?"

I nodded.

"Well, your father was in the wrong place at the wrong time. He was in Giordano's office when Big Angie ordered the hit."

Tree plunked his mug down with a thud and drummed his pencil eraser on the desktop in a syncopated rhythm. "Big Angie is old-school, Jake, and getting the cocaine back is a matter of honor for him. But it's not only the drugs. Louisiana uses lethal injection for capital crimes. Your father's testimony could put Giordano on death row. Overhearing Big Angie order a murder and not reporting it makes him an accessory—and a dead man walking. Out on the streets, he'll have the life span of a mayfly. Unless we find him, they'll hunt him down and kill him. From what I know about Giordano, he'll torture him and kill him personally to set an example for his gang."

His eyes went to a photo of his wife and three daughters on his desk.

"Your daddy was a delivery boy for Big Angie. He made drops in all the dives he played in. He always hid the stuff in his sax case. One day he failed to show up for a gig and left the state with Giordano's coke. He must have stashed the shit he stole somewhere near the Diplomat hotel, because when I inspected the case in your father's hotel room, there was no dope. Now your daddy and the cocaine are back in the wind, and all I got is theories."

Tree shook his head. "When I squeezed Willy, he confirmed that your father stole uncut cocaine. Quite the entrepreneur, your old man. Or maybe he saw it as his retirement plan. Willy said your dad had a buddy in Ohio with connections. James Sole." Tree paused for effect. "Yeah, the dead guy in the dumpster without his hands. Giordano's troops found old Jimmy before your father did. And your dad ended up with no buyer, and with some very pissed off Louisiana foot-soldiers hot on his heels."

"Tubby and Muscle."

"Yeah. Jackson Romig and Stefan Keteltas. Not to worry. Now that we know who they are, with the hatchet-job you did on Muscle's face, we'll nail 'em. Some street snitch will give them up. But who knows how many other guys Giordano sent?"

"Besides the sax, Tree, what else was in the case when you examined it?"

"Not much. Loose change and a few bucks, cough drops, a couple keys, cigarettes. Not sure what else. Some junk."

"Wait, Tree. You saw *keys* in the case? What did they look like?"

"Just … keys."

"Were there numbers printed on them?"

"I don't remember any numbers. Why?"

"I'm wondering if one was a key to a storage locker. There's a bus station and a gym not far from the hotel. Maybe my old man rented a locker and stashed the drugs. He wouldn't have walked any farther from the hotel than he had to."

Tree pondered that for a second. "Come to think of it, one key did have a plastic grip similar to locker keys. Shit!" He slammed a fist on the desk. "It would be nearly impossible to get legal access to those lockers quickly. The stuff will be gone before I can get a warrant. What I *can* do is put undercover agents at all the public lockers near the hotel along with your father's description. If they haul ass, there's a chance they can get there before your dad does."

He held up a finger, made a few calls, and set his plan into motion.

"So what now, Tree?"

"While you get ready for tonight, I'll have my deputies fill the case you brought with baggies that can pass for cocaine, put some real coke on top for them to test, and set up the operation at Cascade Park with the FBI and DEA."

I gave him the saxophone case, tracked down Father Vargas, and made my confession, knowing it might be my last.

CHAPTER THIRTY-SEVEN

Monday, December 9, 2002, 12:30 a.m.

Inside a mobile tactical command vehicle filled with electronics, Special Agent Keri Novak and Tree Macon finished their last minute pow-wow. They stood below a low-voltage bulb that spilled a useless puddle of pale yellow light.

Novak was dressed all in black with a sidearm the size of a howitzer. Her forehead was wrinkled with worry. She put on a Kevlar vest and said, "I still think he should wear a wire, Sheriff."

"No way, Keri. They frisk him, he's toast."

Agent Novak grumbled, picked up a satellite phone, and left.

My insides were churning. Tree strolled over to me, remarkably calm. He handed me paperwork.

"Here. Sign these."

"What's this?"

"One's a hold-harmless waiver and the other deputizes you. Got to keep my boss and the D.A. happy."

"Sure. I wouldn't want any of the honchos to fret about a lawsuit or suffer any guilt if this all blows up tonight." I signed without reading and handed him the forms.

"The GPS tracking device in your car and the one sewn into your jeans are both working fine. Remember, Jake, keep your pants on at all times." Tree smiled. "Seriously, drop off the saxophone and get the hell out of there. The stuff inside it will pass for the real thing long enough for us to swoop in and bust 'em. I added an open pack of cigarettes, a few cough drops, and three keys to empty lockers from Amtrak and bus stations. Between the Feebies and DEA, we got enough ground troops and helicopters to take out a third world country, so don't be there when it goes down. No hero-shit, okay?"

I did my best impression of a clucking chicken. "The *hero* went AWOL ages ago."

Tree walked me to my car. The night was deep in silence. Then an owl screeched nearby and I nearly jumped a foot off the ground. A light dusting of snow sifted through the pine boughs. The sky hung low above us, as black and blue as a celestial bruise. I put the saxophone case in the trunk next to the broken statue of St. Joseph, slammed the trunk closed, and got into the car. I lowered the window, slid the key in the ignition— and tried to slow my breathing.

"One thing, Tree. If this all goes to hell tonight … look after RJ for me. Please buddy."

Tree nodded slowly and said, "Hold on, I want to give you something."

He glanced around, slipped on a latex glove, pulled a small handgun from under his coat, and shoved it through the open car window.

"Take it. It's a throw away, untraceable. Serial number's been filed off. Use it if you have to, wipe it down, and toss it."

The priest and the ex-soldier in the back of my head were screaming at each other. I hesitated.

"These fuckers are bad-ass, Jake. You should have a piece. Hide it under the driver's seat in case they frisk you."

"No. I left that life a long time ago. An eye-for-an-eye makes everyone blind." I started my car and switched on the defroster. "They want the case and my dad. I'm just the delivery boy. I'll be okay."

"C'mon, man. You sound like Don-frickin'-Quixote's more optimistic brother." Tree spat and thrust the revolver toward me. "Sometimes the meek inherit the grave, Father. Take the damn gun."

I waved him off.

Keri Novak stepped around the tactical van and headed our way. Tree hid the revolver under his coat, snapped off his glove, and stuck his head in the driver's window.

"Be careful, Jake. It's Monday Night Football at eight tonight. Browns vs. Bengals at your place." He punched me gently in the arm. "I'll bring pizza and beer. Be there, buddy."

Tree slapped the roof of my car twice and walked toward Agent Novak. In my rearview mirror, I saw him turn and stare.

I drew a lung-full of frigid December air, closed the window, and fired up the heater. The dashboard clock read 1:30 a.m. City lights slid behind me as I followed the sallow beam of my headlights through the darkness across the flat Ohio landscape, feeling like I was about to plummet off the edge of the earth. When I reached the drop site, I nearly did.

CHAPTER THIRTY-EIGHT

Monday, December 9, 2002, 1:55 a.m.

The entrance to Cascade Park was a very steep hill with a hairpin turn. Covered with snow and ice, it resembled a toboggan run. My heart pounded against my ribs as I pumped the brake pedal and inched my way down the slope, hoping my car would not become a sled and crash into a tree or the icy river. One thing was certain; no way would my car climb up that hill fast if I had to make a run for it. First gear down, and first gear going back up.

When I finally arrived at the water's edge, I realized that I had been praying the rosary the entire way down using the steering wheel bumps as beads. I stopped near two picnic tables and waited with the engine running. A gnarled cluster of chestnut oaks along the other side of the ravine swayed and groaned in the chill wind. Darkness poured down the steep bank. A fierce, distant roar grew louder as a single-prop plane swooped in low over the park, then rose up until its running lights vanished into a bank of clouds.

My eyes strained to part the night until a blanket of clouds lifted from the moon. I saw no one. My sole companion was the river. It twisted like a snake before me, laboring toward Lake Erie, its gullet choked with ice chunks.

After a few minutes, I stepped from the car into air colder than the inside of a meat locker. The only sounds were my breathing, the crunch of snow under my shoes, and the ice floe cracking. I trudged to the picnic tables, inspected each one from top to bottom, looking for further instructions. Nothing.

The west wind escorted the clouds toward Pennsylvania and the sky grew freckled with stars. A spill of moonlight painted a shimmering silver stripe across the river.

The air smelled of pine. Above me, naked tree branches tried to grasp the heavens, their ice-covered fingers glistening in the moonlight.

A sudden wind gust beat the leafless twigs together and ice chips rained down like shattered crystal onto the picnic table nearest to me.

I was slogging back to my car when something rustled to my right and a high-pitched shriek broke the stillness. I grabbed the handle and threw the door open. A large coyote scampered from a stand of trees, its muzzle red with blood. The body of a cat dangled from its jaws. It stopped when it saw me. Two more of the pack loped into the clearing and growled, yellow teeth flashing.

Jumping into my car, I slammed it into reverse and backed up ten yards. The trio calmly trotted back into the undergrowth to enjoy their feast. I shoved the gearshift into park and slumped over the wheel. On the food chain tonight, I was that cat—prey, not predator. I hoped Tree's police buddy in Toledo was providing protection for RJ. And I would not even begin to relax until Emily called to let me know that she and her father had landed safely in Boston.

My breathing was beginning to slow when Handel's "Messiah" filled the car. I had come to loath that damn ringtone.

I answered, praying it was Tree calling with some good news. It wasn't.

Hospital parking garage roof. Now. You and the sax. Got my Glock pointed at your daddy's noggin, so you best hurry. Or maybe I'll just toss his skinny ass from the roof and watch him go splat. No cops, no bullshit. Got it?

Garage rooftop? My father? What the hell? I was speechless.

You still there, dipshit? You don't hustle here, maybe I waste the blind lady too. Throw your cell from the car. No calls. We're watching. Do it now!

Click.

Crap! As I rolled down the window, I lowered my phone out of sight, decreased the volume, and speed dialed Emily. It went straight to voicemail. Damn it!

I heaved my cell into a snowdrift and carefully crept my car up the steep, icy hill, hoping Tree's GPS trackers were working.

Driving as fast as I could on the slick roads, dark thoughts swirled through my mind. Nothing made sense. Could they really have Emily? How? And if they had my father, why didn't they already have the saxophone case with the cocaine? Maybe the mob grabbed him before he got to the locker, or maybe he had spotted the cops and bolted before he could retrieve the coke. Could my old man have hidden his case somewhere else? And did the damn money and drugs mean more to him than my life? Sadly, I knew the answer to that question.

The caller's voice bothered the hell out of me. His speech pattern and intonation sounded familiar. I leafed through a mental list of friends and associates from the church and hospital, but no one was a match.

I reentered the city, and the hum of metal bridge grating beneath my tires rattled me back to reality. Streetlights and neon signs slid past the car window. Near the hospital, I rolled through a stop sign, touched the small crucifix I wore, and eased into the parking garage.

The ground level was half full. I drove cautiously up the ramp buying time, passing a few cars on the second floor and only one on the third, a white SUV. It pulled out and swerved sideways, blocking the ramp to the roof. In my rearview mirror, I saw Muscle leap out and point his automatic weapon away from me. He was the reception committee for anyone tailing me.

I couldn't believe how stupid these guys were. How did they expect to escape if the police arrived? They had trapped themselves on the roof. Did they think Muscle could hold off a SWAT team? Or was I there as an insurance policy, a hostage to be traded?

When I arrived at the top of the ramp, I saw that they were neither trapped nor stupid.

A helicopter rested on the roof, its engine purring, its blades slowly spinning. Shades Gingrich sat in the pilot's seat adjusting the controls. It had been his voice on my cellphone. He briefly illuminated my old man's face with a flashlight. My father sat next to him in the passenger's seat, his mouth gagged.

Shades pointed his weapon at me and waved it, indicating that I should drive closer. No turning back now.

CHAPTER THIRTY-NINE

Monday, December 9, 2002, 2:45 a.m.

As I neared the chopper, Shades held up a hand. I stopped, opened the car door, and listened for the wail of sirens. All I heard was the hiss of traffic far below and my heart beating itself to death.

There would be no doubt when the cops arrived. Muscle's automatic would unleash hell on them and the fireworks would be louder than the Fourth of July. But if the cavalry was not close behind me, my father and I did not have a prayer. I could identify Shades, so there was no chance he would let me walk away.

Then it hit me. Something was off. They already *had* my father. If he had witnessed Angelo Giordano order a hit and his testimony could put Big Angie on death row, why was my dad not already dead? Maybe Giordano wanted to personally skin him alive and use him as gator bait in a Louisiana swamp? Or had my father's death sentence been postponed long enough to entice me to bring the cocaine? An even darker thought occurred: Could my old man still be loyal to the mob? Maybe he wasn't even tied up. Doubtful, given all that had happened, but not impossible.

The other thing that bothered me was why they wanted the sax case so badly. For a big-time operator like Giordano, the amount of coke in the case was chump change. Why not fly off with my father and forget about the coke? Was it worth the extra risk? Or was there something else at play?

The hospital security camera on the roof had been disabled, its power cord swaying impotently in the breeze. A few low storm clouds sailed overhead, propped up by city lights. Atop an institution devoted to healing, I stepped from the car, hands in the air, and awaited the crack of a gunshot. The wind made a mournful noise.

A stairwell door opened. Tubby appeared. I held my breath, praying he would not drag Emily out by the arm. The situation was already untenable, and I wasn't sure I could save myself, let alone both Emily and my father. I waited. He finally slammed the door and sauntered toward me, a revolver leveled at my gut. He examined me like a bug collector about to mount his next specimen.

"Well, if it ain't Mr. Tough Guy." He sneered. "I was hopin' you'd be the delivery boy. Where's the case?"

Fear twisted in my belly. "In the trunk."

"Get it. Real slow, asshole. You even think about being a hero, I'll end you, right here, right now."

Cursing myself for not taking the gun Tree had offered, I popped the trunk lid and leaned in. St. Joseph's disembodied head stared up at me with vacant plaster eyes. The statue had worked its way free of the towel it had been swaddled in. I picked up the saxophone case in my left hand, wrapped my right one around the figurine, and turned back to Tubby, concealing St. Joseph behind me.

Remembering that Tree had told me Tubby's identity, I conjured up a smile and said, "Easy does it, Mr. Romig." At the mention of his name, Tubby flinched, surprise on his face. I hoped my voice was not as shaky as my hands. "You don't want to drop the case and blow Mr. Giordano's coke across all of Ohio, do you? Big Angie'd be upset."

"What the—"

"Catch!" I lobbed the case at him. He reached for it, his weapon tilting to the side when he attempted to catch it with both arms. I stepped forward and swung the statue.

Tubby looked up in time to see St. Joseph's feet hurtling toward him like a karate kick. The statue split his scalp, showering the white snow with his blood. Tubby's eyes opened wide, rolled up, and he collapsed without a sound.

His revolver lay at my feet. I snatched it and jumped behind my car. The weapon felt heavy and cold. I aimed it at Shades. He leaned back in the pilot's seat, his automatic pointed at me.

It had been decades since I had fired a gun, but I was both scared and mad as hell. I raised the revolver, sighted down the barrel, and my finger tensed against the trigger. The helicopter was too far away for a clear shot. Even if I had been a marksman with steady hands, I was liable to hit my father rather than Shades.

I waved the weapon. "Don't screw around with me! You want the drugs? How about a trade? My dad for his saxophone case."

"No deal, dipshit," he said in the same cocky voice I had heard on the cellphone. "I like the cards I'm holding."

The case lay between my car and the chopper. I forced a laugh. "Fine. Come over and get it."

"Wake up and smell the Napalm!" He snickered. "I hear you're a priest, Jake. Now'd be a good time to start praying." His gun drifted from me to my father. "How about I just blow your daddy's head off if you don't drop the piece and bring me that case? I've killed enough dinks and towel-heads, one old geezer won't cost me a minute's sleep. I ain't bluffing. Do it."

I listened again for any sign of police backup, but heard only silence. Had these thugs somehow jammed the GPS trackers? I couldn't stall much longer.

If this became a gun battle, I was outnumbered and overmatched—and my father and I were both dead. And for what? Money? Drugs?

I was out of time with no chance of escape. This was a standoff, me verses Shades. No one was going to bail me out now.

"How about I punch your bird full of holes, Shades, and you don't fly anywhere?"

"And frag your daddy? Or blow up my chopper with him in it? Horseshit! Hand over the case."

What I really wanted to do was run to the stairwell that Tubby had come out of and make sure Emily was not in there, but that was suicide. And what the hell was I even doing here? Trading a life with RJ and Emily for the dirt-bag who had discarded me as a child? What an idiot I was.

I glanced at the ramp, grateful that there was no sign of Muscle. He was still protecting the getaway chopper from below. If he charged up here, I would be outflanked and in deep shit.

Without warning, the parking garage erupted into the roar of engines and the screech of tires.

Shades heard it and stiffened. "Times up, Jake. Quit fuckin' around. Gimme the case, or say goodbye to Daddy." He pointed the gun barrel at my father's head. "I'm counting to three. One... Two..."

"All right, all right. You win."

CHAPTER FORTY

Monday, December 9, 2002, 3:00 a.m.

The night air filled with the crack of gunfire and the clang of lead striking steel.

I hesitated.

"Don't be stupid, Jake." His expression was killer-calm. "Do it now, or I'll blow your old man into tomorrow."

I lowered the gun to my side but did not release it. Stepping over the bloody statue of St. Joseph and Tubby's motionless body, I picked up the saxophone case and walked toward the helicopter. Shades revved the engine and the slowly spinning blades picked up speed. He yelled something that I couldn't make out over the noise.

Being on the rooftop put me at a tactical disadvantage. I would be looking *up* into the chopper, which protected Shades and made me an easy target. To have any chance at all, I had to move to higher ground.

I was approaching his door and nearly out of options. Any closer and he could just shoot me, jump out and grab the case, hop back in, and take off. I planted my foot, cut right, and took off at a run. Burning up the last of my adrenaline, I sprinted full-out and ducked under the tail section, using it for cover, then scrambled up onto the low, snow-covered wall at the edge of the roof. The location gave me a better angle if I had to open fire in self-defense and it was closer to the chopper's passenger door and my father.

I hunched over to avoid the spinning blades and tight-roped along the wall toward my dad. It was hard to use my arms for balance with the saxophone case in one hand and the revolver in the other. Fluffy white sheets of snow tumbled to the ground four stories below. I did not dare peer down. With each footstep, I prayed the next would not land on a snow-covered patch of ice.

When I reached the copter's door, the window was open.

"Gimme the case, Jake, and you can have your old man."

"The window's too small. Open the door and I'll toss you the sax. Otherwise, no deal. I'm not coming any closer."

With his automatic pointed at my gut, Shades reached over and threw open the passenger door. My father was bound hand and foot, his eyes wide and wild, his head shaking a warning. Bruises and cuts covered his chin and swollen cheek. I pointed my weapon into the chopper.

Confusion crossed Shade's face. "What the fuck you doin' asshole?" He leaned back, using my father as a shield. "Gimme the damn sax!"

I should have tossed him the case—hell, I should never have tried to help my old man in the first place—but when I saw the beating they had given my father, I tasted bile and something coiled inside me like a viper. I pulled the hammer back with my thumb, my finger tensing on the trigger. A primordial spore from the war, long buried in the rubble of bombed out buildings and nightmares, germinated. Shades, my one-time friend, was now not only a drug dealer, but he soiled the very military uniform I had been proud to wear. I was overcome by the urge to blow him into a bloody mist.

My father turned his head toward me and rubbed his gag against his right shoulder.

"Don't test me, Shades." I dangled the saxophone over the edge of the roof. "If you shoot my dad, I'll open fire, toss the sax, and scatter Giordano's cocaine all over downtown. Shoot me and the drugs go over the edge with me. Either way, you've got nothing and *you're* dead. Big Angie will feed you to the bull sharks."

"Damn you to hell, Jake!"

"I'm good with God and not afraid to meet my Maker." Blood pulsed behind my eyes. Complete BS. I was terrified. "How about you, Shades?"

While Shades was focused on me, my dad continued to loosen his gag against his shoulder.

Shades balked. "That what you want? To die a martyr? Saint-friggin' Jake? Be happy to oblige."

He spoke slowly with an eerie serenity that scared the hell out of me. He swung the gun from my father's head to mine. The black void of the gun barrel loomed large.

"Do it, Jake. Toss in the sax or I'll blow a hole in your world."

"The drugs for my dad. That's not negotiable."

I could not imagine why a couple pounds of cocaine was so important, but from what Tree had told me, they wanted my old man more. Giordano had something particularly grisly in mind for him. No way could I allow Shades to fly him to Louisiana.

Sirens bansheed in the night. Another burst of gunfire. Shouting. Muscle could not hold off a SWAT team forever. Shades was running out of time.

"Gimme the sax, Jake, *then* I give you the old man."

"Not a chance! If you deliver my father to Giordano, he's dead." As long as I had the case, I didn't think Shades would shoot—but I wasn't sure. I could identify him and that made me a liability too. "This is your last chance to fly out of here before a small army storms onto the roof."

Another salvo of gunfire came from the garage below, followed by a guttural cry, a brief silence, and another volley.

Shades waved his automatic. "The case, *now!*" he screamed and cranked up the rotors. Snow leaped up around my feet and the wind slapped me, nearly knocking me off the edge.

My father had the gag partially off and he tried to talk. I looked at him and noticed that he was not strapped into his seatbelt. When he spoke again, I heard him say, "No, the *list!* Don't give him the list!"

I had no idea what my father was talking about but did not have time to think about it. I had only one play left. All my chips were on the table, and the dice had left the cup. I prayed they would come up seven, not snake eyes. *Thy will be done.*

"Okay, you win, Shades. The case first." I needed a split second of distraction and feigned a confidence I did not feel. "But you're not going to shoot me. Not with the safety still on."

Shades glanced down at his weapon, and I threw the case directly at him, grabbed my father's coat sleeve, and yanked him out of the door. With his arms and legs tied, he tumbled through the air and hit the concrete with a loud thud.

A police car bounced over the ramp onto the roof, bathing it in pulsating red and blue light. Shades gawked at it, and for an instant I had a clear shot—but couldn't pull the trigger.

He turned back to me and opened fire. I nose-dived from the ledge onto the roof. My wrist and forehead hit the concrete hard. The world became scarlet for a second, but I managed to crawl on top of my father to shield him with my body.

Muzzle flashes lit the night, loud as cannons. Shades gunned the engine and the bird lifted off the rooftop, the downdraft whipping an arctic wind at me.

Warm blood poured down my face. My head thumped like a bass drum. The front of my coat was stained dark red. Had I been hit? I expected pain to flare in my chest, but it was my forearm that burst into flame.

I rolled onto my back and watched the helicopter shrink in size above me. No way could I allow the slimy bastard who sold poison to kids to get away. I shook cobwebs from my vision, gritted my teeth against the pain in my forearm, raised my weapon, and fired at the copter's belly.

The recoil was unbearable. A fiery-hot agony raced from my wrist up my arm. I cried out. In the cruiser's headlights, I could see jagged white bone poking through the bloody sleeve of my coat.

More shouting, another salvo. The smell of gunpowder filled the air. I tried to move, could not find the strength, and surrendered to gravity.

My mind grew soupy. For one terrifying moment, my past and present fused and I was back on the battlefield. The soldier I had killed in the war floated toward me, then drifted back to the heavens. The moon became a spinning toy top. Three helicopters circled the star of Bethlehem. I tried to call for a medic. No sound came out. A tinny voice echoed in my ears without words as my world shriveled and everything went pinpoint black.

CHAPTER FORTY-ONE

Monday, December 9, 2002, 7:30 a.m.

I was hopelessly lost in a thick mist that had a strange, pungent smell. Unable to see, I listened and heard a woman talking to Tree. Following the bread crumbs of their muffled conversation, I slowly made my way through the dense fog back to consciousness.

When I finally managed to raise my eyelids, I could not tell which blur was Tree. I blinked a few times and made out his weak smile. He was backlit by flickering fluorescent lights. I tried to speak. Nothing came out.

The distinct aroma of disinfectant enveloped me and I drifted off. When I opened my eyes again, Tree was still there, his face wavering in and out of focus. My mouth was dry, lips glued together. I pried them apart.

"You look lousy, Tree."

"Better than you, tough guy. I told you, *no hero shit*, remember?" He released a low grumble. "Hell, you look worse than you did after the Avon game, when you got blindsided and they carried you off the field on a stretcher."

Tree and I were in a small cubicle surrounded by curtains on three sides. Muted voices floated through them. The metal gurney I lay on was cold and a chill slid down my spine. The rails were up and an IV bag hung from a pole to my left, its label an alphabet soup of antibiotics.

Vague images from the hospital rooftop flickered, then faded as my many cuts and bruises found their voices and began to scream. With everything hurting, no single pain could rise above the angry chorus. The percussion inside my skull slowly took the lead and soloed, until my right wrist joined my head in a duet of agony. Fire burned like a torch at the end of my arm. I tried to lift it and groaned. The memory of shattered bone protruding through the sleeve of my coat came roaring back.

A nurse wearing colorful scrubs with the St. Joe's logo threw back one of the curtains and walked over. She took my vital signs and scribbled on my chart.

I recognized her, but the cogs in my brain weren't meshing and I could not recall her name.

"What's going on?" I asked.

"They're almost ready for you in surgery, Dr. Austin."

"Surgery?"

"To repair your right wrist. Here, sign this." She held a consent form on a clipboard in front of me and freed my left arm from the sheets. Without reading it, I scrawled something illegible. As always, all things, including my life, were in God's hands.

The nurse withdrew the clipboard and said, "This'll take the edge off for you." She injected something through my IV and ambled away.

"What time is it, Tree?"

"Nearly eight in the morning. When EMS saw bone poking through your clothes, they snowed you with morphine and you drifted off to dreamland. The sight of it damn-near made me puke. Even *I* got pale."

My mind was pea-soup, my tongue thick and heavy. Then I remembered Tubby coming onto the roof from the stairwell.

"Did they hurt Em?"

"Emily? What're you talking about?" Tree looked at me as if the nurse had injected too much pre-op sedative. "She was never in danger, Jake. She's fine."

"Is my dad okay?"

"Yeah, though he's pretty banged up. He and Tubby are on the third floor, under guard. Two guards. Trust me, no one's going to get to them this time! Your father told us where to find the drugs. He'd just opened the locker at the Greyhound bus station when he spotted Tubby at the entrance. He locked the sax case in with the cocaine, made a run for it, slipped into a men's room stall, and hid the locker key in a toilet tank. The guy's definitely street smart. Muscle grabbed him about a block from the bus station."

I thought about my father loosening his gag and warning me about something. "My dad was mumbling about some 'list.' Any idea what that's about?"

Tree let loose a deep, cavernous laugh. "Oh yeah, the *list*. As Muscle was beating the crap out of him, your father told them he had a list of all Giordano's overseas suppliers hidden in his saxophone case. If he hadn't said that, they would have killed him. But they needed him alive so that you'd bring them the case. And if you had handed it over, you'd both be dead."

"So you got the list of suppliers too?"

Tree laughed again. "No. It was a bluff. Your dad was stalling. For a scumbag drug dealer, he's damn sharp. Don't ever play cards with him or he'll clean you out. The guy must be a hell of a poker player."

"No, but he's a world-class liar."

"You must have rubbed off on him, Jake. I think he got religion. He said after what you risked to save him, he knew he had to protect you and RJ from those goons. Said you were a hero. He jumped at the chance to testify against Giordano." Tree's expression sobered. "He also told me how you charged the helicopter and refused to give up the decoy case until you could yank him out of the copter door."

"What happened to Muscle?"

"He's D.R.T."

"Dirt?"

"Same thing. D.R.T. That's police lingo for *dead right there* … from a severe case of lead poisoning. Keri Novak and her team filled him full of it. Tubby has a skull fracture and a bitchin' headache, courtesy of you and that St. Joseph statue. He's real talkative now that he's facing serious prison time. He's spilling the beans on Giordano's operation. Tells me the copter pilot is some sort of undertaker in Afghanistan."

"A Mortuary Affairs Specialist. His name's Shades Gingrich. I knew him in boot camp and from overseas. He transports the bodies of fallen soldiers back home."

"Did more than that. The bastard hid drugs intended for our troops in with the bodies, and the U.S. Army flew them to the States. Another mob guy in receiving shipped them to Giordano. Morphine and other narcotics mostly. The pilot was Big Angie's main supplier. Quite an operation." Tree shook his head. "Is the military always that careless with its dope?"

"It's hard to keep track of drugs in the heat of battle. That's the last thing we medics think about."

Pain flared in my right forearm again, and the scene on the parking garage rooftop came into sharp relief. I recalled trying to shoot the helicopter as it rose into the sky.

"Did Shades get away?"

"Nope. We, ah, surprised him with an escort of two helicopter gunships."

"Cops have attack helicopters?"

"Nah, but a phone call to the Governor suddenly freed up a couple from Wright-Patterson Air Force Base. I got friends in high places, buddy."

Tree's beeper screeched. He glanced at the number and silenced it. "Anyway, Gingrich flew low over houses where the gunships couldn't fire at him. We didn't want civilian casualties. Past Youngstown, he was running out of towns and gas. He surprised us by taking the chopper straight up, as high as it would go. The gunships followed and watched him bail out."

"Did they catch him when he landed?"

"Didn't have too. He must have realized there was no way out. He jumped without a parachute. The copter crashed in a cornfield, thank God."

I drew a slow breath, trying to make sense of the senselessness.

"Shades once told me he lived life by *his* rules and he intended to go out the same way. He was raised in Youngstown. Maybe he went home to die."

"Or maybe he just didn't want to face a court-martial and death row." Tree sighed. "What *he knew* about Giordano's operation alone would have shut it down but … Tubby and your father will have to do."

My mind was leapfrogging from image to image, and landed on the child with huge chocolate-brown eyes who had died in Urgent Care.

"Tree, please tell me you arrested the S.O.B. who was selling OxyContin to kids outside the high school."

"That clown named Razor? No, I can't tell you that, but I can *guarantee* he won't be selling any more drugs to kids. He decided to resist arrest like a couple other gangbangers. He's also D.R.T."

My life had been filled with violence and carnage, and I felt ancient and very tired.

"Please call Emily and Colleen, Tree, and tell them it's okay to come home." I paused. "It is safe, right?"

"Already done. I called Emily at the airport a few minutes ago and told her what happened. She and her dad canceled their flight, and she's on her way here. RJ's going to stay with Colleen until you're back on your feet. And yeah, it's safe." Tree forced a weary smile. "I had law enforcement locked and loaded, with judges on standby for warrants last night. With an army of DEA and FBI troops, we rounded up half of Ohio while you took your little morphine nap. Tubby gave us names and addresses. Hell, he'd have given us birthdays and favorite colors if I'd asked. Folks around here should be a lot safer, and my life should be a hell of a lot quieter with those bastards off the street."

The pre-operative meds the nurse had injected kicked in. I closed my eyes and pondered the chaos of the past two weeks, and the nightmare that my old man's return had unleashed on those I loved. It must have been the medication, because the next thing I knew I was sitting with Emily in seventh period high school Latin class, as Sister Very Nasty growled her mantra at us: "Ordo ab Chao!"—Order out of Chaos.

For a change, some order in my life sounded like a wonderful idea.

"Buddy, you still with me?"

I fought my way back. "Yeah, Tree, I'm here."

"Now that Tubby's rolled over on his pals and your father has agreed to testify that Giordano ordered the murder of a competitor, I've been arranging witness protection for both of them. Otherwise they're dead men." Tree's face clouded over. "We got no choice, Jake. Your dad has to vanish. Permanently."

"My old man's an expert at that. That's all he's ever done. He won't even notice I'm not around. Not that it matters to—"

I stopped. For the first time in years I felt *something* for my father. Given the short time he had actually spent in my life and how much pain he had caused, it certainly was not love, not even affection, and it didn't make sense to say I would miss him—yet strangely, a part of me would.

It must have been the sedative.

"Your father really wants to meet RJ before the Feds send him away to his new life. He begged me to get your okay." Tree arched an eyebrow and waited.

"The deal was that he'd help you nail Giordano *and* get himself clean. No coke, no booze. I hope they're watching him for DTs."

"They are. He's doing all he can to put Big Angie away, and he's been toughing out his injuries, refusing narcotic pain meds since admission. He's keeping his end of the bargain."

My body went limp. I had gone well beyond exhaustion to something I couldn't even name. I managed to nod. "Then I'll keep my end of the bargain."

An orderly joined us. "Time to wheel you in and get you fixed up."

Tree took a step back and said, "Guess I'll take a rain check on Monday Night Football and pizza at your place tonight. Probably for the best. Got a desk full of paperwork, and I better get to it. See you soon, Jake."

The orderly rolled me into the O.R. Dr. Michael Ritz was being gowned and gloved. He was an excellent orthopedic surgeon. At a teaching hospital, I expected an intern or resident to help him, but Gavin Glade peeked into the room and smiled.

"I asked to assist, Jake." He laughed. "Didn't want some first-year rookie dropping the sterile plate and screws on the floor or sneezing on your wound." Glade took a couple of steps in my direction. "I may have forgotten to tell you, Father. I was raised Catholic. Can't have your immortal soul on my conscience." He chuckled again and left to scrub his hands.

After I had been moved onto the surgical table and draped, the anesthesiologist injected something through my IV that made me float to the ceiling. He placed a mask over my face and asked me to count backward from one hundred. I got as far as ninety-one.

CHAPTER FORTY-TWO

Monday, December 9, 2002, 10:00 a.m.

I could not lift my eyelids, though that didn't seem important. Metal clanged close by and several conversations merged into a generalized background buzz. The scent of disinfectant mingled with the meaty smell of blood and flesh.

An alto voice boomed over the din: "Code Blue—Recovery Room." Someone was crashing, probably having a cardiac arrest. The page operator kept repeating, "Code Blue—Recovery Room."

I knew I should run to help, but it felt as if my head was filled with tapioca pudding and my body made of lead. Pain washed over me, rising and falling like a churning sea. Everything hurt—my wrist, my head, everything, even my chest.

Then the words registered. *Recovery Room*. Was *I* the Code Blue?

My eyes popped open, my vision blurry, as if looking through wrinkled cellophane. People scurried nearby and carts rolled around me. Anxious voices filled the air.

I scrambled out from the dark pit of anesthesia, blinked several times, and recognized the plump, saggy face of Bishop Lucci. Rosary beads rattled in his hands, his expression grim. Was he praying for me?

"Your Excellency?" My throat seemed filled with gravel. "What's going on? How—?"

Dr. Glade appeared. Someone yelled, "Clear!" and he vanished. I heard the unmistakable sound of a defibrillator. I raised my head and focused on the other side of the Recovery Room where a Code Blue team was pushing meds, placing lines, and pumping on a child's chest.

Dear God please, not Anna!

The clamor was loud, but the voices soft and controlled. Glade grabbed a scalpel and inserted a chest tube. A nurse closed the curtains around me to shield me from the commotion. My neck muscles were weary and my head dropped back onto the pillow.

I heard, "Got a pulse!" followed by the sound of a regular EKG heartbeat. Someone turned the monitor volume down and the chatter faded.

Lucci must have sensed my fear. He leaned down. "Relax, my son. Everything's fine. They tell me your surgery went well."

"Bishop, you shouldn't be …. How … how'd you get in here?"

"Special dispensation." He smiled. "Dr. Glade was my altar boy years ago. Professional courtesy, I guess you could call it. He said it was okay for me to be here as long as I stayed out of the way."

He kissed his rosary and sequestered the beads in his robes.

"You visited me in the hospital after the incident in July, Jacob, so I came today to pray for you."

The bishop always referred to his attempted murder as *the incident*.

"I can't repair bodies, my son, but I'd like to think I have some pull with my boss." He pointed heavenward. "Though I'm beginning to think you'll do anything to avoid giving me your decision about where things stand with … your lady friend. I'm dragging my feet as best I can, but the Superior General of your order is pressing me for explanations and updates."

He shook his head and the wattle under his chin flapped from side to side. "I'm sorry. This is the wrong time and place. We can discuss the issue in a few weeks when you're feeling better."

Like some bizarre TV game show, for months I had been standing in front of three doors, one leading to Emily and one back to the Church. Yet I kept choosing door number three to Limbo.

I had dodged enough bullets for one day. No reason to dodge this one.

"I wish I had an answer for you, Your Excellency. I'm afraid this may take more than a few weeks to figure out."

That was not what he had hoped to hear. Lucci looked at me as if I had just drop-kicked the baby Jesus. "God is testing you, my son. You understand that, right?"

I nodded, and he continued. "It's only when our bonds are tested that we learn how strong they are."

Bonds? I didn't know which bonds he meant—to the priesthood or to Emily. They were both fiercely strong.

Lucci stared at the ceiling, then back at me. "You can out-distance what chases you, Jacob … but *not* what stalks you from within."

"I'm sorry to be a burden to you and the Church. I don't understand why I'm so … confused and conflicted."

"Because you're human. The Lord doesn't blame us for our frailties. He judges us on how we deal with them. You won't be content until you find what you're searching for." He must have sensed the irony in his statement and added, "Searching for God, of course."

Lucci cleared his throat. "I can grant you sick leave until you recover, but I can't prolong your Spiritual Retreat much beyond that. Pray about this. Pray hard, for only the Lord can guide you in this matter."

A hand threw the curtain back and Dr. Glade materialized at the foot of my bed, peering like a crocodile over his surgical mask. He removed it and picked up my chart. I was glad for the distraction and a chance to end the discussion of God and Emily. I raised my left hand and pointed toward the other side of the room.

"Please tell me that Code Blue wasn't for Anna Grabowski."

"No, Jake. She's doing fine. Between the chemo and the drainage tube you placed, I may not have to open her up again."

Improbable as it was, I was becoming fond of Glade. In my experience, the best surgeons were the ones who were happy *not* to operate.

"Yep, I think Anna's going to make it." Glade scribbled something on my chart, turned toward Bishop Lucci, and produced a grin worthy of the Cheshire Cat. "Sometimes great surgeons—and a little prayer—can work miracles."

I said, "I can't ever remember seeing you so cheery, Gavin. What's up?"

"I performed an emergency bowel resection early this morning on Dr. Guo. Got in before it ruptured and saved her—and I did it all without new-age hocus pocus or voodoo. She'll be recuperating for quite a while, which should set the Department of Leeches, Spiders, and Alternative Medicine back a few months." He shrugged. "Hate to admit it though. I'm beginning to like her. She's a pretty tough lady."

"Who would have guessed you were an old softy, Gavin?"

"Yeah, yeah. You hungry?"

"Starved."

He filled a plastic cup with water and handed it to me.

"Good. Drink this. Soon as you pee, we can move you outta here. You're way too healthy to be taking up space in the Recovery Room." Glade placed my chart at the foot of the bed and added, "Gotta run. Plenty more lives for me to save." As he began to walk away he added, "Get well soon, Jake. I'm tired of covering your shifts in Urgent Care."

CHAPTER FORTY-THREE

Monday, December 9, 2002, 1:30 p.m.

DeQuan Kwame wheeled me into my hospital room. Emily sat in a chair, her fingers flying across the pages of a book. This was the second time in six months she had been waiting for me after surgery. Given our recent turmoil over the missing letters, I was thrilled that she had come.

"Hey, Em," I whispered. My throat was sore and my voice raspy from the endotracheal tube used for anesthesia.

"Jake!"

In that single word, I heard relief, pain, and a plea in her voice.

She snapped the book closed and laid it on the tray table. Not her usual romance novel, but a braille edition of the Holy Bible.

After DeQuan helped me into bed, Emily removed her sunglasses, extended her collapsible cane, and tapped over to me.

I forced a smile. "We really have to stop meeting like this."

She found my face and planted a quick kiss on my lips.

"Shut up, Jake. Just shut up." She kissed me again, this time slow, soft, and deep.

I was almost as stunned as DeQuan and pulled back. Even as a teenager, Emily had always avoided public displays of affection, but a PDA right here, in the rumor mill that was the hospital? I was dumbfounded.

That kiss, however, was better medicine than anything dripping into my IV. I wrapped my good arm around her in a quick embrace. To hell with the gossip. I was grateful to be alive, and glad to be with her.

Never one to miss an opportunity, DeQuan gave me a mischievous look and a thumbs up, then headed toward the door.

I said, "DeQuan, please don't—"

He raised a hand to stop me. "Have no concern, Doctor. *All your secrets* are safe with me." He left the room and closed the door.

A nurse entered and Emily returned to her seat near my bed. While the nurse checked my vital signs and the dressing on my wrist, I studied Emily's dour expression and watched her nibble on one arm of her sunglasses, her hands trembling. I wanted to rejoice at surviving the rooftop apocalypse and talk about RJ and happy things, but something was very, very wrong.

After the nurse left, I said, "Your hands are shaking. What's up?"

She moaned and a tear rolled down one cheek.

"Come on, Em, tell me. What's going on?"

She fixed watery eyes on me. "I can't ... can't do this anymore. It's too painful."

"Sorry to put you through this again, Em. I had no choice. If I hadn't made the drug drop, they'd have killed my father."

"Not that, you big dope—us. What we are, what we've become. This terrible Purgatory." She set her sunglasses on the tray table. "The one Mary Oliver calls *a love that leaves, yet never leaves.*"

Purgatory indeed. I knew exactly what she meant.

I had been certain for a long time that this day would come. What woman would *want to be* in a frustrating and fruitless relationship with a priest?

I had no desire to leave the priesthood, but I'd fallen short in the first real test of my vows. The fact that I had even explored our relationship was proof that I should submit my resignation to Bishop Lucci, with or without Emily in my life.

My arrival in town had upended both our lives, and the resulting chaos and violence had made hers a living hell—twice. I was about to apologize and promise to ask Lucci for a transfer out of town when she spoke.

"I'm such a fool, Jake, and so very sorry."

"You? For what?"

"I've been thinking about the letters you sent me from overseas. All those years, I was convinced you'd forgotten me and didn't care. I was so hurt, so angry. I'd completely given up on us. I'm sorry I've wasted the past six months with my fear and doubts." She drew a breath. "We're at a fork in the road. As Robert Frost said, two paths are diverging in the woods—and you and I have been standing there paralyzed, deciding for far too long. Enough."

I stared at the face of my first and only true love, the face of a love that never *would* leave. Trying to deny my feelings for her was like telling a leaf not to blow in the wind.

"It wasn't your fault or mine. Your father intercepted those damn letters."

"There's more to it, Jake. Dad couldn't bring himself to tell me what he'd done, so," she paused, "he saved the letters. He knew I'd find them after he died and hoped I would figure out that he was trying to protect me."

"He what?"

"He kept your letters in a shoebox all these years. They broke my heart!" Her words poured out, so crowded together that they blurred into one long word. "If only I'd read them sooner—"

"Read them? How?"

"I asked Todd. He read them all to me."

"Todd? You're joking!" I sat up, then stood slowly on wobbly legs. "You let that clown read my private thoughts? I don't even *know* the guy!"

I was shouting and a nurse peeked into the room. I lowered my voice, but it came out as a snarl. "Who the hell is Todd to you? Your lover?"

"Stop it, Jake! You have no right. He's just a friend, and when I needed one, he was there for me. He was also my eyes." She stood and whispered, "Todd is gay, so let it go. This isn't about him. It's about your letters."

"I ... I assumed...."

She waved me off. "When I realized what had happened and heard what you wrote ... it changed the way I feel." She reached out and found my good hand. "Can we go for a walk?"

She helped me put on a hospital robe, and we strolled slowly off the medical floor and into the research wing. We were both out of words. In the silence, the invisible wall that had separated us for years seemed to collapse and fall away.

She stopped and leaned into me. I was still slightly woozy from anesthesia and slipped an arm around her waist. We fit together like two pieces of a jigsaw puzzle. I wanted to hold her forever—and at the same time, I wanted to run far away from her.

But I didn't. I couldn't.

She took my hand and we walked again.

"What now, Jake?" she asked in a wind-soft whisper. "Where do we go from here?"

I was certain I loved her, but there are as many kinds of love as there are stars in the sky. The problem was that I was not sure if we were becoming a binary star system, two luminous bodies revolving around each other, or a supernova about to explode. I was sure Bishop Lucci strongly favored the Big Bang.

I took her chin in my hand, gently raised her face, and searched it for the answer to her question—and saw what? Pain? Regret? Hope?

"Now what? I have no idea, Em. Friends?"

"Always—but I think those letters change everything."

I was sure of that, but had been afraid to say it out loud.

"Is it possible to start over, Jake, and ... become *us* again?"

I had wondered the same thing ever since we had been reunited.

"Do you?"

"Maybe, in time. I hope so."

Time.

I took her hand and we ambled together from the research corridor through the administration hallway, my mind churning with questions. Harvey Winer stepped from the CEO office, stopped, and shoved his hands into his pockets. He studied us briefly and disappeared back inside. I did not tell Emily. We had only been holding hands, but I was glad she had not seen his look of disapproval.

She ran a finger over her braille watch. "Sorry, I have to get back to the snack shop and relieve Dad."

"Sure. Probably best if I don't walk you there."

"Hold on a second. Is there anyone in the hall?"

"No."

Her hands wandered up my arms, found my face, pulled me to her.

When she kissed me this time, I did not resist. Hesitation became surrender, then complete commitment. We eased into a slow, Sunday morning sort of kiss, soft and so tender it almost hurt. It was deliciously sweet and intoxicating, like drowning in an ocean of champagne. She was my life preserver, and I wrapped my arms around her.

Without words, Emily had said it all.

Her breath feathered my cheek when at last she stepped away. She aimed her luminous blue eyes at me, lit by a mysterious source within, and I knew I could fall into them and never escape.

A door deep inside me opened, letting in a sliver of truth—and I recognized how desperately I loved her. I slammed it shut, maybe an instant too late. I wanted to find a way to say that we could never do that again. At the same time, I desperately wanted to do that for eternity.

Yes. No. Yes.

Can. Can't. Can.

Emily must have sensed my turmoil. Her expression crumbled. "Oh my God! No, no Jake. I didn't mean …."

"Me either. We can't …."

"No, never again."

I don't think either of us bought into the lie.

"I'm sorry," I whispered. And I was. Very, very sorry. What was I doing? What had I done?

"This is madness." She took a step backward. "I *won't* do this. Friends yes, this… no way! Not because I don't love you, Jake. I do. But I won't be the reason you leave the priesthood. You'd never forgive me, and I'd never forgive myself."

"We're in deep trouble, aren't we, Em?"

"So very deep." She took my hand again. "And if I fall backward, Jake?"

I answered with a hug, and she slid back into my arms as if the space was made for her, filling me with a strange calm. "If you tumble, I'll catch you this time."

I released her while I still could, leaving me with the scent of her perfume and a growing sense of hope. She was crying, but the tears found the upturned corners of her lips.

"You need to be certain, Jake. We both must be certain, and that won't happen overnight. Do what you can with the bishop to buy us more time."

"I'm already working on it." I pointed to my surgical dressing. "He extended my leave of absence this morning. I think he's grateful that I won't be his problem for a while."

"There's one thing you should understand, Jake." She grinned. "I'm actually after that boy of yours—so don't mess this up." She squeezed my hand. "I better relieve Dad in the snack shop."

She extended her cane, walked down the hall, stopped, and called out to me.

"About your last letter, the marriage proposal?" A smile played on her lips. "The answer would have been *yes*." Then she vanished around the corner.

CHAPTER FORTY-FOUR

Wednesday, December 11, 2002, 1:00 p.m.

On a diet of all-you-can-eat painkillers, a hazy Tuesday somehow drifted into a more lucid Wednesday. I thought of Emily and could only wonder how much of our romantic moment in the hallway had been drug induced.

After a decent lunch, I began to feel human again, cranked up the head of my bed, and grabbed the Lorain Journal from my tray table. Tree Macon's photo graced the front page above the fold. He was in uniform, standing before a microphone, flanked by the governor and Special Agent Keri Novak. Tree looked more rested and relaxed than he had for weeks. His reelection as Sheriff was assured.

I read the entire article, grateful that my name did not appear this time. When Tree and I had stopped the serial killer in July, it had been my picture on page one. Tree had been the real hero and had saved my life. The newspaper should have featured his courage, not mine. But a headline about a priest "exorcizing a devilish killer" attracted more readers and sold more advertising space.

The latest update on the pedophile priest scandal swirling through the archdiocese in Boston filled the rest of the front page. After reading the first two paragraphs, I became frustrated and disgusted, and skimmed the rest of the newspaper. The Cleveland Browns were on another losing streak, the stock market remained volatile, and the Middle East was on fire. Who would have guessed? Although the world had kept on spinning since my father returned to town, mine had stopped revolving and been turned upside down.

Next to the crossword puzzle, my horoscope indicated that my planetary alignment predicted upheaval in my future. Not what I was hoping for. Because my life had been nothing but upheaval since coming back to town, I checked the date to see if the paper was six months old.

The advertising section was peddling a wide selection of toys for Christmas. 'Tis the season. I combed through my options and decided to buy the new Harry Potter LEGO set as RJ's present. I still had no idea what to get for Colleen. Failing any creative ideas, I could always fall back on her favorite color, green, and give her cash.

I was reading about the Cavaliers game against the Knicks when Dr. Ritz stopped in on rounds. A small amount of blood had seeped through my bandage. Ritz removed the gauze, examined my incision, redressed my wound, and pronounced me ready to go home. He handed me written post-operative instructions and prescriptions for Vicodin and an antibiotic.

As he left, Keri Novak entered the room. She had led the assault on Muscle in the hospital garage and I heard that she had been wounded.

"Agent? What a pleasant surprise." I pointed to the sling on her left arm. "Are you okay?"

"Oh this? A mosquito bite. I'm fine."

With or without a gun, she was one intimidating woman.

"Maybe you should consider entering a convent. You were a natural in that habit, Sister Keri. Forget smacking delinquents with a ruler, I prefer a nun who packs heat. If you ever decide on a quieter life, I have connections."

"I wouldn't exactly call Sunday quiet, Father."

"True. By the way, I saw your picture on the front page of the paper, looking chic and photogenic. Now that you're famous and hang out with the governor, I'm honored you stopped in to see me."

"Chic and famous, huh." Novak scoffed. "Yeah right, my girlish heart is all a pitter-patter." She strode over to the bed and extended her hand. "Thanks for your help. You've got guts. You ever need a favor, call me."

My painkillers were wearing thin, and she was a strong woman. I hesitated and she glanced at my surgical dressing and withdrew her hand.

"Sorry. Forgot about your little boo-boo." She shrugged. "I fly out tonight and wanted to tell you that your father gave us a boatload of info. We arrested Big Angie in New Orleans an hour ago, and we're shutting down his drug operation in six states." She laughed. "Giordano's the same as the rest of the punk-ass crime bosses. He didn't get it either."

"Get what?"

"That our gang," Novak said tapping her badge, "is bigger than his gang." She paused. "Anyway, I also wanted to tell you that your old man *knows* they'll come after him. He didn't flinch. He said he's like his son … fearless. Said you made him proud."

Novak waited for a response. I didn't have one. My eyes got moist. My dad had never said he was proud of me. Ever.

"Well, now I understand where you get your guts." Novak turned to go, then stopped. "Your dad will be in good hands in Witness Protection. I asked a friend in the Marshals Service to be his handler. I'll update you when I can." She let a few seconds pass, then added, "I guess I owe you an apology. I was wrong to accuse the local medical community of opening pill-mills here. That flood of prescription drugs was all Giordano and his gang. My bad. Well, take care of yourself, Padre, and stick to preaching the Good Word from now on, okay? See you around."

I hoped not. The last thing I wanted was to have the FBI back in my life.

After Novak left, I called Colleen and asked her to drive me to my apartment. I had had enough drama and couldn't wait to leave the hospital and go home. As if on cue, the last person in the world I wanted to see knocked on the doorframe.

Rudy VonKamp entered the room. What now? The last time we had spoken, he had implied that I might be a drug dealer and threatened to revoke my hospital privileges. I should have added 'lawyers' to my list of allergies.

"I'm sorry to intrude, doctor, but I felt clarification was required." He cleared his throat and looked down. "In light of recent events, the board of directors and I have reviewed your credentials, and I wanted to assure you that your medical staff privileges are not in jeopardy and have been renewed in full." He raised his gaze. "I won't take any more of your time. Get well soon, doctor," he added and disappeared to wherever lawyers go when they are not harassing other people.

An apology? Probably as close to one as I would ever get from him.

I closed my eyes. Since I'd come back to town, I had sustained more physical and mental trauma than I had during the war. Yet, I'd found RJ and reconnected with Emily and Tree, and the cost seemed … acceptable.

I must have dozed off, because the next word I heard was the one I loved most.

"Daddy!"

RJ sprinted to the chair, climbed up, and leaped onto the bed. He landed on my incision, of course, awakening the pain in my forearm. I was getting used to the small hurts that inevitably accompany the great joys of raising a child.

Colleen stood in the doorway.

"Are we safe now do you think, Father? Can we go back to a normal life again?"

I was no longer certain what a *normal life* was, but said, "Yes, Colleen."

"And my sister in Toledo too, mind you? Is she out of danger?"

"Definitely."

"Grand. That's settled. Time for us to be off." She assumed her role as the one-time queen of the rectory and gave me my marching orders. "Get yourself dressed, Father, and I'll fetch the car."

"Wait, Colleen. I need a few more minutes." My nephew discovered the electric bed controls and my mattress contorted. I stared into his silver-blue eyes, my sister's eyes. "There's someone RJ has to meet."

CHAPTER FORTY-FIVE

Wednesday, December 11, 2002, 2:30 p.m.

RJ clutched my good hand and we walked down the hallway. He was babbling with the usual enthusiasm of a four-year-old about the approach of Christmas, Santa, and of course, the presents he hoped to receive.

When we entered my father's room, he was asleep, looking older than God and as fragile as Waterford crystal. The head of his electric bed was in the semi-recumbent position. Several lacerations on his face had been sutured. An angry bruise seeped out from under the sleeve of his gown, painting his stringy bicep in various shades of deep blue and purple. His EKG softly beeped an irregular but benign, syncopated rhythm—oddly appropriate for a jazz musician.

My nephew's chatter woke him. My dad opened his eyes and grinned.

"Well, I'll be. Y'all must be RJ. Come on over here and give an old man a hug."

The stitches on my father's forehead and cheek gave him a Frankenstein-like appearance. My nephew's expression morphed from a question mark into terror.

I smiled at him. "It's okay, you can go over. He's my … ah, your …."

I could not find the right word and hesitated. My old man shifted his gaze to me. I did not want to use the term "grandfather," and then have him vanish from the child's life forever into witness protection. With the death of his mother, my nephew had already suffered too much unexplainable loss in his four short years.

My dad cleared his throat, but before he could object I said, "He's a good friend of mine, RJ. His name is Jacob."

The corners of Dad's lips turned up and he nodded.

My nephew walked to the bed with tiny, cautious steps. He gawked at my father's cuts and bruises, and froze when my old man reached out and tousled his red hair.

"Boy's the spittin' image of your sister, Jake. Same hair and eyes." Pop pointed to the sweatshirt that Emily had purchased for my nephew, which had BOY GENIUS printed on the front. "Know what that says, RJ?"

He fixed his eyes on his sneakers. "Yup."

"So, you're a genius?"

"Yup."

"How'd you know?"

"Emily said so."

"That right? What's 'genius' mean?"

RJ shrugged.

"Guess were gonna have to work on that a touch." My father patted the bed. "Hop on up here, son. Let me get a look at you."

Instead, RJ ran back to me and grabbed my leg. Resignation replaced my father's look of anticipation.

"It's okay. Don't be afraid," I said. "Let me tell you a secret. Jacob *loves* to play with toy soldiers."

"Really?" RJ's bright eyes moved from me to my father.

"Yeah, I was just layin' here, real sad-like," my father said, "because I got nothing to play with."

Dad did the worst impression of a 'gloomy' face I had ever seen, but apparently RJ bought it. He clambered onto my father's bed, marched his troops from his pockets, and handed over a plastic soldier. My father pretended to sight down the rifle barrel.

"Well, I don't rightly know 'bout this," he said, trying on a pouty expression. "I'm a loyal son-of-the-South, and I wanna be General Lee, not some darn Bluebelly. Got any Confederate Calvary in them pockets of yours?"

"Give the kid a break, Pop. The Civil War's over. I guess you'll have to accept that and join the good guy's side."

"Didn't you learn nothing in that Yankee school of yours?" He scowled. "Twern't nothing civil about it. That was flat-out a war of Northern aggression. And the Greybacks *was* the good guys, fightin' for their farms." He let out a rebel yell. "Guess I'll hafta school the boy some."

Within minutes, my nephew had my old man's army on the run. I plopped onto the chair and watched my two remaining blood relatives play together until I heard a cane tapping at the door.

Emily entered and waved at us. "Hi, RJ. You can take your daddy home now."

RJ mumbled hello, went back on offensive, and blew up a Kleenex mountain protecting my father's troops. Getting me home was obviously of secondary importance to my boy.

"Hey, Em. How'd you find us?"

"I passed Colleen in the hall. She's getting the car now, so you guys better wrap up this party." When no one moved, she lightly tapped the bed frame with her cane and added, "Are you two kids going to play all day?"

My father eyed Emily with no sign of recognition. Not surprising. The last time they had been in the same room, she had been wearing pigtails, sighted, and was watching cartoons—and he had probably been drunk or stoned. I knew how Em felt about my father for deserting me, so I let the reunion slide. Forty years was too much history to bridge. Besides, Dad would soon disappear again.

Emily glanced from my father to me, then back at him. "Looks like you've performed an *absolution* that I missed, Father. Guess C. S. Lewis was right."

"About what?"

"Being Christian means forgiving the inexcusable, because God forgives the inexcusable in us if we ask Him."

"Bullseye."

I stood and kissed RJ on the top of his head. "Sorry, sport. Time to go."

"Aw, Daddy!"

I shook my head and his expression withered.

He gathered his soldiers and turned to me with pleading eyes. "Can I play with Jacob again sometime? Pleeease. He's fun."

"The boy's right. I'm a regular hoot." My father raised his eyebrows. "So can we?"

I lifted RJ off the bed with my good arm and deposited him next to me. "We'll see, Pop—next time we meet."

Next time probably meant never, and a part of me felt as disappointed as RJ was. Like all raging fires, my hatred of my old man had burned itself out. Continued anger and bitterness simply required too much energy, and I would need all I had for my nephew.

As we walked from my dad's room, the hollowness inside me expanded. I had finally forgiven my father for the sins of the past, and in a strange way I would actually miss him—and his second impending departure from my life hurt more than I thought possible.

CHAPTER FORTY-SIX

In my room, I dressed in a sweatshirt, jeans, and was slipping on a light coat when DeQuan Kwame entered with a wheelchair. I protested being wheeled to my car, but he gave me his trademarked *I've-seen-you-with-your-pants-down* grin.

"Hospital policy, doctor. Sit."

I sat.

We joined Emily and my nephew in the hallway. She took RJ's hand and said, "I think I'll walk my two gentlemen to the door."

DeQuan rolled me into the elevator, and I asked her, "How are things with your father?"

She hesitated. "Getting better … slowly."

"Did you tell him about our last conversation about the two roads diverging in the woods?"

"I did."

"Did he go ballistic?"

"No. He likes the new, updated, 2.0 version of Jake Austin much better than the original."

I lowered my voice. "That's because he can't see the way I look at you."

Emily gave me a gentle slap on the back of my head. "Dad may be blind, but he has eyes all over this hospital, so watch it."

"Ouch! A smack in the head? That'll teach me to associate with domineering women."

I noticed that DeQuan was smiling. The cat had already vacated the bag when he had seen Emily kiss me, so there was no point in putting on an act in front of him. I hoped he had been sincere when he promised to keep our secret.

"That wasn't a smack, Jake; it was a love-tap." She smacked me again. "And I'm not domineering. I'm *concerned*. I realize that you and Superman were both born in Cleveland, but I will not tolerate a guy who's being shot at or tossed from buildings on a regular basis—so stop it. I'm tired of visiting you in the hospital. No more playing superhero."

"That was never part of my plan, believe me."

RJ gazed up at Emily and his eyes grew wide. "Is Daddy a superhero?"

She chuckled. "You know, I think he just might be."

She leaned down and whispered in my ear, "Little pitchers have big ears. I guess we'd better be careful about what we say around Boy Wonder."

Too late. RJ was literally bouncing up and down as if he had springs on the bottoms of his sneakers.

"A superhero? Oh boy, Daddy! What are your superpowers?"

In the past few months, all I had learned was that I could take a butt-kicking better than most. I couldn't think of any other abilities, shrugged, and gave my boy a quick hug.

Emily bent down to RJ. "I guess you and I will just have to find out together, young man."

The elevator door opened and DeQuan rolled me through the hospital entrance into an unusually warm late afternoon, a pleasant surprise after the early winter blizzards we'd had. The air tasted as sweet as honey. The sun had finally vanquished the cloud cover, and God had airbrushed a flawless western sky in misty shades of scarlet and fuchsia. It was the kind of December day we dream about up north, and to me it seemed like a sign from the Creator.

Another orderly wheeled Anna Grabowski outside, and she popped up from the wheelchair, her ragged teddy bear dangling from one hand. She did a happy dance, said something to her mother, and they both laughed.

Her scalp was wrapped in an elaborate green headscarf to mask the hair loss. Her jaundice was fading, and she appeared stronger and to have gained weight despite her last round of chemotherapy. Anna still had a long, rough road before her, but at least it headed home for a while. I prayed that road would never lead her back to the oncology ward.

I stood and thanked DeQuan for the wheelchair ride, and for not doing any wheelies along the way.

He patted me on the shoulder. "Take care of yourself, Doctor." He paused, glanced at Emily, and leaned in. "Not to worry. Mum's the word," he added and reentered the hospital.

Emily gave me a quick hug. "I have to run. Bye RJ. See you soon." She began to walk away, then stopped. "By the way, Jake, Dad and I really enjoyed the Episcopal wedding we attended on Saturday. Nice church. The service was a lot like Mass. Maybe you can join us sometime."

Episcopal, huh. Very subtle. The woman was always two steps ahead of me.

"Maybe." I sighed. "We'll see."

She flashed a radiant smile and reentered the hospital.

Colleen pulled the car up to the curb, and I opened the door for RJ. He jumped into his car seat, but with my surgically repaired wrist and forearm, I fumbled with the latch and could not quite buckle him in. Colleen swept me out of the way.

"Would you let me do that, Father? And please put this on." She handed me a scarf. "You'll catch your death out here. And *I* will be doing the driving home, so let there be no confusion about that!"

I climbed dutifully into the passenger seat. It appeared that my future would be filled with strong, dynamic women and one rambunctious child. Strangely, I liked the idea.

ABOUT THE AUTHOR

Born and raised in the Cleveland, Ohio, area, John Vanek received his bachelor's degree from Case Western Reserve University, where his passion for creative writing took root. He received his medical degree from the University of Rochester, did his internship at University Hospitals of Cleveland, and completed his residency at the Cleveland Clinic. During the quarter century he practiced medicine, his interest in writing never waned. Medicine was his wife, but writing became his mistress and mysteries his drug of choice. He began honing his  craft by attending creative writing workshops and college courses. At first pursuing his passion solely for himself and his family, he was surprised and gratified when his work won contests and was published in a variety of literary journals, anthologies, and magazines. John lives happily as an ink-stained-wretch in Florida, where he teaches a poetry workshop for seniors and enjoys swimming, hiking, sunshine, good friends, and red wine. For more information, go to www.JohnVanekAuthor.com.